THE
DUKE
OF
DISTRACTION

USA TODAY
BESTSELLING AUTHOR
DARCY
BURKE

The Duke of Distraction
Copyright © 2019 Darcy Burke
All rights reserved.

ISBN: 1944576460
ISBN-13: 9781944576462

Book design: © Darcy Burke.
Book Cover Design © Hang Le.
Book Cover Font Design © Carrie Divine/Seductive Designs.
Photo copyright: © Period Images.
Editing: Linda Ingmanson.

For siblings

I am so grateful for my big brother.
Except for the time he hid my favorite purple clogs.
We never found them.

Chapter One

⋅ε·3⋅

London, May, 1818

"Is THAT ANOTHER new hat, Miss Colton?"

Sarah brought her hand to the side of her poke bonnet trimmed in Pomona green and persimmon-striped ivory ribbon and bright yellow flowers with persimmon-colored centers. "Yes."

Mrs. Wetherell clucked her tongue. "It's absolutely stunning. Wherever did you buy it? I must have something just like it."

"Well, not *just* like it, I hope." Sarah smiled demurely, and her mother's friend laughed gaily.

"Of course not just like it," Mrs. Wetherell said. "But that striped ribbon is gorgeous. It pulls the green from your gown so beautifully."

Sarah's walking dress was Pomona green with an ivory sash. The striped ribbon and yellow flowers were a bold choice according to her mother, but Sarah thought they worked together perfectly.

"Thank you," Sarah said, inwardly beaming.

Lavinia, the Marchioness of Northam and Sarah's dearest friend, approached with a wide smile. "Why, Sarah, you look particularly fetching today." She nodded toward Mrs. Wetherell. "Good afternoon. I hope you don't mind if I steal Miss Colton away?"

Mrs. Wetherell dipped a brief, shallow curtsey. "Not at all, my lady."

Sarah looped her arm through Lavinia's and walked her away from the group of ladies that had gathered to watch the afternoon's races. "Thank you for rescuing me. I need to place my wagers."

Lavinia narrowed her eyes slightly as she cast a sidelong look at Sarah. "How much money have you made on these races?" It was the third week of a tournament, with two more weeks after this one.

Sarah shrugged as she steered them toward the table where Mr. Kinsley was collecting and recording wagers for the five races taking place that day: two for the women and three for the men. "I'm not getting rich, if that's what you're wondering." She was, however, accumulating an adequate purse and might just achieve her goal today. If she was lucky.

"I presume you'll be wagering on both Lucy and Dartford," Lavinia said.

"Of course." Their friend Lucy, the Countess of Dartford, was racing in one of the women's heats, while her husband was racing in the men's. "I will also place money on Lady Exeby and Mr. Wakeham."

"Indeed?" Lavinia sounded surprised. "Mr. Wakeham over Lord Ponsford?"

"It's a bit of a gamble, but that's the point of it." If Wakeham won, it would surely fatten Sarah's purse to precisely where she needed it to be.

"I'm surprised you haven't taken to gambling with Lucy." Lavinia waved her hand. "Never mind. Your parents would be horrified."

Livid was perhaps a better description. They'd notice her wagering at social events, but not on these races. Her father rarely came to the park, and her mother stayed far away from the races, which were for the younger set anyway.

"The only reason Mother allows me to attend these is because there are bachelors." Now on her fourth Season,

Sarah felt an intense pressure to marry. From her parents. From herself, she felt only an intense pressure to be happy, and marriage alone wasn't enough. Now, marriage to a man she *loved*…

But she wasn't holding out for that. She was tired of holding out for anything. Of waiting for something. Or someone. She was ready to make her own future.

"You didn't say who you planned to place your wager for in St. Ives's race," Lavinia said, arching an auburn brow.

The Earl of St. Ives had seemed to be on the verge of courting their friend Fanny, but then she'd left town abruptly, retiring to the country with her sister who was expecting her second child.

"St. Ives is by far the better racer," Sarah said.

Lavinia scowled. "But we're annoyed with him because it seems he might have driven Fanny away."

They'd discussed it, and that was their estimation. They'd written to Fanny, asking about her relationship with him, but had yet to receive a response.

Sarah exhaled. "Even so, I will bet on him."

Lavinia looked at her shrewdly as they arrived at the wagering table. "You are definitely trying to make money."

Letting out a nervous laugh, Sarah withdrew her arm from Lavinia's when the handsome Mr. Kinsley, who was also the Earl of St. Ives's secretary, took her wagers.

He winced when it came to his employer's race. "I'm afraid St. Ives has forfeited his race today."

Sarah frowned. "Why would he do that? It was almost certainly going to be him and Dartford in the final in two weeks."

"He had to leave town."

Sarah exchanged a look with Lavinia, whose elevated

brows surely mirrored Sarah's. Sarah returned her attention to Mr. Kinsley with a murmured "Indeed?"

"Did he go to Yorkshire?" Lavinia, who often lacked subtlety, asked.

Mr. Kinsley gave a bland smile. "I'm not entirely certain."

Sarah and Lavinia shared another look that silently communicated their extreme skepticism about *that.* "Well, we shall hope he went to Yorkshire," Sarah said as she handed him her money.

Mr. Kinsley finished recording her wagers, and Sarah turned from the table with Lavinia.

As soon as they put some distance between themselves and Mr. Kinsley, Lavinia asked, "Should we write to Fanny and tell her he's left town?"

"What if he isn't going to Yorkshire? We mustn't interfere."

Lavinia pushed out a frustrated breath. "You're right. I didn't like it when Beck tried to interfere in matters of the heart."

Her husband, Beck, had been the self-described Duke of Seduction, penning poems to young ladies with the goal of elevating their popularity on the Marriage Mart so that they would gain the attention of marriage-minded bachelors. He'd written about Lavinia and Sarah before Lavinia had put a stop to his "help." While some ladies had appreciated the assistance, others had not.

Sarah's mother had loved the attention Sarah had received for a few weeks. However, it hadn't lasted. Sarah had liked it at first too, but then she'd realized she was a novelty and that the men were less interested in her than they were in joining in the fun created by the Duke of Seduction's notoriety.

Sarah looked over at the vehicles gathered for the races,

then glanced toward Lavinia. "Are you sad you're no longer racing for the championship?"

Lavinia, who had lost her race in the second round, lifted a shoulder. "A bit, but I was never really in the hunt. These other ladies have far more experience than I. Next year, I shall be a formidable opponent." She waggled her eyebrows and smiled.

"You think Felix will do this next year?" Sarah asked.

"Why not? What else would he do? It's not as if he'll be married."

That much was true.

Sarah's gaze found the man in question. Felix Havers, the Earl of Ware, stood beside the platform from where he would make his announcements and was flanked by Lavinia's husband, the Marquess of Northam, whom they all called Beck, and Sarah's brother, Anthony. She and Anthony had known Felix most of their lives, having met him when he and his father had come to stay when he and Anthony had been eight. Sarah had been just four, and the only thing she remembered about the occasion was the boys hiding her favorite shoes. They'd hidden them so well that they'd never been found. Sarah had cried for days.

"But what of you?" Lavinia peered at Sarah. "Are there any bachelors here who've caught your eye?"

Sarah pressed her lips together. "You'd know if there were."

"The right man will come along," Lavinia said with great confidence. "Likely when you least expect it, as happened with me and Beck." Her gaze traveled to her husband, who just happened to be looking her way, and they shared a long, intimate look that made Sarah's gut tighten with envy.

Then she promptly admonished herself. She didn't

begrudge her friend's happiness one bit. She'd find her own happiness, and she didn't need a man to do it.

"Shall we go join them?" Sarah said with a smile, knowing Lavinia wanted to be with her husband.

"If you don't mind," Lavinia said a bit sheepishly.

Sarah laughed softly. "Not at all."

A pair of women arrived before them. The purpose of their visit became immediately apparent. "Why did you cease asking for the offer of favors?" one of them asked Felix. Her voice held a hint of a whine, and she looked rather disappointed. Her friend, on the other hand, gazed at Felix with an edge of hostility.

The first two times they'd convened for races, Felix had called for favors to be offered to the drivers. At the first tournament, only women had been invited to offer a favor to the male drivers—if their favor was chosen, they rode with the driver. After the women had complained, Felix had called for men to offer favors at the next set of races.

Felix smiled warmly at both women. "While that was incredibly diverting, a couple of the drivers confided to me that it was distracting to have a passenger with them, so in the interest of safety, I decided to end the practice. I do hope you aren't terribly disappointed. I shall be most upset." He placed his hand against his chest and looked at them with solemn regret.

Both ladies seemed to melt beneath his charm, and they spoke over each other in their effort to assure him they understood. Sarah rolled her eyes. If they were hoping to attract Felix in any way, they would be sorely disappointed.

After the ladies departed, Lavinia blinked at Felix. "Did anyone other than me complain?"

"Actually, someone else did," Felix admitted. "Though

in his case, I'm not sure his passenger had anything to do with his loss."

"Well, Beck was entirely the reason for mine." Lavinia slid her husband a heated glance. "Very distracting," she murmured.

Beck inclined his head in apology that seemed to somehow be lacking in remorse.

Anthony looked to Sarah. "I see you were placing wagers again. Do Mother and Father know you're doing that?"

Sarah gave him a dark stare. "What do you think? You'd better not tell them either."

Anthony chuckled. "I wouldn't dare. But I must ask what you're going to do with all your winnings. Seems as though you've been rather lucky the last two weeks."

"Luck has nothing to do with it," she said primly.

"Your sister's got an eye for winners," Felix said, his green eyes sparkling in the warm sunlight. He winked at Sarah, and she nodded in appreciation.

"It's a shame St. Ives forfeited," Sarah said.

Felix nodded. "He told me last night at the club, and I did try to convince him to stay."

"Is he going to Yorkshire?" Lavinia asked.

"He didn't say," Felix said with a touch of apology to his tone. "Nor did I ask."

Lavinia shook her head. "You men are terrible at gathering information."

"We aren't gossips," Anthony said with a laugh.

"It isn't gossip. We're all friends. We share information." Lavinia briefly pursed her lips. "Or at least, we should."

Sarah blinked at Lavinia, who hadn't always shared all the information regarding her and Beck. Lavinia seemed to comprehend Sarah's silent communication as her cheeks turned a faint shade of pink and she muttered, "Never mind. It's none of our business."

It wasn't, but like Lavinia, Sarah cared about their friend Fanny and hoped that she and St. Ives would find their way to a happily ever after.

Then that would just leave Sarah alone.

"Time to get started," Felix said. He lifted the horn to his mouth and announced the first women's race, featuring their friend Lucy and Mrs. Jermyn.

The track was shaped like a three-sided box with sharp corners that required expert turning. The course had been lengthened after the first week, which had more resembled a U. It took skill and nerve—two things Sarah lacked when it came to racing a vehicle. She could ride a horse as if she was escaping a fire, but driving was something she preferred at a sedate and orderly pace.

Lucy and Mrs. Jermyn positioned themselves at the starting line, which was to the right. Felix's platform was in the center of the open side of the three-sided box course. He could view the entire track and call out a commentary as it progressed.

Anthony handed him a bell, which Felix rang loudly to signify the start of the race.

Sarah held her breath as the two phaetons lurched forward. Mrs. Jermyn took the lead as they headed toward the first turn. Lucy was devastatingly efficient on the turns, and this time was no different. Though she was on the outside, she took it at a faster pace and was able to drive abreast of Mrs. Jermyn on the straight track as they raced to the second turn.

"The Duchess of Daring is poised to take the lead. Mrs. Jermyn will need to make up some time on this next turn," Felix yelled through the horn.

The spectators were gathered in the center of the three-sided box, with most of them standing near the finish. Lucy's husband, the Earl of Dartford and the owner of the nickname, the Duke of Daring, couldn't seem to stand still as he watched his wife take the second turn. As with the first, she was faster and this time leapt out ahead as they sped toward the finish.

In the end, it wasn't terribly close as Lucy crossed the line first.

"And we have our first participant in the women's championship," Felix called. "The Countess of Dartford!"

The cheers were loud and boisterous, and Sarah joined in. She mentally calculated her winnings. If she could win the Wakeham race, she'd have what she needed.

Sarah and Lavinia went to congratulate Lucy, whom they knew—she was a close friend of their friend Fanny's sister. The countess was overjoyed, and the pride shining on her husband's face was nearly as bright as the sun.

Felix announced it was time to ready the next race between Lady Exeby and Mrs. Childers. Both women were in their thirties and were admirable drivers. Mrs. Childers possessed a more dashing style and was faster, but Lady Exeby's skill and quiet confidence were the reasons behind Sarah's wager.

Sarah migrated back to the platform where Felix stood. "You have the best view, you know," she said.

"I do." He smiled down at her. "Come see." He held his hand out to help her up the steps.

Sarah put her hand in his and climbed onto the platform. It was only three or so feet off the ground, but it did provide a better vantage point. She looked out over the crowd and the track. "You should build platforms for everyone to stand on next year."

He slid her a sly glance. "You think there will be a next year?"

"Why not?"

He shrugged. "You know me, I always find something else to occupy my mind. Besides, I don't think I'd be allowed to build something that large. This thing is portable but, as you can see, barely large enough for two."

It was indeed. She had to stand quite close to him, not that she minded. Felix was the only gentleman around whom she felt utterly at ease, probably because he was the only gentleman she didn't have to worry about impressing.

"Did you wager on Mrs. Childers or Lady Exeby?" he asked. "Let me guess—Mrs. Childers."

"I did not, in fact," Sarah said.

"I'm surprised. You've made some daring wagers the past two weeks, and from reviewing the ledgers, you've earned quite a sum."

Sarah flinched, then looked up at him, for he was at least six inches taller and perhaps more like eight. "Please tell me you haven't shared that information with Anthony."

"I haven't. People's wagers are private and not mine to disclose." He shot a glance toward the track. "Are you saving for something specific?"

"Merely planning for my future of spinsterhood."

His gaze snapped to hers. "Why would you do that?"

"Because it seems prudent?" She laughed. "If I have enough money to support myself, my parents can't force me into a situation I don't want."

Felix looked mildly horrified. "And what would that be?"

"Marriage to a man I don't love."

"Mmm, that *would* be rather odious," he murmured, looking toward the starting line where Mrs. Childers and Lady Exeby were preparing themselves.

Sarah snorted in a most unladylike fashion, but she never felt the need to censor herself in front of Felix. "You think all marriage is odious."

He grinned down at her. "I do indeed."

"But surely even you will have to relent—you've a title to pass on."

"My cousin is more than capable of becoming earl," he said. "My uncle is making sure of it."

Sarah hadn't ever met his uncle. "That seems rather presumptuous of him."

"I don't mind. In fact, it makes things simpler knowing I don't *have* to marry." He gave her a pitying look. "I'm sorry you feel as if you do."

She let out a hollow laugh. "*All* women feel that way because it's our duty."

"It's bloody ridiculous. You should be able to invest your money and live your life as you see fit."

"How forward thinking of you, Felix."

"Yes, well, independence can't be overestimated." He straightened his coat. "And now I should begin the next race. Do you want to stay up here to watch?"

A thrill shot through her. "Yes, if you don't mind."

He slid her a half smile. "I wouldn't have offered if I did."

Felix lifted the horn to his mouth and announced the race was about to begin. The participants took their marks, and Anthony approached the platform.

"What are you doing up there?" he asked Sarah.

"Watching the race. Isn't it obvious?"

Anthony narrowed his eyes with a smirk as he handed the bell to Felix. "You've never invited me up there to watch."

"It's not a very large space, and your sister is far more petite," Felix said. "She's also much prettier." He winked at Sarah, and she laughed before giving her brother a superior look.

Anthony shook his head but smiled.

"Now we race!" Felix called. "Ready. Go!" He rang the bell, and the women started from the line.

Lady Exeby seemed to have a bit of difficulty getting going, and Sarah suffered a moment's concern. Perhaps she *should* have wagered on Mrs. Childers, who was off to a rather fast start. In fact, it seemed the fastest start of any of the women over all the races.

"That was an incredibly fast start by Mrs. Childers!" Felix yelled through the horn.

"I thought so too," Sarah said, her heart speeding up as the racers approached the first turn. "She's not slowing down at all."

Mrs. Childers was mad to take the corner at such a speed! Sarah held her breath as she turned. One of the back wheels of her phaeton came off the ground, and the entire vehicle teetered. Sarah had heard of accidents where the vehicle tipped over but had never seen such a thing. Without thinking, she grabbed Felix's forearm and squeezed.

The phaeton went over, and the air filled with screams.

"*Bloody hell.*" Felix's whispered oath reached Sarah's ears, and she turned to see that he'd gone completely white.

⋆ဒ•3⋆

HORROR SLAMMED THROUGH Felix, and he abruptly turned, nearly knocking Sarah from the platform. She clasped his arm more tightly, and he grabbed her by the waist, pulling her toward him so their chests almost touched.

"My apologies," he murmured. "I need to go."

"Of course." She moved around him so he could descend the stairs. He handed her the horn before he flew from the platform, his feet barely touching the steps. Then he dashed across the grass toward the site of the accident.

His insides churned, and he prayed Mrs. Childers wasn't terribly injured. Or worse.

Others had rushed toward the accident, and many more were heading in that direction. However, Felix was still one of the first to arrive.

Mrs. Childers lay on the grass, her face pale, and appeared to be unconscious.

Lady Exeby had stopped her phaeton and exited the vehicle. She knelt beside her opponent with a stricken expression as Felix squatted down on the other side.

"Why did she go so fast?" Lady Exeby asked, lifting her dark, tear-filled gaze to Felix's.

"Charlotte! My Charlotte!" Mr. Childers practically fell to his knees beside Felix. In his early forties, Childers was an affable fellow with a penchant for drink. Indeed, he seemed as though he'd already imbibed quite a bit, if the color in his cheeks and stench from his breath were any indication. Childers cupped his wife's head and shot a venomous glance toward Felix. "This is your fault! These bloody races!"

Felix was horrified by what had happened, but was it his fault the man's wife had taken a reckless pace?

"You should have at least had a surgeon present!" Childers raged as he stroked his wife's face. "Wake up, my dear."

Mrs. Childers's lids opened. She blinked up at her husband. "Did I go over?"

"Yes. You were driving much too fast, you silly

woman."

"You needn't call her silly," Lady Exeby murmured.

Felix looked over at the toppled vehicle but more importantly at the pair of frightened horses still attached to the phaeton. Dartford and a few other gentlemen, including Felix's friend Beck, were tending to the animals and working on freeing them from the vehicle, as well as trying to return the phaeton to its upright position.

"How are the horses?" Mrs. Childers asked. Her eyes seemed a bit unfocused, the pupils larger than normal.

"Hopefully not damaged!" Mr. Childers handed his wife over to a surprised Lady Exeby, then leapt to his feet to see to the animals.

Mrs. Childers turned her befuddled gaze to Felix. "Will you help me to stand?"

"Of course." Felix clasped her hand and exchanged a look with Lady Exeby, who assisted her from the other side.

Felix did most of the work, pulling Mrs. Childers to her feet. She wobbled, and Felix slid his arm around her to keep her steady.

She flashed him a smile. "Why, thank you, my lord. You are most attentive."

Lady Exeby let go of her, much to Felix's chagrin. He didn't particularly want to stand here holding on to Mrs. Childers.

"It looks as though I've given your races some extra excitement," Mrs. Childers said.

Felix kept his touch light. "Not on purpose, I hope."

She laughed in response. "Certainly not. My head feels as though it might split in two. I'll have to see if Childy's headache tonic will work as well for this as it does for him after a night of excessive spirits."

Childy?

"Are you able to stand on your own?" Felix asked.

"I'm sure I'd rather not find out." She batted her lashes at him, then leaned close, lowering her voice. "I've often hoped to have a moment alone with you, my lord. To show you my…*inclination*."

Good Lord. Felix knew he had a bit of a reputation with married ladies, but he kept those affairs to a minimum, and they were only for one night. Furthermore, he was quite satisfied with his current mistress.

Felix summoned a pleasant smile. "I'm sure now isn't the time to discuss such matters. Your head." He glanced toward her husband.

"Don't think Childy would mind, my lord," she whispered. "He can barely perform and wouldn't slight me for looking elsewhere."

Felix doubted that. He spoke loudly, "Lady Exeby, would you mind helping Mrs. Childers? I must see to the races."

"You can't mean to continue them?" Lady Exeby asked.

He was about to ask why they shouldn't when Sarah arrived. "Everything all right, then?" She looked toward Mrs. Childers. "You appear to be in excellent hands. I'm so pleased you weren't injured. My brother went to fetch a doctor. They should be along in a moment. In the meantime, you should sit down."

"She's right," Lady Exeby said. "Let's find a bench."

"I should see to my horses…"

Felix watched as Lady Exeby led Mrs. Childers away.

"You can't continue with the races," Sarah said grimly.

"But Mrs. Childers is fine."

"Seemingly, but at the very least, you should postpone the rest until next week."

He scowled. "That would drag them out another week.

The men's event already needs another week."

"Is that a problem? It's not as if anyone has grown bored with the event." She cocked her head to the side. "Unless you have."

"Maybe a little." Indeed, he hadn't really thought ahead when he'd come up with this scheme. He'd committed himself to coming here five weeks in a row, weather permitting. And so far, the weather had more than permitted.

Sarah exhaled. "Typical of you to grow restless, I suppose. Perhaps you'd rather arrange a liaison with Mrs. Childers when she's feeling better."

He locked his gaze with Sarah's. "Why would you say such a thing?"

"Because the two of you were flirting, and I'm not the only one who noticed. Mr. Childers was glaring daggers at you. That's why I came to intervene."

Felix hadn't noticed that. "I wasn't flirting with her. She was throwing herself at me."

"Well, whatever the specifics, might I suggest you stay away from her for a while?"

"You don't need to." He narrowed his eyes at her. "I'm not sure I like you playing the role of manager with me."

"Manager? I thought I was rescuing you." She laughed softly, and he let out a low groan because she was right.

"Whatever you're doing, it isn't seemly. We shouldn't be discussing my... Never mind." He looked toward the horses, which were now free of the phaeton. Several of the gentlemen were working to right the vehicle. Mr. Childers was not one of them. He was glowering at Felix.

Bloody hell.

And now he was stalking straight for Felix.

Thankfully, Anthony arrived at that moment with a physician in tow. "I've brought a doctor," he said.

"I'm glad someone is thinking," Childers grumbled.

"Where is the patient?" the doctor asked.

"This way," Childers said, leading the man toward his wife where she sat on a bench beside Lady Exeby.

Felix exhaled with relief—at least for now.

"Shame the races are over for the day," Anthony said. "Sarah, it looks like you won't be fattening your purse any more today."

"It does not." She sounded disappointed. Felix knew how much she'd made and wondered if she was really just saving for a lonely future.

Lonely. Was that how he thought of spinsterhood? He didn't plan to wed. Why couldn't she make the same choice? Furthermore, he didn't expect to feel lonely, so why should she?

Alas, none of it mattered because women and men weren't afforded the same choices. He could be a bachelor and she'd be a spinster.

"Felix isn't certain the races are over," Sarah said, eyeing him.

Anthony stared at him. "Are you mad? You can't mean to continue. Not today. Why not carry on with the men's races tomorrow?"

Because he had appointments tomorrow. "Do you people think I have nothing better to do than host entertainments?"

"No." They answered in unison, and he was torn between growling at them and laughing. What came out of his mouth was an unfortunate mix of the two. Anthony laughed in response, and Sarah merely arched a brow.

It was true that he spent most of his life in the pursuit of entertainment and diversion. "Well, tomorrow I'm busy. I'm sure Dartford and the others would prefer to continue."

"Let's ask him," Anthony said.

Before they could do so, Childers marched back over to them, not stopping until he was nearly in Felix's face. "My wife has suffered a concussion, you dolt. I'm going to make sure these races of yours are finished. I'll petition the Regent if I have to."

Felix exhaled with boredom. "He will likely attend the final, so I wish you luck with that."

"I doubt that. Mrs. Childers's uncle is a special friend of his. When he finds out she was injured and you didn't even have the sense to ensure a doctor was at the ready, he'll shut these races down faster than you can say *go*." Spittle had gathered on his lip and then leapt onto Felix's coat with the vehemence of the man's last word.

While he was skeptical of Mrs. Childers's uncle's importance, Felix didn't say so. Perhaps it *was* time to move to a new amusement.

Or perhaps he should move them to a new location and ensure only certain people were invited. Then they would be quite exclusive... Even better, he'd have one final race—the women's final between Lady Dartford and Lady Exeby and a madcap six-man competition with the remaining gentlemen. They'd have to hold it somewhere quite large... Felix's mind was already working.

He smiled at Mr. Childers. "You are quite right that the races should be finished."

Felix went to Sarah. "May I have the horn?"

She placed it in his hand. "Certainly."

He announced that the races were concluded— permanently. There was much upset, with many people voicing their displeasure, which only made Felix relish his plan even more.

Childers wandered back to his wife, and Sarah took a step toward Felix.

"That was the right thing to do," she said softly, from right beside him. "Probably."

He looked her in the eye, the corner of his mouth trying to lift of its own accord. "Just wait."

Her brow arched again—it was a fetching expression on her, particularly with her hat.

"Your hat is lovely," he said.

Light color stained her cheeks. "Thank you."

Beck and his wife, Lavinia, joined them. "Shame you had to cancel the races," Beck said.

Lavinia frowned at Felix. "I disagree with this decision wholeheartedly. We deserve to know who would win."

Felix clenched his teeth together lest he spoil the surprise. "It was necessary, I'm afraid."

Anthony nodded. "Still disappointing. If only that Childers woman hadn't gone so damn fast."

"I'm just glad she's all right." Felix didn't know what he would have done if she'd been seriously injured—or worse. For a brief moment, his heart had stopped and he thought about the poor woman's children no longer having a mother… But then he wasn't even sure she had children. Surely she must?

"Yes, we all are," Sarah said. "And now I suppose we should go." She looked at Lavinia with a resigned expression.

"We may as well. Do you want me to walk you to your mother, or shall I just convey you home?"

"I'll ride with you, if you don't mind." Sarah turned to Anthony. "Will you tell Mother?"

"Now I'm your secretary?"

Sarah gave him a saucy smile that made Felix laugh. He'd always enjoyed their sibling antics, probably because he didn't have any brothers or sisters. "Why not?"

Anthony groaned. "Fine. Just don't expect me to dance

with you at whatever ball we're going to tonight."

"I'll dance with you, Sarah," Felix said.

She gave him a prim nod. "Thank you, my lord. It would be my honor. Until this evening." She gave him an exaggerated curtsey and left with Lavinia and Beck.

"You're kind to dance with her," Anthony said. "Not that it will help. I don't understand why she can't land a husband, but our parents are adamant she must do so soon. You sure you don't want the job?" He looked askance at Felix and laughed. "Are we still going to the Red Door?"

Felix was—that was where his mistress, the incomparable Meggie, lived and worked. "Yes."

"Excellent. I've a mind to visit a certain redhead." Anthony waggled his brows and chuckled.

"I'll see you at the ball." Felix turned and went to the platform—rather, where it had been—where his footman was waiting for him.

"I've already put the platform in the coach, my lord," Glover said.

"Thank you." Felix started toward the coach, and Glover walked alongside him.

"A shame to see how your hard work ended today."

"Yes." But Felix wouldn't dwell on that. He was already too fixated on the secret race. First, he had to decide where to hold it. Dartford's estate came to mind. It was less than a day's ride from London, and Felix was certain he would enthusiastically agree.

Perhaps he'd talk to him at the ball tonight or maybe at Brooks's afterward. In between dancing with his best friend's sister and spending the night in his mistress's arms.

Chapter Two

SARAH MADE SURE her mother was busy speaking with Mrs. Kyle at the front of Marsden's Millinery before stealing to the very back corner of the store where Mr. Marsden's primary assistant, Dorothy Hinman, stood. She'd been eyeing Sarah since her arrival.

"Good afternoon, Dolly," Sarah said with a smile. Since the races several days ago, she'd been looking forward to seeing Dolly.

"Good afternoon, Miss Colton. I'm so pleased to see you."

Sarah could tell that Dolly was trying not to look expectant, and that she was also failing miserably. Her light brown eyes were alight with anticipation, and the barest of smiles curved her lips.

"I've done it," Sarah whispered after casting a look over her shoulder toward her mother. "I have enough saved to start the shop!"

Dolly's mouth opened, and a small gasp escaped before she clapped her hand over her lips. "My apologies." She looked toward Sarah's mother in horror and then glanced toward Mr. Marsden, who was consulting with another client at the counter.

"Don't be concerned," Sarah said softly. "They can't have heard anything, and it is exciting, isn't it?"

"I can hardly believe it." Dolly shook her head as tears filled her eyes.

Sarah touched the woman's shoulder. "Now, don't cry. They're bound to notice *that*."

"You're quite right." Dolly sniffed and pushed her

shoulders back with a determined smile. Though she was in her early thirties, Dolly looked younger than that. However, the fierce look in her eye at present gave an air of maturity—and experience.

Good, they'd need both in this new endeavor.

"I still have much work to do," Sarah said. "But hopefully, we'll have the shop up and running by fall."

Dolly shot a glance toward her employer and winced. "I hope Mr. Marsden isn't terribly cross with me."

"How can he be after all your years of service? Besides, he can't possibly fault you for wanting to better your position and increase your income." It would be Sarah's shop, of course, but not as far as anyone could tell. Dolly would be the outward face of Farewell's—that was the name Sarah had chosen. It sounded dignified, and she hoped they would "fare well." Behind the scenes, Sarah would manage things. But most of all, she would design hats to her heart's content. And *best* of all, she would get paid for it.

Husband hunting be damned.

Her parents would hate this enterprise, which was why Sarah hoped to keep them ignorant of it until it was far too late for them to stop it. Or to ignore how lucrative it was. Which would in turn nullify the need for Sarah to marry. Though she suspected her mother would still want that.

It was more than the financial aspects. The viscountess took it as a personal failure that her daughter hadn't yet wed.

Sarah's gaze drifted to her mother. She took that moment to look toward Sarah too, and their eyes connected. Mother's brow furrowed, which meant it was time to end this brief but necessary meeting with Dolly.

"I must go," Sarah said. "I'll send word when I've

property for us to tour."

Dolly nodded enthusiastically. "I'll look forward to it."
Her focus moved upward to Sarah's hat. "I like this
design very much. That's an excellent interpretation of a
cavalier."

The brim on the right side was low, but pinned up on
the right in the cavalier style. However, instead of
installing feathers where it was pinned, Sarah had affixed
them to the top, which added height and volume. "I'm
pleased you like it. I've attracted a few stares. I was
worried it was a bit daring." She grinned, then left Dolly
before her mother came to interrupt.

Sarah joined her mother and chatted with Mrs. Kyle for
a few moments before they made their excuses and left
the shop.

As they walked to the coach parked just up Bond
Street, Sarah's mother glanced in her direction. "Were you
discussing your new hat with Mr. Marsden's assistant?"

"I was. She was very complimentary."

"It's rather fetching." Her mother's blue-gray eyes kept
fixating on Sarah's hat. "I still can't believe you made that
entirely on your own, but then I know you didn't
purchase it. Come to think of it, when was the last time
you purchased a hat?"

"It hasn't been that long," Sarah said. It had, but she
tried to distract her mother from realizing how long Sarah
had been creating her own hats. At first, she would
purchase the basic hat and trim it herself as many women
did, but in the last couple of years, she'd taken to making
them entirely herself. Forming the hats without attracting
more than her maid's notice was the most challenging
part.

"I might ask you to make me one in that fashion,"
Mother said as they reached the coach.

Sarah's chest swelled beneath her mother's praise. Typically, Sarah disappointed the viscountess in most ways and was glad to know she didn't do so in everything.

They returned home, and as soon as they stepped into the hall, Sarah's good mood was torn to shreds.

Mother announced, "Sarah, please join me in the library with your father." Summons like these were never good.

After handing her gloves and hat to the footman, she dutifully followed her mother to the library at the back of the house. Expecting to find her father seated in his favorite chair near the fireplace, she was surprised to see him standing instead. And he wasn't alone.

Anthony sat in a chair near the window that looked out to the garden, and Felix—Felix?—stood near the corner wearing a look that could only be described as confused.

"Ah, there you are." Father glanced toward the clock on the mantel before straightening to his full height. "I've an appointment in a little while, so let's get right to it." He looked toward Sarah. "It's time you—"

"Let her sit down first," Sarah's mother said with a touch of heat before ushering Sarah to the settee.

Sarah didn't really want to sit. She wanted to flee. In compromise, she perched, her backside barely grazing the edge of the cushion so she could slip off and run at a moment's notice.

Mother took the space beside her, although in a much more secure manner. "Now you may proceed," she said, smoothing her skirt and looking up at her husband with a bland expression, as if calling their daughter in for a lecture were an everyday occurrence.

Well, it wasn't unusual, Sarah had to admit. However, this time felt different somehow. Because Anthony and Felix were here. She could almost understand Anthony's presence, but Felix? Sarah slid a glance toward him and saw that he continued to appear befuddled. Or perhaps uncomfortable was a better description. Yes, she'd feel uncomfortable too if she were him.

As if that mattered. She *wasn't* him, and she still felt uncomfortable.

"It's time for you to marry," Father said, surprising no one. Or so Sarah assumed. Anthony knew how desperately they wanted her to marry, and she had to think Felix did too. Of course he did. Sarah was the first person to complain about the pressure they applied.

"Past time, one might say," Sarah murmured and tried not to send an exasperated look toward her mother.

"There's no need to be saucy," Mother said tartly.

"Why must Felix and I be privy to Sarah's humiliation?" Anthony asked.

Humiliation? Sarah had been annoyed, mildly embarrassed even, but not humiliated. At least not until *now*. She tossed a withering stare at her brother. He had the grace to wince and look away.

"There is a reason," Mother said before inclining her head toward Sarah's father.

Father coughed. "Er, yes. We wondered if it might make sense for you, Felix, to wed Sarah."

Humiliation didn't begin to describe the emotion swirling inside Sarah and erupting in her cheeks. Surely they were about to catch fire.

She would have snapped at her father or mother or both, but words simply wouldn't come.

Anthony stood. "You can't ambush Felix like that!" At Sarah's intake of breath, he added, "Or Sarah."

Sarah didn't bother sending him another acid glare.

Their mother pursed her lips at Anthony. "We're not ambushing him. Felix is like family. He's well aware of Sarah's sad state."

Oh, this was just getting better and better. Now she was in a sad state?

"Furthermore, Felix is in need of a wife. Your father and I discussed it, and we think this is an excellent match."

Sarah couldn't bear to meet Felix's gaze, so she stared at the floor. Had the patterned carpet always had that odd mushroom shape next to the leg of the settee?

"I'm glad you discussed it," Anthony said with a great deal of sarcasm. "You might have discussed it with Felix, however." He looked toward Felix. "Did they?"

Now Sarah chanced a look at him. Felix shook his head. To his credit, he didn't look surprised or annoyed or pale or anything other than what he'd appeared since she'd arrived: uncomfortable.

Father frowned at Anthony. "Never mind your outrage, Anthony. In fact, you don't really need to be here." He looked toward his wife. "Why *is* he here?"

"We thought he might help us persuade them of the match. It doesn't look as if he'll do that."

That they'd thought he would almost made Sarah laugh. In fact, why *would* they have thought that? She opened her mouth to ask, but Anthony beat her to it, practically leaping from his chair.

"Whyever would you think that?" Anthony shook his head. "I'm not going to match my best friend—who has no desire to wed—with my sister." He turned a pained expression toward Felix. "Please accept my deepest apologies for this…error."

Mother stood. "Why not think about it, Felix?" she asked. "Sarah would be the perfect wife for you. You already know each other quite well. There will be no awkward expectations or discomfort."

Sarah snorted. There was already awkward discomfort.

"Mother, please don't put Felix—or me—in this position."

"You, my girl, are already in this 'position.' I simply do not understand why you aren't married. You're pretty, you dress exceptionally well, you possess many talents, and you're of at least average intelligence." Mother placed a hand on her hip, and her neck turned pink with agitation. "Felix, you're a man—and apparently one of many who won't marry our daughter. What is wrong with Sarah?"

Oh dear God. Sarah prayed she would simply melt into the floor, into very oblivion, and never emerge.

"There's nothing wrong with her." Felix turned his attention to her. "She's beautiful, exceptionally talented, and brilliant."

A bright sense of pride filtered through the horror of the moment and filled Sarah with warmth. Brilliant? She looked toward Felix, who gave her a subtle nod.

"You've just convinced me you should marry her," Sarah's mother said, looking pleased.

"*Mother*." Anthony growled the word.

The viscountess shot an irritated glance toward her son. "Since you *aren't* going to help, this doesn't concern you."

Sarah had suffered quite enough. She stood from the settee, and now they were all standing. "I'm not marrying Felix."

Mother and Father swiveled their heads toward Sarah and gave her matching expressions of annoyance. "What's wrong with Felix?" Father asked. "He's an earl." Nothing about his looks or talents or intelligence. Apparently, a title was all a man needed to be marriageable.

"We don't want to marry each other," Sarah said. "If we did, don't you think we would have done so already?"

"It's not a question of want, dear." Mother's tone held a note of condescension. "You're both in *need*. It's a perfect solution, you must agree."

"It isn't. And I mustn't agree to anything. You can't force me to marry him. You can't force me to marry anyone." And with that, Sarah was finished with this farce of a discussion. She turned on her heel and exited the library through the closest door. Which meant she was heading to the garden.

Anger and frustration raced through her, making her shake as she propelled herself into a circuit of the small walled garden. The roses had begun to bloom, and they filled the air with a lush, spicy scent. She took several deep breaths in an effort to calm her racing heart.

On her second time around, she saw Felix leave the house and walk toward her, his expression pulled into a somber mask.

When he caught up to her, she said, "I'm sorry about that."

"No more than I am." He steered her to a bench that was situated next to her mother's favorite rosebush. They sat, and Sarah arranged her skirt around her ankles.

She glared at the plant as a proxy for her mother. "That was absolutely humiliating. And unnecessary. Who says I have to marry at all." It wasn't a question but a defiant statement. More than ever, she wanted to open her shop and become a truly independent woman.

"Your parents, but I would argue their opinion is not all-important," Felix said softly.

Sarah rotated herself to face him. "But you think it's somewhat important."

Felix lifted a shoulder. "I don't have parents anymore, so don't ask me. I know you love them, and they love you. That's all I meant."

"Parents can be a pain in the arse." She gave him an apologetic look. "I didn't mean to suggest you were better off."

His mouth curled into a half smile. "I didn't take it that way."

"I'm sure you miss your parents very much." She realized he never mentioned them. Perhaps he didn't miss them.

"My mother died when I was born. How can I miss what I never knew? And my father…" He glanced away, and she found herself waiting expectantly for the rest of what he would say. Only he didn't continue.

"Your father what?"

He looked back at her, his green gaze carrying an edge of steel. "My father has been dead a long time." When he said nothing more, she accepted that was all he wanted to express on the subject.

"I'll help you find a husband," he said, startling her. "If that's what you want."

She blinked at him, surprised at the offer. "Why? Did my parents ask you to?" She narrowed her eyes at him.

"No. I did suggest it, and they were both relieved and pleased. It at least alleviates the pressure they've put on you."

"Why, because now I'm your problem instead of theirs?" She let out a soft snort.

"You're not a problem. I meant what I said about you earlier. You'll make some man an excellent wife."

Some man. "I don't want to marry 'some man.'"

"Whom do you want to marry?" He tipped his head to the side. "No, the first question you must answer is whether you truly wish to marry at all. You told me at the races that you were planning for spinsterhood, and just a bit ago, you wondered why you had to marry. It sounds to me as if you might prefer to remain unwed."

"I'd be a pariah—particularly in my mother's eyes."

He hesitated before answering. "Not necessarily. Plenty of women never marry."

She exhaled. "Yes, and aren't they pariahs?"

"I admit I don't know." He shifted his gaze to the side. "My experience with, er, spinsters is rather limited."

"Is it? And here I thought you'd carried on with a few." She noted his discomfort and laughed. "I'm teasing. But you are a bit of a rake."

"I suppose I am." He looked at her without apology.

"Yes, you should not be ashamed. We should embrace who we are. Would you like to know who I am?"

He leaned toward her, his gaze a bit...rapt. "Tell me."

She took a deep breath. "I'm a hat designer, and I only wish to marry for love." There, she'd said it out loud. She turned away from him, readjusting herself on the bench so she faced straight toward the garden. "I've never told anyone that before."

"Not even Lavinia?"

Lavinia was her dearest friend, so of course it seemed she would have. Or should have. "She knows I like hats. And she knows I want to fall in love, especially now that she has." Watching her with Beck had transformed love from an intangible dream into a real possibility.

They were both quiet for a moment. Both staring at the garden. Or so she thought from the limited view she had of him from the corner of her eye. He'd come out without a hat, so the breeze stirred a lock of his dark hair, brushing it against his temple.

Then he turned his head toward her. "How about I try to help you find a gentleman to love?"

"Beck tried this with Lavinia. He introduced her to his friend from Oxford."

"Yes, Horace. I don't mean like that," Felix said. "I don't actually have anyone in mind. But if I go out of my way to invite every single gentleman in London to one of my entertainments, then you'll at least have a better field to choose from."

"Don't you invite them already?"

"I don't base my invitations on marriageability," he said wryly. "But I will for the rest of this Season. Everything I do will be for the primary purpose of finding the man worthy of your affection."

When he said it like that, how could she refuse? He didn't assume she was faulty or that this was a difficult task. And he didn't treat her desire for love as if it were foolish.

"Why would you want to help me like this?"

"Because you're my best friend's sister."

"And because by helping me, you avoid being snared in a parson's trap."

He laughed, but his gaze was dark. "It would take more than your parents' pleas to cage me."

"I believe that. If I could wager on you remaining unwed, I would."

"You're a gambler at heart. Would you prefer a gentleman who shares your adventurous nature?"

He thought her adventurous? Even if it only pertained to wagering, she'd take it as a compliment. Still, it wasn't entirely accurate. "I'm not sure I'm a gambler at heart—or anywhere else. I wagered on your races because it was an opportunity to increase my purse."

"To prepare for spinsterhood."

"Would you like to know how?" she asked softly. For some reason, she felt emboldened to share everything. At his nod, she continued. "I plan to open a millinery shop. I design all my hats—and make them too."

He turned toward her, staring, his gaze drifting to the top of her head, which was bare because she'd rushed from the library without sending for a hat. "You're very talented."

She laughed. "There's nothing on my head!"

"Not at present, but I do pay attention."

Yes, apparently he did. He had, in fact, complimented her hat the other day. And today, he'd called her beautiful. Did he really think so? That wasn't something she was bold enough to ask. Besides, it didn't signify. *He* wasn't the man she was looking for.

"Your parents won't want you to open a shop any more than they would want you to become a spinster."

"Obviously." She angled her body toward him once more. "I don't plan for them—or anyone else—to know. I already have an assistant who will manage the physical shop. She'll live there and oversee a small staff. I will design and create some of the hats, but neither I nor my name will be associated with the enterprise."

"You've thought this through," he said. "How did you obtain the property?"

"I haven't yet. Now that I have enough money—because of your races—I'd planned to ask Beck or maybe even Anthony for help."

"You can't put Anthony in that position with your parents."

She frowned at him. "Why not? I'm confident he would help me."

"I am too. However, he shouldn't. It's better if he knows nothing. I'll help you."

"You're already helping me."

"Precisely. May as well fulfill everything you require." He flashed her a smile, and she couldn't help but grin in return.

"What will you get from this arrangement, besides my eternal gratitude?"

He leaned forward again briefly. "That will be enough."

"What are you two conspiring out here?" Anthony called out as he strode toward them.

"Talk of the devil," Felix murmured, rising to his feet.

Sarah bit back a smile and stood alongside Felix. "Felix was merely offering moral support."

"Isn't he going to help you find a husband? That's what he told Father."

"He's going to do what he can," Sarah said. "But Anthony, I won't be forced."

"Of course not. I pledge to care for you in your spinsterhood after Mother and Father are gone." He laid his hand over his chest. "I give you my word." His eyes danced with mirth.

"Joke all you like, but I'm holding you to that."

He sobered. "I only wanted to inject a bit of levity. That was a disaster inside, and I'm very sorry."

She knew he was. He'd been as outraged as she was. "Thank you."

He put his arm around her and gave her shoulder a squeeze. "We'll find you a worthy husband." Had he and Felix discussed this? She looked between them—of course not.

"One she can love," Felix said firmly. "She deserves nothing less."

"I couldn't agree more." Anthony smiled at her, then dropped his arm to his side. He looked to Felix. "Ready to be delivered from this asylum?"

Felix nodded. "I do need to pay a call. Until later, Sarah." He inclined his head, and they left the garden where Sarah contemplated hats, love, and rakes with hearts of gold.

Chapter Three

❦·3·❦

"AFTERNOON, WARE," GREETED the Earl of Dartford as he strode into his drawing room, where his butler had led Felix to await the earl.

"Afternoon, Dart. Thank you for seeing me." Felix hadn't run into Dartford since the races, so he'd decided to pay a call.

"I sincerely hope you're here to talk about how to wrap up the races. Not for me, mind you, but for Lucy. My wife deserves to take the championship."

Felix smiled. "I will try to remain impartial," he said judiciously, which earned him a chuckle from Dart. "That may be difficult if you agree to my proposal, but I daresay no one will care if it means the races will have the opportunity to conclude."

"I'm thoroughly confused," Dart said with a laugh, his dark eyes crinkling at the corners. "Sit." He gestured to a chair while he sprawled at one end of a settee.

Felix took the chair Dart indicated. "I think it best to act as though the races are finished."

"Because of that dolt Childers?" Dart shook his head. "His wife was foolish, and now everyone else is paying the price."

"I don't know if he'd really get the Prince Regent involved, but I'd just as soon not find out."

"A wise decision." Dart stared at him with interest. "What is your proposal, and what has it to do with me?"

"I should like to continue the races—in secret."

Dart leaned forward, his eyes alight. "Ha, you did say 'act as though' they're done. What do you plan?"

"We'll need to stage them out of town, and I thought Darent Hall might be the best location. Furthermore, I didn't think you'd—" Felix didn't get a chance to finish.

"Yes. *Hell* yes. When?"

"Whenever we can manage? In a week perhaps?"

"I can manage it. Just tell me what you need."

Felix had considered a possible schedule, and now that he was using the event to help Sarah, he'd come up with what he hoped would be an enjoyable social occasion for everyone involved. "I'm envisioning a two-day affair. Guests will arrive in the early afternoon, and we'll have the next men's heat followed by the women's final. That evening, we'll celebrate the winner with a feast. The following morning, we'll have the men's semifinal and then the final in the afternoon. We'll finish off that night with another celebration. I will provide additional staff and pay for the celebrations."

"Nonsense. It's my house party, I'll pay."

"But they're my races," Felix said.

"You can contribute, but it will be a shared expense," Dart said firmly. "Those are my terms."

"How can I possibly refuse?" Felix asked with a smile. "As I said, this event will be secret. I will invite very select people and no one in possession of a flapping tongue."

"This may be your most successful endeavor yet. The races were terribly popular, and now to have them become *exclusive*? The Prince Regent may be annoyed that he wasn't invited." Dart said this with a grin. "Next Wednesday through Friday, since Wednesday was race day?" Dart asked.

"If you can organize it that quickly. I've calculated about forty guests." Ten of them would be bachelors for Sarah to consider, but Felix wouldn't point that out.

"It's a bit tight for Darent Hall, but we can make it

work, particularly if we can put unmarried guests like you and Anthony Colton in the same room together."

"That's more than acceptable—and there will be a decent number of unwed guests. I'll let you know a final count and rooming situation as soon as I speak with each guest."

"You plan to invite them all personally?"

"I refuse to write it down—it's *secret*."

Dart laughed. "Brilliant!"

"What's brilliant?" The Countess of Dartford swept into the room. She was an attractive woman with ink-dark hair and a shrewd gaze. Felix rose.

Dart stood and turned toward his wife. "I'll let Ware explain. It's his secret."

"It's *our* secret since you're sharing hosting duties."

"I'm merely providing the location," Dart said.

The countess looked at him in confusion. "Location for what?"

Dart smiled at her. "You're going to love this. Ware will finish his races—in secret—at Darent Hall next week."

Her face lit up like a bonfire. She turned her head toward Felix. "How wonderful!"

"Now you can truly become champion," Dart said, putting his arm around her.

"*If* I beat Lady Exeby. What's this about it being secret?" she asked.

"I think it best to keep people like Childers away," Felix explained.

The countess nodded. "Good idea."

"I'll apprise you of the specifics, my dear," Dart said to her.

"How exciting." She glanced toward Felix once more. "Thank you for planning this. It will be nice to finish it."

"Happy to," Felix said. "I'll be in touch." He excused

himself and left their town house, stepping out into the bright mid-May afternoon.

A short while later, he made his way home and summoned his secretary to his study. He'd barely sat down at his desk when she breezed in the door carrying her typical ledger in which she kept all her notes and information. She called it her bible.

"How did it go?" Felix's secretary, Georgiana Vane, sat in her usual chair beside his desk. A pencil jutted from the blonde pile of hair twisted atop her head. Just a bit younger than him, she was astonishingly efficient and organized. She was also exceptionally beautiful—a fact that hadn't been lost on Felix's valet, who had married her last year.

"As expected. The party will begin next Wednesday."

George opened her bible and scratched her pencil across the paper. "Two dinners?"

"Dartford insisted on sharing the expense. Draft a letter asking for the menu—I'll buy what's needed, and his staff can make it."

"Wine?" She didn't look up.

"I'll let him provide that."

"Shall I do the same for other meals?"

"Whatever you think is best," Felix said. He was renowned for his entertainments, and yet without George's oversight, they wouldn't be nearly as successful as they were. Hell, they probably wouldn't happen at all.

She snapped the ledger closed and slid the pencil back into her upswept hair. "Have you completed your list of guests?"

He hadn't seen George since visiting the Coltons earlier. "Not yet. And there's been a bit of a change. This will be forty people instead of thirty."

"I suspected as much," she said with a hint of a smile.

"You always think of people you've forgotten."

"In this case, I need to think of people. Bachelors, specifically. I need to find a match for Sarah Colton."

George had met Anthony before but not Sarah, though she'd heard enough about her to know who she was. "You're adding matchmaker to your activities? Why am I not surprised? In fact, it's a wonder it's taken you this long."

"I am not becoming a matchmaker. I'm helping a dear friend." And escaping the parson's trap himself. In truth, the Coltons' suggestion that he marry Sarah wasn't terrible. If he had any interest in marriage, he would consider it. Or at least he would have before he'd known Sarah wished to marry for love. Now he would help her fall in love.

Hell, he *was* a matchmaker.

"I'm only doing it this one time," he said firmly.

George pressed her lips together and nodded. "Mmm."

"Help me think of bachelors to invite."

George laughed. "As if I'm acquainted with any of them in your circle."

She had a point, but he grumbled anyway. "You take care of everything."

"True, but I can't take care of this. The Brixcombe ball is in a few days. Surely that is a good place to find eligible bachelors."

So was the club. Felix had only to pay attention. "I'll rely on that if necessary. In the meantime, I'll look at the club later."

"Should I draft an advertisement to place in the newspaper?" George possessed a fair amount of cheek.

"Yes, let's proclaim to all of London that Miss Colton is looking for a husband, and I'm to find him for her." He shook his head, half smiling.

"Always happy to be of service," George said, rising from her chair. "Is there anything else?"

He shook his head, and she left.

Felix leaned back in his chair and stared at the empty doorway, his mind going back to earlier at the Coltons. He'd been shocked as hell when her father had suggested Felix marry Sarah, but he probably should have seen it coming. He'd known their family for years, and since both he and Sarah were not yet wed, it made sense.

Except it didn't.

She wanted to fall in love, and he wanted to stay as far away from that emotion as possible. It had brought nothing but grief to his family, and he'd no wish to suffer its pain and disappointment.

She also wanted to sell hats. *Secretly.* This made him smile. Whomever she chose to marry would have to support that. Or she could remain unmarried, an option that didn't seem distasteful to her. She was, he realized, a unique and special woman.

Sarah was going to make some man blissfully happy.

"THERE'S A NEW gentleman here tonight," Lavinia said, prompting Sarah to scan the Brixcombes' ballroom.

"How did you hear this?" Sarah had just arrived with her mother and had left her to join Lavinia in their favorite position near the wall. Lavinia wasn't a wallflower anymore, of course, since she was now married, but she still stood with Sarah.

"Oh, you know how that sort of information travels." Lavinia rolled her eyes. "I'd scarcely been here five minutes before I heard of him. He's just returned from several years in India."

"I don't suppose he has a title?" Sarah asked. "My parents do prefer a title."

Lavinia pursed her lips. "This isn't about your parents. This is about you."

"Is it?" she muttered.

"There he is. And no, he doesn't have a title. His name is Mr. Silvester Fielding." Lavinia gestured toward a gentleman walking toward the doors open to the terrace. "He's a bit ordinary, isn't he?"

He wasn't particularly tall, and his build was best described as stocky. His clothing was clearly very fine, however, and he wore a pleasant, welcoming expression. "One person's ordinary is another's superlative."

"You are correct," Lavinia said. "Shall we wander toward the doors?"

He hadn't gone outside, but was merely standing near them, as if he was hoping to catch a bit of the cool night breeze. It had been a warm day, but the temperature had dropped as clouds had moved in. There would be rain tomorrow.

"I suppose, but who will conduct an introduction?" Sarah wasn't entirely in the mood to meet a new gentleman. Or even be at this stupid ball. She was rather fixated on her hat business and was frustrated that Felix hadn't communicated anything on that front. But then he hadn't communicated anything regarding a husband either, so perhaps he'd changed his mind.

"I'm a marchioness," Lavinia said with a touch of hauteur followed by a grin. "I'll introduce myself and then introduce you."

Sarah exhaled. "Let's go."

Lavinia touched her arm, her eyes sympathetic. "We don't have to. We can stay here all night if you prefer. Well, until Beck arrives, that is." Her gaze turned sheepish.

Sarah knew Lavinia sometimes felt bad that she'd found happiness and Sarah was still alone. And sometimes Sarah felt bad about that too. Which was why she focused on her millinery shop. It wasn't Lavinia's fault that she'd fallen madly in love. Furthermore, Sarah was thrilled for her and never failed to regret the envy she felt from time to time.

Summoning a smile, Sarah squeezed her friend's hand. "We should go. For all we know, Mr. Fielding is having a terrible evening, and we're about to improve it."

Lavinia laughed. "Of course we are." She adjusted her spectacles on her nose and linked her arm though Sarah's, then they made their way to the gentleman.

His complexion was a bit dark, as if he'd spent a great deal of time in the sun, and his hair was light brown and quite thick. He seemed close to Anthony's twenty-eight years, perhaps a year or two older.

As they approached, his gaze shifted to them, and he quickly dabbed a handkerchief at his brow before slipping it into his coat pocket. His lips curved into a welcoming smile.

"Good evening," Lavinia said. "I'm the Marchioness of Northam. I hope you don't find me impertinent, but I understand you are newly returned to London and wished to welcome you home. Assuming this is your home?"

"Surrey. And thank you," he said. "I take it you already know I am Silvester Fielding? I returned last week, and this is my first social engagement, so I do appreciate your impertinence." He laughed, a low rumbling sound. "Not that you're impertinent at all. It's actually quite astounding that I had a moment's respite. People seem very…welcoming."

"Allow me to present my dearest friend, Miss Sarah

Colton," Lavinia said, withdrawing her arm from Sarah's. "Her father is the Viscount Colton."

Mr. Fielding bowed first to Lavinia and then to Sarah. "It is my very great pleasure to make both of your acquaintances."

"Good evening, Mr. Fielding," Sarah said, dipping into a curtsey. "Have you been dancing?"

"Guilty, I'm afraid." He lowered his voice. "I had to step over here into the cool air for a moment. One would think I would be accustomed to being overheated after the past three years in India."

"I imagine so," Sarah said. "Did you enjoy India?"

"I did. In fact, I plan to return in a couple of years. Had to come home to take care of some family business. My father is ill."

"I'm so sorry to hear that," Sarah said.

"Thank you. I don't mind sharing that he's quite old— my mother is his third wife. Alas, I have five older sisters and no brothers at all, so it was up to me to return home and oversee matters." He waved his hand. "Listen to me, going on!"

"We came to meet you," Lavinia said. "And we're happy to get to know you. Are you a member at Brooks's? I'll ask my husband to look for you later."

"Boodle's," he said. "Though I may try for a spot at Brooks's."

"Then I shall definitely introduce you to my husband," Lavinia said.

Mr. Fielding turned to Sarah. "I'm feeling much more restored. Would you care to dance the next set?"

"Only if you promise to tell me about India."

He laughed again, and she decided she liked Mr. Fielding. He was far more genuine than most gentlemen she met. "I will tell you about India until you beg me to stop. Or to take you there." His sherry-colored eyes danced with flirtatious merriment.

Lavinia chuckled. "It seems as though you're in excellent hands," she murmured to Sarah. "See you later." She turned and walked away, leaving Sarah to take Mr. Fielding's arm as he guided her to the dance floor.

"I must warn you that my dancing is average at best. I didn't do much of it in my travels."

"My dancing is only slightly above average, so we are well matched."

He laughed again, and they managed to execute themselves well enough. When he wasn't focusing too hard on the steps, he spoke of India, and she could hear his affection for it. While he was charming and witty, she didn't think she could take him seriously as a potential suitor. Not when his future was meant to be in India.

"It sounds like a very nice place to visit," she said as they left the dance floor.

"It is indeed. I may decide to move there, depending on whether I can secure a government appointment."

She glanced toward him. "Is that a possibility?"

He nodded. "It seems to be."

Sarah looked about for Lavinia, but her gaze found Felix instead. He came toward them and offered a bow. "Miss Colton." Then he turned to Mr. Fielding. "I don't believe we've been introduced."

Taking her arm from Mr. Fielding's, Sarah angled herself toward both gentlemen and gestured to Felix. "Allow me to present the Earl of Ware. Felix, this is Mr. Silvester Fielding, newly returned from India."

"Welcome," Felix said. "Have you been gone long?"

"Three years. A bit more than, actually. Pleased to make your acquaintance, my lord." He bowed and discreetly wiped a finger over his dewy temple as he rose.

"He may be interested in joining Brooks's," Sarah said.

Felix looked at Mr. Fielding with interest. "Indeed? I'd be happy to help, if you require it. If you'll pardon us, I have a bit of business to conduct with Miss Colton."

"Of course." Mr. Fielding turned to Sarah with a warm smile. "It was my honor to partner you this evening. I look forward to doing so again in the future."

"Thank you. I do as well."

Sarah put her hand on Felix's arm, and he led her on a circuit of the ballroom.

"A potential suitor?" he asked when they were some distance away.

"Doubtful. He's keen to return to India, perhaps with a government appointment."

Felix lifted a shoulder. "You don't wish to relocate to India?"

"Not particularly."

"It's quite sunny there. Also rainy. Think of the headwear you could design."

She sent him a wry glance. "Speaking of headwear, have you anything to share regarding my shop?"

"Precisely why I wanted to speak with you," Felix said. "Do you mind if we go out onto the terrace?"

"Not at all."

He guided her outside. "I'm not certain you can afford Bond Street, but I did find a small space on Vigo Lane that might work."

Excitement danced through her, and she turned toward him with enthusiasm. "That sounds splendid! When can I see it?"

"I'll need to set an appointment. It will have to be after the races. Which brings me to my next topic." He led her to the edge of the terrace and stopped.

She took her hand from his arm. "Matchmaking."

"You're going to call it that too?"

Sarah laughed softly. "What else should I call it?"

He shook his head. "Call it whatever you like—so long as it remains between us."

She inhaled sharply. "Can you imagine if people learned of this…arrangement? Actually, it would be far worse for you than me, especially if you're successful. You'd have to pick up where the Duke of Seduction left off."

"Quash that thought right now," Felix said. "I am helping *you*, my best friend's sister whom I've known for twenty years. It is like helping my own flesh and blood. I wouldn't dream of doing this for anyone else."

She could see from the determined glint in his gaze that he meant it quite wholeheartedly. "Have you found me a suitor already?"

"I'm not going to find you a suitor," he said. "I'm bringing bachelors into your orbit that you may not otherwise meet."

"I am not the sun," she said.

"You will be to your husband."

She stared at him. "Why, Felix, that's lovely. I do believe Beck is rubbing off on you."

He let out a dark laugh. "Hardly. I just hope you marry someone who values you in every way."

"Thank you." She hoped so too.

"I've scheduled the races for Wednesday and Thursday at Darent Hall."

She frowned. "That's a long drive two days in a row."

"Yes, which is why it's a miniature house party. I will ensure several bachelors are in attendance."

"That's…wonderful. However, I am not sure my mother will allow me to attend—and she won't want to go. She didn't like the races." Sarah rolled her eyes.

"Which is why she isn't invited," Felix said with a

delight that provoked Sarah to laugh. "This is a *private* party. I'm inviting select people in person and swearing them to secrecy."

She held up her right hand. "I solemnly swear to keep it secret. Except I have to tell my mother."

"Yes, you do." He looked out over the garden for a moment. "Tell her Lucy is hosting a short party for her friends, and that you'll be going with Lavinia."

"That could work."

"If not, tell her it's a Bachelor Forum."

Sarah laughed again and couldn't stop for a moment. "You really ought to consider opening such a place."

"It already exists. I believe it's called Almack's," he cracked.

Another giggle escaped Sarah. "You're in rare form tonight, Felix."

"Thank you." He inclined his head. "I think."

"Please invite Mr. Fielding," she said.

Felix arched his brow at her. "I thought you weren't interested in him."

"Not particularly, but he was very charming, and since he's newly back to town, he could do with some engagement."

"You've a generous heart," Felix said.

"No more than you."

He snorted. "Hardly. As I said before, I am helping you and only you. Indeed, you're the only unmarried woman I can suffer."

"Well, now you're just flattering me," she said.

"Always. Shall we go back inside?"

She took his arm. "If we must. You'll let me know when you schedule the appointment to see the shop in Vigo Lane?"

"As soon as I know, you will." He steered her toward

the ballroom, inclining his head at another gentleman who escorted a lady onto the terrace. "And I'll invite Mr. Fielding."

"Thank you. I'm quite looking forward to the party." She turned to look at him. "I assume I can discuss this with Lavinia?"

"Of course. And Anthony. And the Dartfords." He peered down at her. "I trust you to know whom to talk to. There's your mother. Do you want me to take you to her or somewhere else?"

The latter, but she supposed she should talk to her about the party. "To her."

He chuckled. "You sound as if she's wielding an executioner's axe."

"Very droll."

A moment later, he delivered her to the viscountess and then took his leave. Sarah's mother watched him go and clucked her tongue. "I still say he's a fool not to marry you."

"Mother, keep your voice down," Sarah said, though she hadn't spoken loudly. "I don't want to marry him."

Mother gave her a resigned, somewhat disappointed look. "You don't want to marry anybody."

"Not yet." Sarah shook away her annoyance. "There's to be a small party at Darent Hall next Wednesday and Thursday. I'd like to go with Lavinia."

"What sort of party?" She sounded suspicious.

Given her mother's fixation on Sarah finding a husband, she blurted, "The matchmaking kind. Felix has arranged for many bachelors to attend."

"Then I should go with you."

"You don't really need to—Lavinia will chaperone, as will the Countess of Dartford. Furthermore, Anthony will be there."

"No, Anthony will be traveling to Oaklands to oversee the repair to the stables."

He was? "Still, I will be well chaperoned." She didn't want her mother to come—she'd loathe the races and put a damper on the entire event.

"I suppose," her mother said slowly, her eyes narrowing. "I expect you to return to London with a suitor—a titled suitor, if at all possible—by whatever means necessary."

Sarah let her jaw drop momentarily. "Are you suggesting I arrange to be compromised?"

The countess lifted a shoulder and moved her gaze about the ballroom. "Excuse me, dear. I must go speak with Lady Ellensworth." She departed, leaving Sarah to stare after her—and wonder if she'd been serious.

Surely she wasn't. And yet…

Perhaps the shop in Vigo Lane had lodgings large enough for Dolly *and* Sarah, for she began to think that was where she'd end up.

Chapter Four

❦

DARENT HALL WAS a nearly four-hour drive from London. The late-May day was bright and warm—perfect for travel and a race. Not that Felix had traveled from London that morning. He'd arrived the day before along with the racers so that their horses would be rested before today's event.

The guests, however, were arriving today and had begun doing so shortly after noon. The staff at Darent Hall, under the direction of the Dartfords, had everything well in hand with regard to accommodations and the afternoon's activities. There would be a picnic along with the races.

Felix surveyed the picnic area, a grassy space with blankets scattered about. Baskets with food and drink sat in a corner of each large square of fabric awaiting the guests who would arrive shortly.

The racecourse was visible from the picnic. Felix had worked to keep it as close to the shape and length of the one they'd used in London, so as to keep things fair.

He went to the wagering table manned by Kinsley, whom he'd persuaded to come for the event despite his employer being out of town. "I do appreciate you coming out," Felix said.

Kinsley looked up from his ledger. "My pleasure. How can I resist such a fine day?"

Felix's attention was drawn to the first group of guests cresting the hill separating the course from the house. "Here they come."

"Why do you do it?" Kinsley asked, squinting up at

Felix. "The races and other events you host, I mean."

It was a question Felix heard from time to time, and he gave the same nonanswer he always did, "Why not?" The reason he hosted such events was of no interest to anyone, including Felix.

Kinsley laughed. "Why not indeed."

Felix grinned and walked away from the table to greet the guests and invite them to find places on the blankets.

Beck and Lavinia, along with Sarah, were among the first to arrive. "I do love a picnic," Beck said, eyeing his wife. "But where is there a copse of trees?" He glanced about, and Felix stifled a laugh.

Before Beck had married Lavinia, Felix had put on a picnic at which Lavinia had shown everyone ancient rock formations. She was an amateur geologist, and it had been one of Felix's more fascinating events. It had also given Beck and Lavinia occasion to escape into the trees for a tryst.

"Yes, this is an excellent addition," Sarah said. "Where is the wagering table?"

"Right this way," Felix said, offering her his arm.

Sarah put her hand on his sleeve, and he escorted her to where Kinsley sat. Felix waited while she placed her wagers, then guided her back toward the blankets.

"What sort of activities do you have planned for tonight?" Sarah asked.

"After dinner?" At her nod, he continued. "Cards, dancing, perhaps some parlor games."

"Will any of them include kissing? Kiss the Nun, maybe, or Le Baiser à la Capucine."

Felix slowed to a stop. "I hadn't considered that. Do you want to play kissing games?" He watched color bloom in her cheeks, and she glanced away.

"It seems we should since I'm in search of a husband.

I've, er, never kissed anyone."

He stared at her in a mixture of outrage and disbelief. "How is that possible?" She was nearly four and twenty, for God's sake. And she was eminently kissable. Why her lips alone, dark pink and bow shaped, should have beckoned any number of men.

Her blush deepened. "You'd have to ask every man I've ever met." She gave him a pointed stare that seemed to scream, *Including you.*

"Then there will be kissing games."

"Thank you." Her shoulders relaxed a bit, and he realized that had taken a bit of courage for her to ask.

"Is there anything else I can do for you?" Felix asked softly. "Anything at all?"

She thought for a moment, then shook her head. "No, I think that will suffice for now. Oh, Anthony won't be coming, I'm afraid. He had to go to Oaklands to oversee something."

Felix was surprised Anthony hadn't mentioned it. "Did this just come up?"

"I don't think so. Mother told me as soon as I informed her of the party." Sarah exhaled. "Well, I'm going to find a place to sit." She went toward the blankets and joined Beck and Lavinia.

Shame that Anthony wouldn't be here, especially since there was now going to be a plethora of kissing games. Felix could think of several, including the ones she'd mentioned, and maybe he'd come up with one of his own… He'd done it before. His mind conjured a series of potential ideas…

"A picnic, eh?"

Felix, startled from his reverie, blinked at the sound of Anthony's voice. "You're here."

Anthony looked around. "Should I be somewhere

else?"

"Oaklands, apparently. Sarah said you had to go and look after something."

Anthony waved his hand. "It will wait. I wasn't going to miss this event."

"That can't have pleased your father." Felix knew the viscount was always trying to get Anthony to take a more active role in managing their estate. Anthony wasn't a slouch compared to some other gentlemen they knew, but he loved his life in London and didn't like to miss a thing.

"No. Between his anger at me and my mother's desperation about Sarah, they were both in a fit."

Felix glanced toward Sarah, the skirt of her coral-colored dress spread across the corner of the gray blanket. "Desperation?"

"She made it clear that Sarah had better return from this party with a suitor."

"And if she doesn't?" Felix asked. He knew the Coltons well, but really had no idea what they would do if Sarah didn't marry. Why did they care so bloody much? Wasn't it enough to ensure she was happy? The millinery shop would do that, not a husband.

Anthony shrugged. "They claim they'll arrange a marriage, but I don't know if they will. They've threatened that before. Granted, there is an interested party."

"Is there?" Felix would have invited him here if he'd known. "Who? I can send a message to London and get him here by tomorrow."

Anthony stared at him for a moment. "You've taken this matchmaking role quite seriously."

"Does everyone need to call it that?" Felix muttered.

"You can't send him a message in London. Allencourt lives in Epping. And he wouldn't ever come to a party like this. He's nearly my father's age, has already been married twice, and has three daughters, one of whom is older than me."

"Age is just a number. As are daughters and marriages."

"Says a man who has none of the latter two." Anthony chuckled. "Allencourt also despises London and spends most of his time in Epping. He is the magistrate for the surrounding area and takes his duties quite seriously. I have to think Sarah wouldn't get to spend much time in town."

Felix didn't think she'd like that. She had friends and enjoyed social engagements. Furthermore, where could she show off her hats in Epping?

"Sounds as if we need to find her a husband, not just a suitor."

"We?" Anthony barked out a sharp laugh. "That's your cross to bear." He clapped his hand on Felix's shoulder.

"Fine, just don't be angry when I launch a set of kissing games during the party."

"Why in the devil would you do that?" Anthony sounded a trifle horrified.

"As if you've never played them," Felix scoffed. "Why do you think? Your sister shouldn't choose a suitor without seeing if they're worth a damn sexually."

"First of all, a kiss tells you next to nothing about a person *sexually*. Second, I do not want to discuss my sister in this way." He looked as if he'd eaten a bad pudding.

Felix gave him a wry look. "If you think a kiss tells you nothing about a person's sexual nature or abilities, you haven't been doing it right."

"I said next to nothing," Anthony said, rolling his eyes. "Can we please talk about something else?"

Felix smiled as he suppressed a laugh. "It's nearly time for me to get the races started anyway." He turned and scanned the picnic area for Dartford. Seeing him standing near a blanket several yards away, Felix started toward the earl.

Dart made eye contact and met him halfway. "Ready?"

"I was just going to make the announcement."

"I'll help usher people toward the starting area," Dart said. "My grooms are tending to the vehicles and horses."

In truth, it was a better situation than the park—they had staff, a larger platform for Felix and the spectators built by Dartford's retainers, and, of course, a picnic. Felix climbed onto the platform, and a footman handed him the horn to amplify his voice. "Thank you," Felix said before lifting the horn to his mouth. "Welcome to the exciting conclusion of our races! First up is the men's heat, followed by the exciting women's final race!"

Felix waited for the applause to diminish before continuing. "Drivers, report to your vehicles. We will begin shortly. I invite spectators to watch from the picnic area, or if you'd like to join me on the platform, please do so."

Several guests, mostly gentlemen, joined him on the platform. He noted that Sarah remained in the picnic area along with Beck and Lavinia. And Mr. Fielding. He'd joined them and now sat beside Sarah. They seemed to be laughing about something. How interesting.

Felix's mind reverted to thinking of kissing games. By God, he'd make sure Sarah received a kiss at this party— even if he had to do it himself.

He froze for a moment. Would he do that? *Of course not.* She was…Sarah.

Shaking his head, Felix focused on the impending race and made another announcement for the drivers to position themselves.

Because the Earl of St. Ives was still out of town, there would be two men's races—one with three vehicles and the other with two. The top two finishers in the three-way, along with the winner of the two-way, would move on to the men's semifinal tomorrow morning, with the top two finishers of that race moving on to the final in the afternoon.

The first race was between Mr. Wakeham and Lord Ponsford. Felix asked the footman for the bell, then called for the race to start before firing it into the air. Ponsford should have won easily, but it was close. In the end, Wakeham beat him by half a length. A gleeful cry from the picnic area drew Felix to turn his head.

Sarah was on her feet with her hands clasped together in front of her chest. Even from this distance, he could see the triumph on her face. She'd wagered on Wakeham, and she'd just made a tidy sum. Well done, her.

She turned toward Fielding, who edged closer and said something next to her ear that provoked her to laugh. Felix frowned. She'd said she wasn't terribly interested in Fielding. Felix hoped he wasn't being a nuisance.

He didn't seem to be, if Sarah's smile was any indication. Felix would keep an eye on the man.

"The next race is set, my lord," the footman said from the ground in front of Felix.

Felix nodded and announced the race would start in a moment.

"So glad you put this together, Ware," Oliver Sherington said. He was one of the bachelors Felix had invited. He didn't frequent many balls or go to Almack's. He was young and possessed a sporting nature. As well as a decent-sized fortune. What he lacked in title, he made up for with investments. Though from what Anthony had said, Felix wasn't sure a title was necessary. It seemed the Coltons simply wanted their daughter *wed*.

"Hear, hear," Sir Rupert Ashburnham said. Another

bachelor, he was actually a widower and a few years older than Felix. He had two small children and was actively seeking a wife. Felix wasn't sure if he and Sarah had met, but Sir Rupert was always exceedingly well-dressed, and Felix wondered if they might find a common interest in fashion.

Good God, he *had* become a matchmaker.

Eager to empty his head of such thoughts, he brought the horn to his lips and told the racers—Dart, Baron Tyrrell, and Mr. Redmond—to prepare. A moment later, he called the start and rang the bell.

Dart took an early lead, which Tyrrell and Redmond couldn't manage to overcome. But the finish between the two of them was incredibly close, with Tyrrell beating Redmond across the line by perhaps a foot. In fact, the two drivers were arguing at the finish line, with Dart trying to keep the peace.

Around Felix, spectators were voicing their opinions. To a one, they declared Tyrrell the winner. Felix lifted the horn and announced, "From the platform, it is clear Tyrrell crossed the line first. He and Dartford will advance to tomorrow morning's semifinal. Redmond, there's a glass of whisky waiting for you in the picnic area."

The last was greeted with cheers, and one of the men around Felix clapped him on the back. Felix called for Lady Dartford and Lady Exeby to ready themselves for the final race of the day.

A palpable excitement settled over the crowd, and nearly everyone in the picnic area moved closer to view the race.

Anthony joined Felix on the platform, cutting through the other gentlemen to stand at his side. "Exciting day! Should be a rousing party later, even without kissing games." He kept his voice low for the last bit.

"Perhaps you should stay upstairs?" Felix suggested.

"I'm just not sure you need them," Anthony said. "Sarah seems quite cozy with Mr. Fielding. He's a rather pleasant fellow. I haven't seen her laugh like that with any gentleman. Save you, but you don't count."

No, he didn't. Felix scanned for Sarah and found her standing near the platform next to Fielding. Perhaps Felix's matchmaking would be over before it even began.

He turned back to the race and announced for the drivers to get ready. "This is the championship!"

"What do they win?" someone yelled.

"The right to brag and the eternal adoration of everyone here. Save perhaps the drivers they defeated on their road to victory." Felix accepted the bell from the footman.

Laughter filled the air, and Felix waited for it to quiet before he shouted, "Ready, drivers. Go!" He sounded the bell, and the vehicles surged forward.

Lady Dartford jumped ahead as they drove toward the first turn. She slowed a bit more than she had in London, and Felix couldn't help but hold his breath. He tried not to pick favorites, but he liked Dart's wife, and they were, after all, hosting the event.

Felix lifted the horn. "Lady Exeby takes the lead as they leave the first turn. Lady Dartford is ducking her head and driving the team a bit faster. There they go, gaining on Lady Exeby."

Lady Exeby led into the second turn, but she was perhaps the most cautious driver in the entire field when it came to corners. Lady Dartford did not make the same mistake twice. In fact, she went into the turn at a rather intense speed, and there were gasps as one of her wheels lifted from the ground. Felix heard someone murmur,

"Mrs. Childers," and could feel the tension in the air.

But she rounded the turn without incident and drove into the lead. She didn't look back as she thundered toward the finish, easily beating Lady Exeby.

The crowd rushed toward the finish line as Dart swept his wife from the phaeton and swung her around before setting her on the ground to greet the well-wishers. Felix handed the horn to the footman and thanked him for his assistance.

At the finish line, Dart's retainers poured ale and wine, and the revelry lasted for some time. When the crowd finally thinned, Felix saw Sarah standing with Beck and Lavinia and decided to join them for the walk back to the house.

"What an exciting day!" Lavinia said. "Well done, Felix."

He inclined his head with a small smile. "Thank you. But the excitement was due to the talented drivers."

"Yes, but there would be no race if not for you," Beck pointed out. "People are already talking about next year's matches, and we aren't even finished with this year's."

Felix still wasn't sure he would continue them.

"Felix may be too bored to repeat them," Sarah said, sending him a teasing smile.

He laughed and offered her his arm. "You know me too well."

She placed her hand on his sleeve, and they all started back toward the house. Sarah walked slowly, allowing Beck and Lavinia to precede them. Felix took the hint and followed her pace, assuming she wanted to speak with him about their objective of finding a suitor.

"What do you have in store for this evening?" she asked him.

He noted the faint color in her cheeks. "In terms of the

kissing games, you mean?"

"I've begun my, er, assessment."

Felix turned his head toward her. "You kissed someone?"

She nodded, the pink still highlighting her cheeks. "Mr. Fielding."

"I see." Felix was surprised, but he shouldn't have been. They'd looked rather cozy together all afternoon. "I hope you were covert about it."

She peered at him sideways. "Did you see it?"

"No, but that doesn't mean someone else didn't."

"We were *very* surreptitious. It wasn't difficult— everyone was focused on celebrating."

That much was true. It seemed Fielding knew how to take advantage of a situation. Felix hoped he hadn't done the same of Sarah. "You were amenable to his advance?"

"Who said it was his advance?"

A sound that was part laugh and part gasp leapt from Felix's lips. "You're incredibly saucy."

"Thank you. I'm trying to be." She flashed him a small smile. "In the hope that it will make me more attractive."

"I think you've always been this saucy. You've just been hiding it. Be yourself." The recommendation burned the back of his mind where he hid all his own secrets and fears. Just because he gave advice didn't mean *he* had to follow it.

They were nearing the house, and Lavinia seemed to notice that Sarah and Felix had fallen back. She looked over her shoulder at them and slowed.

Felix rushed to ask, "And how was it? Is Fielding still a possibility, or should we focus our energies elsewhere?"

"Oh, he's still on the list. But I should like to compare." She winced and shot him a slightly pained look. "Is that bad?"

He laughed. "Not to me, but again, you must be covert."

"Or disguise my objectives with a kissing game." She gave him a faux look of innocence that made him laugh again.

"We'll play Kiss the Four Corners. That will give you another four *observations.*"

"Brilliant." .

Lavinia and Beck waited near the door, and Sarah and Felix were nearly upon them. Sarah stopped several feet away and took her arm from Felix's. "Thank you. I really do appreciate your help and support."

Then she turned and went to join Beck and Lavinia before the trio headed inside. Felix watched her go and wondered at the odd sensation in his gut. He felt a bit...unsettled. *Because you're playing matchmaker,* his mind reasoned.

Or maybe because things better left forgotten were nearly stirred to the surface.

Either way, he shrugged the feeling away. It was time to plan the specifics for this evening.

⊷℈⊶

THE FOLLOWING AFTERNOON was not as bright and warm as the morning had been, and certainly not as glorious as the day before. It was still quite pleasant, however, and no one cared about the clouds moving in when they were too excited for the final race to begin.

The morning semifinal had been another three-way contest between Dartford, Wakeham, and Tyrrell. Tyrrell had fallen out of contention rather quickly, but Wakeham had given Dartford a good run. Dartford was the favorite for the final, but no one was completely discounting

Wakeham.

Sarah wasn't at all sure whom to place her wager on. She'd gone to Kinsley's table three times so far, and on each occasion had retreated without taking action.

Lavinia joined her as Sarah contemplated what to do. "I hope you wagered on Dartford."

"I haven't placed one yet." Sarah's stomach twisted into a new knot. Her mind was telling her to bet on Dartford, both for safety and because he was a closer friend than Wakeham. Indeed, she didn't know Wakeham very well at all.

"You really are trying to make money," Lavinia said, cocking her head. "For the future? It seems as though there are several potential suitors here. I don't know how Felix did it, but he managed to recruit an excellent group of gentlemen with charm and wit and whom you haven't really met before." She shook her head in bemusement.

"Felix has a gift." And he truly did. He was able to read people and give them what they wanted. Or maybe what they didn't know they wanted. Several of the gentlemen here were confirmed bachelors, but that hadn't stopped them from flirting with Sarah last night.

"He does indeed," Lavinia murmured. She fixed Sarah with a direct stare. "And is it working? You kissed no fewer than four gentlemen last night."

"Don't forget Fielding yesterday afternoon," Sarah said with a laugh. She'd briefly mentioned all this to her best friend earlier in the day, but they hadn't had a chance to discuss anything in depth.

Lavinia narrowed her eyes slightly. "I want details. Which one was the best kisser?" She shook her head. "No, never mind, how was it to go from kissing no one to kissing five men in one day. Good God, have you become a light skirt?" She asked the question in jest, but kept her voice low and glanced about to ensure no one was listening to their conversation.

"In truth, the kisses last night were very brief and rather perfunctory. I will say that Mr. Lytton smelled the best."

Lavinia laughed. "Your kiss with Fielding was a bit more involved, I take it?"

"A bit." Sarah tamped down the rush of heat flooding her neck when she thought back to the way he'd kissed her. "I'm glad you told me to expect to use my tongue."

"Excellent." Lavinia grinned, looking thoroughly pleased. "I'm glad you enjoyed it."

"I think I did. I mean, I don't really have anything to compare it to, do I?"

"No, but I'm not sure that matters. When the right man kisses you, things just…happen." Her gaze glassed over in a lovesick manner, and Sarah followed her gaze to Beck who stood talking with Anthony several yards distant.

"I will take your word for that." Sarah wasn't sure what had happened with Fielding. Her heart had raced and her insides had…quickened. Perhaps that was what Lavinia meant.

"Do you look forward to kissing him again?" Lavinia asked after shaking herself from her self-inflicted trance.

"I—yes, I think so." She hadn't really considered it, which was maybe her answer. "It was very nice." That much was true. Perhaps she was so overcome by finally being kissed that she hadn't experienced the proper reaction. Yes, another kiss was likely in order. But she'd also like to kiss someone else. Viscount Blakesley, perhaps. He was the most attractive bachelor in attendance, with wavy golden hair and eyes the color of sapphires. He was purportedly uninterested in marriage at the present time, but Sarah thought she might like to kiss him anyway.

Goodness, maybe she *was* a light skirt.

Lavinia swatted an insect away from the vicinity of her head. "What does Felix have planned for tonight?"

"I'm not entirely certain, but I would guess it involves kissing games." Because she'd asked for them. She looked toward the platform and saw him standing in the center, the horn in his hand, ready to announce the race.

"How I wish I could come to your side of the house instead of the boring saloon with cards." Lavinia rolled her eyes.

Sarah laughed. "Is there any reason you can't?"

"I don't know, but I plan to find out. You're my best friend. I'd rather be where you are even if I don't partake in some of the entertainment. I can't imagine *all* the games involve kissing."

They hadn't last night. "You're correct. You should come."

"Now I won't have to die of envy." Lavinia grinned.

"Envy? I'm the one who should be envious." And she was when she watched Lavinia and Beck together. Or the Dartfords. Or Sarah and Lavinia's friends Nick and Violet, the Duke and Duchess of Kilve, who were also here.

Lavinia's gaze softened with empathy, and she touched Sarah's arm. "You're going to fall in love. I just know it. You may already have met him. Or kissed him." Her mouth quirked up in a smile, and Sarah chuckled.

"Maybe. And maybe not. Maybe I'm not meant to fall in love. Plenty of women don't, and plenty of women remain unwed. You were once prepared to become a spinster, and I still am. Hopefully, you will still be my friend." She said this with a lilt of humor. She knew Lavinia would always be her friend.

Lavinia took her hand and squeezed it. "Always."

"I have to tell you something," Sarah said, wincing. "I've been a bit of a bad friend."

Lavinia's dark eyes clouded as she released Sarah. "You could never be a bad friend."

"I've been a bad friend in much the same way you were when you didn't tell me about your and Beck's relationship." Sarah was referring to when Lavinia had learned Beck was the Duke of Seduction and hadn't told Sarah about it—or the fact that she and Beck had become friends and then more than that.

"Well then, you aren't a bad friend at all. You're merely paying me back. What have you been keeping from me?" Her eyes widened. "Does it involve a gentleman here?" She glanced around.

"No," Sarah said with a laugh. "You know how I like to make my own hats from time to time." At Lavinia's nod, she went on. "I've been increasing my purse so that I may open my own millinery shop."

Lavinia's jaw dropped. "You're going into trade?"

"Quieter, please," Sarah whispered as she looked about to see if anyone had heard. It didn't seem so. "I won't work there, and the shop won't have my name on it. Dolly from Marsden's Millinery is going to manage the shop and will execute my designs."

"So you won't claim credit for them?" Sarah shook her head, and Lavinia frowned. "That's a shame. An outrage, really."

"It's not about gaining accolades," Sarah said. "It's about securing my future. And doing something I love." She smiled then, as she always did when she thought of building something of her very own.

"You will have the best millinery shop in the history of millinery shops," Lavinia said, her eyes bright with pride.

"The drivers should prepare to begin," Felix announced

through the horn.

"It's almost time," Sarah said. "I'd better place my wager." She dashed over to the table and blurted the first name that fell from her lips. As she made her way back to Lavinia, she prayed she'd made the right choice.

A moment later, Felix called for the start and clanged the bell. Dartford and Wakeham raced forward, their vehicles all but even as they dashed toward the first turn. Sarah's heart pounded as both drivers took the curve as fast as they dared, faster than they'd seen in any race yet. Both phaetons tipped, and there was a collective gasp followed by exhalations of relief once the eight wheels of the vehicles were back on solid ground and racing toward the second curve.

Wakeham seemed to take this turn just a bit more cautiously, while Dartford pressed even faster. His phaeton teetered again, but he kept masterful control and then drove into the lead as they rounded toward the finish.

"Come on, Dartford!" someone yelled as Wakeham seemed to gain on him as they neared the end. But it was Dartford who finished first, and Sarah finally exhaled fully.

Lavinia laughed. "I take it you wagered on Dartford?"

"I did." Sarah grinned, and they made their way—along with everyone else—toward the finish line.

As with yesterday, there was ale and wine and much revelry for some time. A pair of men hauled Dart up onto their shoulders and paraded him around to the cheers and adoration of everyone present. No one was prouder or more pleased than Lucy, however, as she gazed at her husband with glowing pride—and love.

Sarah caught sight of Felix a few feet away and went to congratulate him on a successful event. "You really will have to do this next year."

"So I keep hearing. It was terribly fun, wasn't it?" he asked with a smile. "Did you win again?"

"I did."

"Did you ever lose?"

She shook her head.

"Perhaps you should join the married couples in the card room tonight," he suggested wryly.

Sarah laughed. "Lavinia asked if she could join us instead."

"Hmm, I'm thinking I should have come up with a game that involves gambling for kisses," he said.

"Why, because I would win them all?"

"Exactly." His eyes glinted with humor. "How is everything going today? I saw you with Mr. Lytton earlier. Is he in the hunt?"

She shrugged. "He smells nice."

"That is your chief requirement?" He waved his hand. "I'm joking. I have a special game organized for tonight. Tell me who you most want to kiss—in private."

Sarah blinked at him. "In private? How are you going to manage that?"

He gave her a devilish grin. "You'll see. It's a variation on Guess the Kisser."

"It sounds rather daring. Will everyone want to play?"

Felix gave her a sardonic look. "You were there last night, weren't you? I think this group is more than eager for a game like this."

He was right. They were a rather audacious company, if last night was any indication.

"You need only tell me who you want to kiss, and I'll make it happen."

"Truly?" Her gaze found the athletic form of Viscount Blakesley.

"I see where you're looking. Blakesley, then?"

She fought back a blush and answered before she could change her mind. "Yes."

"Consider it done."

"Who are you going to kiss?" she asked.

"No one. I have to oversee the game—and Anthony has offered to help me. The men outnumber the women by two, and we'll need exact numbers for this game."

"Well, Lavinia would be glad to help too. Anything to rescue her from the card room. She's envious of our fun."

"Then perhaps she should not have wed," Felix said, waggling his brows. "Perhaps you'll change your mind about marrying too."

Change her mind... As if it were her decision. Her parents would ensure she wed, whether she fell in love or not.

Chapter Five

⟡

AFTER A ROUSING game of charades and several hilarious rounds of the Toilette, most of the guests had accumulated a number of forfeits, which would need to be repaid at some point, typically after the games concluded.

Felix had earned only one forfeit during the Toilette. He'd taken the role of hairbrush and had failed to jump up fast enough when the acting Lady had requested his assistance. Others had fared far worse. Sir Rupert had at least five forfeits from both games.

Everyone seemed to be having a jolly time, and Felix was keen to unveil the game he'd concocted to ensure Sarah would kiss Viscount Blakesley. The former sat on the settee beside Lavinia, their heads bent together as they whispered. The latter stood near a corner with two other gentlemen, glasses of whisky dangling from their fingertips.

Felix softly rang a bell to gain everyone's attention. "And now for the premier game of the evening, a new version of Guess the Kisser."

"The Ware Version!" Mr. Walter Pratt called out, generating laughter and agreement.

Felix bowed. "If you want to call it that. In this version, we will have the same number of gentlemen and ladies. For that reason, I and Mr. Colton will be excused." He looked toward Anthony, who stood nearby with Beck, who, along with his wife, had preferred to join their entertainments this evening, save any kissing games.

"That's a shame," Mrs. Alnwick said, eyeing Felix. She

was the only widow among them and the younger sister of Lady Exeby. She'd been flirting with Felix all night, and he was beginning to consider meeting her for an assignation later.

However, he didn't react or respond to her comment before launching into the explanation of the game. "There are nine young ladies and nine gentlemen. Dartford's footman and I will distribute a slip of folded parchment to each of you who are playing. On that parchment is a number. There are two of each number—one for a lady and one for a gentleman."

"What are the numbers for?" Lord Crawford asked, slurring. Thankfully, he was not drinking whisky like Blakesley and his companions.

"The numbers will tell you which room to go to. My staff will direct you if necessary. Everyone must keep their numbers secret. The gentlemen will go to their rooms where they will be blindfolded and wait in total darkness for their lady to arrive. The ladies will then find the room with their number and step inside. Once the door closes, the couple will have one minute to kiss—or not. A bell will ring to indicate the minute is over, and the ladies will depart. The gentlemen will wait until one of my staff fetches them to return here, where the players will attempt to guess their kisser. If they are correct, they win! If they are incorrect, they will earn a forfeit."

"Oh, this is delightful!" Miss Reynolds said.

"Scandalous," Fielding murmured. "And utterly captivating." He grinned, and those around him chuckled.

"The game will be far more entertaining if you don't cheat—gentlemen, keep your blindfolds on, and ladies, don't try to discern the gentlemen in the dark. You must base your guesses on the kiss alone. And try not to speak. If you must, disguise your voice." He looked around at the assembly. "Are there any questions?"

"What if one minute isn't long enough?" Blakesley asked, eliciting a few titters around the drawing room.

"If you take too long, I'll have the staff interrupt you," Felix said. He hadn't given them that instruction, but he would. "Let us begin." He went to Gerald, who held two trays, one of which he handed to Felix. Felix exchanged a look with the footman, who'd been instructed to give the parchment with the rumpled corner—number nine—to Blakesley. Felix would ensure Sarah got the same number. Everyone else's numbers would be random.

Felix began to distribute the numbers to the ladies, careful to save the one with the rumpled corner for Sarah.

When he reached Mrs. Alnwick, who was seated in a wingback chair, she gave him a catlike smile. "I thought of a question after all. Are all the rooms nearby, or are some *upstairs*?" Since the bedchambers were upstairs, she seemed to be asking if any of the rooms contained beds.

"They are all nearby—a couple are closets used by the staff," he said, handing her the paper.

"How…close." She seemed to purr the words as she opened the paper. "Oh, look, number two," she whispered.

"You're supposed to keep it secret," Felix said, amused at her brazenness.

"And I will. From everyone else." Her lashes fluttered, and her lips curved coyly before he moved on.

"What a deliciously inappropriate game, Felix," Lavinia said as he arrived at the settee she shared with Sarah.

Felix handed the parchment with the rumpled edge to Sarah with a purposeful look. Her eyes widened slightly, and she glanced, ever so briefly, toward Blakesley. Felix allowed his lip to twitch up the barest bit. "Should I have allotted a room for you and Beck?" he asked Lavinia, smiling.

She laughed. "We have one, thank you."

Felix handed out the last slip of parchment and turned to address the room. "Gentlemen, please step out, and the staff will show you to your rooms and blindfold you."

The men shot eager glances toward the ladies before leaving, some of them smoothing their hair or straightening their cravats. The ladies gathered at one end of the room and chattered excitedly about the game.

"How will we ever know?" one of them asked.

"Scent," Sarah said.

"My lord?" Gerald interrupted Felix's eavesdropping.

Felix turned. "Is there a problem?"

"Yes. If you'd come with me?"

Felix followed him out, pausing near Anthony on the way. "I need to see to a problem. Keep the ladies in here for now."

Anthony nodded.

Outside the drawing room, Gerald informed Felix that Crawford had become ill and could no longer take his place in room five.

Felix frowned. "That leaves us one short. I'll just take his place," he said. "I know where it is."

Room five was the smallest, barely more than a closet next to the library. He greeted the footman assigned to the closet before going in. Once inside, the footman blindfolded him. "All right, my lord?"

"Fine, thank you," Felix said. Then he was plunged into darkness, and he waited. Who would it be? It wouldn't be Sarah, of course. Or Mrs. Alnwick. She'd said she had number two. That left one of the Misses Conwyn or Christie, Miss Reynolds, Miss Saunders, or Tyrrell's daughter, Miss Smithson. None of them were particularly remarkable in Felix's mind, though the elder Miss

Conwyn was very attractive, if quiet.

It was several minutes before he heard murmured voices and then a light knock followed by the opening of the door. Experienced as he was, his heart picked up speed. This was a rather scandalous game, he realized. When he'd thought of it, he hadn't imagined playing it himself. He'd thought he'd be the organizer and nothing more. Now he found himself basking in the thrill of secrecy.

Another body joined him in the small space, and the door clicked shut. He recalled what Sarah had said about scent and inhaled deeply. He didn't smell anything.

He felt the brush of skirt against his leg, and then he smelled her—the faint scent of roses, which he could attribute to many women.

She moved, and her hand brushed the front of his pantaloons. His cock jumped at the sensation. They only had one minute, so he might as well make it good.

He felt for her, finding her waist and sliding his arms around her to pull her flush to his chest.

Her soft gasp filled the small space. He moved one hand up her spine and felt her shiver. He searched for—and found—her nape, then cradled her neck to establish where she was. Brushing his thumb over her cheek, he tipped her head to the side and pressed his lips to hers.

He meant it to be a gentle, sweet kiss, but it seemed his partner had other ideas. She splayed one hand against his collarbone and curled the other around his neck, pulling at him as her lips moved over his. And then her tongue slid into his mouth.

His body, already succumbing to arousal, came instantly alive. Rational thought tried to intrude and caution him to go slow or, better yet, stop, but he had one minute to kiss this sweet mouth, and he was going to take it.

He cupped her nape and bent her back slightly as he met her inquiring tongue. She hesitated, but only briefly, before she opened herself to him completely. She pressed against him from breast to groin, and his cock hardened. This was not what he'd intended with this game. He hadn't meant to participate at all, and here he was, eagerly locked in an embrace with what amounted to a stranger.

But, God, it was divine. Her fingers curled into his coat, and she grasped his lapel in her fist while her other hand moved up his neck into the base of his scalp, her fingertips massaging his flesh and tangling in his hair. He held her tight against him, relishing the feel of her body perfectly matched to his. Her breasts were full, her waist slender. He moved his hand lower and felt the curve of her hip and behind. At his touch, she twitched, pressing farther into him.

Lost in her embrace, he drove his tongue into her mouth, kissing her more deeply than he'd ever dreamed he might. This was supposed to be a charming, slightly scandalous endeavor, but this was something far more. This was heat and desire and erotic promise.

The sound of a bell broke into his lustful haze. With great reluctance, he pulled his head up from hers, taking in a deep breath. But he didn't let go, and neither did she.

She dug her fingers into his nape, urging him back down. He barely needed her to ask. Angling his head the other way, he kissed her from a new direction, eager to taste her any and every way he could. It was never going to be enough, but it was all they had.

She met his kiss, their tongues tangling as their hands moved over each other. She put both hands on the sides of his neck, beneath the collar of his shirt, and caressed him with her warm fingers.

He massaged her hip, pulling her against him so that

she had to feel his erection. He shouldn't do it, but she moaned into his mouth, and he was absolutely beyond himself. Desperate to make this moment last, he brought his hand up and grazed his thumb along the underside of her breast. She quivered, and her fingers dug into his flesh.

A loud knock on the door interrupted them once more.

"Time to finish," the muffled voice called through the door.

Felix tore his mouth from hers and forced himself back against the wall behind him. "Go," he grunted, his body aflame.

The door opened, and all the heat in the space seemed to leave with her. Realizing he was out of breath from kissing her, Felix fought to regain control of his body, taking deep breaths to slow his heart and hopefully calm his raging cock.

Bloody hell, that had been far more than he'd bargained for. He whipped the blindfold from his face and cursed the damn thing for adding to his incredible arousal.

Once Felix had himself under control, he exited the closet and handed the blindfold to the footman without a word. He strode back to the drawing room and was a bit surprised to see he was nearly the last one back. Only Blakesley came in behind him.

The ladies were all seated while the men stood. Everyone looked about the room in an almost comically surreptitious manner as they tried to determine whom they'd kissed. Felix did the same but had absolutely no idea.

"Now—" Felix sounded as if he'd ridden through the cold, his voice low and raspy. He gently cleared his throat. "Now, I'll go around and ask you to guess your kisser. You do not have to guess the person who guessed you—

not unless you think they're right."

"It's important to note at this point that Crawford took ill, and Ware had to take his place," Anthony said.

"So one of us kissed Ware?" Mrs. Alnwick asked a bit breathlessly.

Anthony nodded. "Yes."

Mrs. Alnwick smiled broadly, and Felix knew she was going to guess him. She would, of course, be wrong.

"Lady Northam, would you mind continuing to record the forfeits?" Felix asked.

Lavinia smiled and nodded. "Certainly." She went to the table that had been moved to the corner and sat down. She'd written down the names of those who had earned forfeits and marked their subsequent penalties. "Ready whenever you are."

"Remember, everyone, the punishments will be assigned after we reveal the kissers and see who was incorrect."

"What will the forfeits be?" Miss Saunders asked.

"A variety," Felix said. "Those earning penalties will draw from a bowl. There is Living Statues, I believe, as well as Quartet and The Dumb Orator."

Fielding laughed. "Splendid."

Ready to get on with things, mostly because he was anxious to learn his kisser, Felix started at the left side of the room and called the first person. "Mr. Sherington, guess your kisser."

Sherington scrutinized each lady, even moving toward a few to study them more closely, before finally saying, "Miss Elinor Conwyn." That was the younger Miss Conwyn.

All heads turned toward her, and she waved her fan in an effort to cool her reddening cheeks.

Felix moved on to the next person and so on until he

reached Sarah on the settee. She took a moment to survey the room, but not as long as anyone else had done. "Viscount Blakesley."

The viscount gave her a wicked stare, and Anthony let out a very low growl that likely only Felix and Beck could hear. Felix shot him a quelling glance, and Anthony frowned in response.

Rolling his eyes, Felix went back to asking the rest of the guests to guess their kisser. He went last and decided to choose the only lady who hadn't been chosen—the game had turned into an exercise in deduction. "Miss Reynolds," he said, wondering if he was right. And also wondering if there was anything to be done about it, for he would certainly dream of her tonight.

"Now it's time to reveal what number room you were in or went to," Felix said. Everyone seemed to lean forward, and the tension in the room climbed. "Number one. Who was the lady?"

Miss Elinor Conwyn raised her hand. "It was me."

"Damn," Sherington said, and everyone laughed.

"And who was the gentleman?" Felix asked.

"Me." Mr. Winston-Whit waved at Miss Conwyn, who blushed profusely again and worked her fan.

Her sister patted Miss Conwyn's shoulder, and Felix continued. "Who was the lady in room two?" He already knew, of course.

"Me." Mrs. Alnwick batted her lashes at Felix.

"And who was the gentleman?"

"I was," Baron Hardwick responded, causing Mrs. Alnwick's eyes to widen and her lips to form a small, brief pout. She quickly recovered and sent a wave to the baron, who chortled with glee. "I was correct in my guess," he said.

"You were indeed," Felix said. "No forfeit for you."

They continued on with the occupants of room three and four, the latter of which the younger Miss Christie and Mr. Lytton guessed each other correctly. There was much laughter over this as well as a few wagers that they would be wed by fall. Both turned pink, and Felix worried he would actually gain a reputation as a matchmaker. Because of that, he said, "I feel bound to remind you that these assignments were completely random." Almost completely.

And now he was to room five. His heart sped as he anxiously awaited the identity of the woman who'd stolen his equilibrium and probably his sleep for at least tonight. "Who was the lady in room five?"

"Me."

The voice slammed into him, upsetting his composure once more. Felix hadn't been looking at her. Why would he? She was one of two women who could *not* have been in that closet. And yet he knew her voice.

His gaze snapped to Sarah. "It was you?"

"Yes." Her answer was hesitant, almost worried. "Who was the gentleman?" But she seemed to already know as the color drained from her face.

"Me." Felix's answer was flat and completely at odds with the storm crashing inside him. How had this happened? How had he kissed *Sarah*?

He didn't dare look at Anthony. He *couldn't*. He'd thoroughly kissed his best friend's sister, and worse? He'd enjoyed it more than any other kiss in his life.

✦❈✦

SARAH STARED AT Felix in disbelief. She'd kissed him. Twice. And touched him places. And he'd touched her. She thought about what Lavinia had told her about what it felt like to kiss the *right* man.

No, no, no. Not Felix. He was like a brother.

Her gaze strayed to Anthony, who was glaring at Felix in what had to be an exact mirror of her own shock. Well, maybe not exact. Anthony's mouth was pulled tight, and there was a slight narrowing to his eyes. He looked…displeased.

It was all her fault. She'd bumped into Miss Reynolds as they made their way from the drawing room, and they'd both dropped their numbers. Sarah had thought Felix had given her number nine but hadn't been positive. Besides, she couldn't have changed numbers because Miss Reynolds had scooped up her number and gone to the footman to be directed to the correct room. Sarah had briefly worried that she wouldn't kiss Blakesley but decided it didn't really matter.

Only it had.

How was she to know Felix was going to be in a room! He was supposed to be overseeing the activity, not participating in it. He certainly wasn't supposed to be kissing her senseless and making her ache for more.

Sarah stared at her lap as Felix continued with the revelations. He sounded a bit off, as if he couldn't focus on what he was doing. Good. He deserved that.

Wait, was she angry with him? It had been a mistake. A complete and utter accident. Surely they could laugh about it.

Someday. Maybe.

For now, she would try not to think about how much she'd liked it. Or about how she'd left the room and prayed she'd have occasion to kiss that man again.

She never, ever would.

And that was maybe the source of her distress. *Oh, bloody, bloody hell.*

Felix finished with room nine, which was Blakesley and Miss Reynolds. "Lady Northam, who escaped a forfeit this round?" Felix asked.

"Mr. Lytton, Miss Christie, Baron Hardwick, and Miss Smithson," Lavinia answered. Her gaze connected with Sarah, and it was clear she was *quite* interested in talking to her about whom she'd kissed.

"Well done," Felix said.

"Mr. Lytton has escaped forfeiture all evening," Lavinia said.

Lytton's good friend, Baron Hardwick, hooted with laughter and clapped him on the shoulder. "For that, he should get to assign the punishments."

There was a wave of agreement, and Felix motioned for the footman to come forward. He held a bowl, presumably full of the penalties. "I'll leave it to you, then," Felix said to Lytton, taking himself to a corner by himself instead of joining Anthony and Beck. Anthony was still sending him perturbed stares.

Lytton went to where Felix had stood in front of the main doorway and rubbed his hands together, grinning. "This will be terribly fun."

"Be kind!" Blakesley called.

"For that, I will be particularly harsh with you, sir," Lytton said with a humorous glint in his eye. This was greeted with laughter, and Lytton seemed to bask in the attention. He turned toward Lavinia at the table. "Lady Northam, will you mark off the penalties as I assign them?"

"I will."

Lytton drew the first paper and chuckled softly. "I should review the list of forfeits to see who has how many," he said, moving to the table to stand beside Lavinia. The footman followed him. "Feel free to set the bowl down," Lytton directed. The footman did so and retreated to the doorway.

"The first punishment is The Dumb Orator, and it's clearly going to be Blakesley doing the talking," Lytton announced. This was met with guffaws as Blakesley moved to the center of the room. He bowed in grandiose fashion and laughed as he straightened.

"I'll choose Miss Saunders to be his arms."

She bounded from her chair with a giggle and moved to stand behind the viscount, who was considerably taller.

"Fetch him a chair," someone called.

The footman produced a chair, and Blakesley sat. Miss Saunders was visible over his head, but that only made it more humorous. "The two-headed Dumb Orator," Fielding cracked, much to everyone's continued amusement.

Blakesley began an incredibly dull, monotone oration on the color of grass, of all things, while Miss Saunders gestured wildly with her arms. By the time they were finished, everyone was laughing so hard, they were crying.

Except Felix.

Sarah glanced toward the corner, and he was staring at her, his mouth in a tight, unforgiving line. Was he angry with her? Why should he be? Because she'd gone to the wrong room? It was an honest mistake.

"Time for the next penalty," Lytton said, drawing another paper from the bowl. "Oh, this is delightful. Le Baiser à la Capucine. Kiss the Monkey." He looked down at the list in front of Lavinia and then circled the room to survey the guests. "I must choose just the right pair." He stopped in front of Felix, and Sarah's pulse sped.

"Lord Ware," Lytton said. Then he spun on his heel and looked straight at Sarah. "And Miss Colton. Clearly, their meeting in room five was unexpected."

Clearly. Because they'd both reacted with utter shock. Oh, this was bad, bad, bad. She didn't dare look at Anthony. Would he try to stop it?

She also ignored Lavinia. Sarah didn't want encouragement or laughter or horror or anything but for this to be over as quickly as possible. Yes, she'd wanted to kiss the man in room five again. But to learn it was Felix and to have to kiss him again in front of so many people was absolutely horrifying.

Sarah stood, her legs quivering. She prayed no one would notice. Felix moved toward the center of the room. Their eyes connected, and she tried to read something—anything—in the depths of his green eyes. But he was utterly inscrutable.

Forcing herself to take a deep breath, she tried to wipe all emotion from her face. She knelt on the floor.

"Do you need a cushion?" Felix asked softly.

"No." She was glad her voice sounded calm.

He knelt with his back to hers, and they both turned their heads toward each other. He was so close... The movement pushed her off-balance, and he twined his arm around hers to grasp her hand, keeping her upright. It was an awkward but also intimate position—their hands clasped, their arms entwined, their backs pressed together, their faces so close, she could see every detail of his dark lashes and the way his green eyes darkened toward the pupil.

Then he closed his eyes, and she did the same. His lips connected with hers, moving softly, gently, so unlike what had happened between them in the dark closet. But for the briefest moment, she was right back there, her body heating with desire.

It was over as quickly as it had begun, and as quickly as it needed to be. Felix pulled his mouth from hers, and she opened her eyes to see him staring intently at her. She caught a flash of something, but it was gone so quickly, she doubted what she'd seen. He went back to being unreadable. She was vaguely aware of people applauding.

He released her hand and unwound his arm from hers, then stood and helped her up. She touched him as fleetingly as possible, too aware of how different it suddenly felt. She'd touched him countless times before, but now it carried a sensual heat that was impossible to ignore.

How were they going to carry on after this?

Sarah again avoided looking at her brother or Lavinia as she made her way back to the settee. She sat stiff-straight as she waited for Lytton to assign the remaining punishments and prayed he wouldn't give her another kissing penalty. Thankfully, she had only one more.

As it happened, Lytton chose her to be one of the Living Statues. Miss Saunders positioned Sarah in a crouching position with her arms wrapped around herself. It was difficult to keep her balance, but fortunately, she was one of the last to be placed and didn't have to hold her statue for long.

During the last set of punishments—a quadrille with eight guests wearing blindfolds and four guests playing the instruments in a quartet—Felix left. Sarah chided herself to stop paying attention to him as Lavinia joined her on the settee.

"I'm so glad to be done with the record keeping," she said. "I never would have agreed had I known what would happen. I've been positively *burning* to come talk to you." She lowered her voice to a soft whisper. "I can't believe you ended up kissing Felix. You had no idea?"

Sarah was torn between wanting to tell Lavinia about the kiss and how she'd felt about it and hoping the floor would open up and swallow her whole. "No."

"I had that impression. It didn't seem Felix knew either."

No, he would have been just as surprised—he'd expected her to be in a room with Blakesley. And even if he *had* known, he presumably wouldn't have kissed or touched her like that. When she thought of the way his tongue had explored her mouth or his hands had caressed her back and neck... She'd best *not* think of it.

"Where did he go?" Lavinia asked, then shrugged. "Anthony looked a bit displeased, didn't he?"

Sarah shot a glance toward her brother. He was still frowning. "Yes," she murmured. "And poor Beck looks bored."

"He is," Lavinia said with a laugh. "He'd rather be writing a poem or creating new music."

"I'm sure he finds the quartet's 'music' rather ghastly." Sarah began to relax in the company of her friend. Maybe it wasn't so bad. Hopefully, they could all behave as if it had never happened.

But then Felix was beside the settee—she hadn't seen him return—and her heart threatened to leap from her chest. *Pretend it had never happened...ha!*

"Sarah, will you come with me?" he asked, offering her his hand.

His demeanor was overtly gentle, his face creased with concern and, truthfully, a bit pale. Curious—and a bit anxious—she put her fingers in his and stood. He kept hold of her, which she found utterly surprising, and led her to Anthony, which she also found shocking.

"Anthony, come out with us."

"Yes," he said sternly, his dark brows dipping over his irritated gaze. He stalked from the room, and Felix and Sarah followed.

The drawing room exited into a sitting room, but Felix didn't stop when Anthony did. "Come with me," he said, and she noted a catch in his voice. What the devil was going on?

"Felix, this isn't necessary," she said, hoping to defuse the tension. "Neither one of us meant for that..." she couldn't bring herself to say kiss, "to happen. And Anthony, you mustn't be angry with Felix. Or me."

"I knew kissing games were a bad idea," Anthony said.

"You were more than happy to participate last night," Sarah said wryly.

Felix led them into the library. Once they were inside, he turned and closed the door. He looked at Sarah with grave concern. "This isn't about us kissing. A note was just delivered. Dartford thought it best that I read it first and then tell you the news. I agreed that it might be easier—"

"What's wrong?" Anthony's voice was flat and completely at odds with the fire in his blue eyes.

"There's been a—" Felix ran his hand through his hair. "Hell, there is no good way to say this. Maybe you should just read it." He thrust the paper, which Sarah hadn't even realized he'd been holding, toward Anthony.

"Tell me," she said, her heart racing for an altogether different reason than it had been earlier. Fear laced through her, chilling her body.

"Your parents are dead." Felix came toward her, his gaze warm with compassion. "I'm so sorry, Sarah. They were on their way to Oaklands, and there was trouble."

"*Trouble?* Fucking highwaymen," Anthony growled. He crumpled the paper and threw it. Then he looked about the room wildly before striding toward the wall.

Sarah didn't pay attention to what he was doing. She could only stare at Felix—and he at her. He reached for her, and she clasped his forearms to steady herself since her legs had begun to shake. "They're dead?"

"Killed," Anthony said from across the room against the sound of clinking glass. "Bloody killed." His voice broke, and Sarah turned from Felix, rushing to her brother, who stood with his hands braced on the sideboard and his head bent.

She gently touched his shoulder, and he turned and wrapped her in his arms.

They gave in to the crushing grief, sobbing, knowing nothing would ever be the same.

Chapter Six

❧·℈·❧

"TIME FOR A walk!" Felix called as he entered the drawing room at the Coltons' London town house. Every day for the past twenty-four days, he'd come here and done his best to cheer Anthony and Sarah, and every day, he left feeling helpless.

Anthony was racked with guilt since he was the one who was supposed to travel to Oaklands. Instead, he'd delayed the trip so he could attend Felix's frivolous party. His anger toward Felix had been white-hot at first, which Felix had been more than willing to endure. It was the least he could do.

Sarah, on the other hand, had withdrawn. Lavinia had visited just about every day, but she'd left feeling as dejected as Felix. And now she was gone, having traveled to Suffolk for their friend Fanny's wedding to the Earl of St. Ives.

Today, Sarah sat near the windows that overlooked the street below. She glanced over at Felix as he entered and offered him a wan smile. "Good afternoon."

She'd grown a bit thin, and her eyes lacked their familiar sparkle. He tried, with every visit—at least every visit when he saw her—to make her smile. Sometimes he succeeded, and sometimes he didn't. That she smiled upon his arrival today was an improvement. He took it as encouragement and decided to see if she was ready to talk about the future.

"The space on Vigo Lane is still available," he said, dragging a chair to sit near her in front of the windows. "Would you like to go see it tomorrow?"

She didn't register she'd even heard him. He said her name, and she turned her head toward him. "I've given up on the shop. It was a silly dream anyway."

He hated hearing the sadness in her voice. "It wasn't. Why are you giving up?"

"Why would I need the shop now? There's no one to care that I become a spinster." Her jaw tightened, and she looked back at the window.

"I care. So does Anthony."

She tossed him a skeptical glance. "Are you certain about that? The only thing Anthony seems to care about is a bottle that holds alcohol."

That much was true. Felix had tried to drag him out of the house, but he simply wouldn't budge. Not even for a trip to the Red Door. Not that Felix had been since the party.

Since the Coltons had died.

They'd been like family to him, but he couldn't possibly feel the loss as deeply as Sarah or Anthony.

Felix tried another tack regarding the shop. "What of your assistant? Isn't she expecting to manage the shop?"

"I sent a note to Dolly explaining everything. She understands."

He let his frustration get the better of him. "I'm sure she said she did. What else is she supposed to say?"

"And what am *I* supposed to do, pretend my parents weren't killed and everything is fine?" Her voice rose, and he was glad to see her display emotion.

"No, but you don't have to stop living just because they did."

She stood abruptly, the dark gray skirt of her gown moving against the chair as she took a step toward the window. "It isn't fair. What happened to them."

He rose and moved to stand next to her "No, it isn't.

But they wouldn't want you to stay in this house forever."

"No, they'd want me to marry. So I should do that." She turned to face him, her eyes sad. "Fanny married David yesterday. At least I think it was yesterday."

"You should have gone." Felix had tried to talk her and Anthony into attending the wedding, but they'd refused.

"I'm in mourning."

He wanted to say, *fuck mourning*. When his father had died, he'd been thirteen. His uncle hadn't forced him to mourn, and Felix hadn't wanted to. But then, he'd felt relieved to finally be free of his father's oppressive despair. That was, he realized, probably why he was becoming so infuriated with Sarah and Anthony. If you couldn't let the dead go, you were no better off than they were.

"That doesn't mean you can't enjoy life. Honor your parents by being happy, by finding joy." That was the only thing that had kept Felix from taking after his father.

"I'm not sure I know how to do that right now." Her gaze found his, and he saw the tears welling in her eyes.

Felix took her in his arms and held her against his chest. She didn't cry, though, not beyond a few sniffs. She was content to rest upon him, though, and he was content to have her there.

"I know this will get better," she said softly. "It has to, doesn't it?"

"Yes."

"Did you feel like this when your father died?"

He tensed but forced himself to exhale and relax. "It was a very different situation. My father was…ill. When he died, it was a relief."

She pulled her head back from his chest and looked up at him. "It was?"

Her surprise reminded him that he'd never told anyone

that before. "As I said, he was ill, suffering. I was relieved to see him free of pain." That much was true. Felix remembered a disconsolate man, one who tried to engage with his son but eventually gave up on that too, as he had with everything else.

"I vaguely remember your father," she said. "I think I only met him three or four times."

That was probably about right. "You were young."

She laid her head back on his chest. "The only thing I recall about him was that he went fishing with us in the pond. Well, I wasn't allowed to fish."

"You weren't?" Felix didn't remember that. He did, however, remember his father swilling brandy all afternoon.

She shook her head against him. "My mother forbade it. She said it wasn't proper for a young lady."

"Neither was climbing trees, but I remember you doing that," Felix said.

"She would have been horrified." Sarah took a deep, shuddering breath, as if she were trying to keep her emotions in check. "I disappointed her."

Felix clasped her upper arms and held her while he looked into her eyes. "No, you did not. You are a wonderful young lady any parent would be proud of. Your mother had expectations that didn't fit you. You can't think she loved you any less because you weren't yet married."

And yet *he* could think so. He knew his father barely loved him, and his uncle had drilled into his head that love was a useless emotion, so what did it matter. But he knew it mattered to her.

"No. I know she loved me. I just wish… I wish they weren't gone."

Felix had spent much of his childhood wishing things

were different, but you couldn't change reality. And this was their new reality. They needed to find a way to live in it. Fortunately, he was a master at that.

He gave her shoulders a quick stroke, then stepped back from her. "Pack your things. We're leaving London."

She stared at him. "To go where? Why?"

"We're going to Stag's Court. You need a change of scenery, and London will soon be too stifling to stay."

"That is certainly true. But I can't go to Stag's Court with you. Not alone." She glanced briefly at his mouth before diverting her gaze to the window once more.

In all the days since they'd left Darent Hall, they'd never discussed the kiss. Kisses. It was as if they had never happened, which he'd decided was for the best. Especially given what had happened to her parents. He'd wanted to be there for her and Anthony as a friend and support, and awkwardness over what had happened during Guess the Kisser would have killed that effort.

Felix had, at first, wondered if it was part of the problem—why she'd withdrawn from him. However, after speaking with the staff at the town house, he'd learned she was like that with everyone.

"We won't be alone," Felix said, addressing her concern. "Anthony is coming with us."

Her brows briefly arched up in surprise. "He is? When did he agree to that?"

"He hasn't yet, but I won't give him a choice. I'll pour him into the coach if I have to." Pour was the best verb to describe it since Felix was fairly certain Anthony was trying to drink his body weight in wine, brandy, whisky— whatever he could find—every day.

"He won't come," she said softly.

"He will. Trust me, Sarah." Felix straightened. "We'll

leave tomorrow morning. I'll be here at eight."

"So early?"

Felix started toward the doorway. "Eight!" He climbed the stairs to the second floor and turned left to Anthony's bedchamber in the front corner. Though it was afternoon, Felix was confident he'd find him there.

Sure enough, the room was dark, and it smelled of stale alcohol. Felix went to the window and opened the drapes. Light spilled over the dark interior, setting dust motes swirling and making the air sparkle with their flight.

"What the bloody hell?" Anthony muttered from the bed.

"Perhaps you should draw your bed curtains next time," Felix offered unhelpfully.

"Perhaps you should stay out of my damn bedchamber," Anthony grumbled.

"Gladly, but it seems to be the only way to reach you of late." Instead of spending less time abed, he seemed to be spending more—according to his valet, whom Felix had interrogated a few days ago.

"Then don't reach me. Go away." He rolled to his side, presenting his back to Felix and the window, and pulled the covers over his head.

"No. It's time you got out of here."

"I do. I go downstairs to the library every night."

Not quite *every* night, but Felix didn't correct him. "Out of London. We're going to the country."

Anthony sat up and glared at him. "I'm not going to Oaklands."

Felix had suggested that last week, which had sent Anthony into a spiral of guilt and self-loathing. That had likely sparked his current penchant for sleeping. When one was asleep, one couldn't be tortured by one's conscious thoughts. "We're going to Stag's Court. We will ride and fish and get into trouble."

Anthony shook his head and winced.

"We'll also dry you out," Felix said. He wasn't going to let Anthony drown himself in liquor as Felix's father had done.

"I can't go. Sarah—"

"Is going, so you see, you *must* go. It wouldn't be proper for us to go alone."

Anthony's heated gaze found his. "Don't think you're going to take advantage of her again."

"Is that what you think happened at Darent Hall? It was a bloody mistake, Anthony. She dropped her assigned number along with Miss Reynolds, and they picked up the wrong ones. Sarah was supposed to meet Blakesley." Lavinia had explained what happened to Felix a few days afterward when they'd encountered each other at the Coltons' town house in their efforts to console Sarah and Anthony. And Miss Reynolds had explained it to Lavinia right after Felix had left the room with Sarah and Anthony. Miss Reynolds had been distressed since it seemed there was a problem between Felix and Sarah, which, of course, had not been the reason for their departure at all. "Believe me when I say that no one was more horrified by the mistake than I was." Or perhaps Sarah.

"You took longer to return to the drawing room than nearly everyone else," Anthony said. "And when I learned you'd kissed...*my sister*, I realized she was the last woman to return." He glowered at Felix again. "So you must have been enjoying yourselves."

Felix most certainly had. And he was fairly confident Sarah had too. If not for the footman interrupting them, he wasn't sure how far they would have taken things. He'd thought of that encounter a hundred times or more, dreamed of it, and in every single instance, he knew he would have taken more if he could.

But he couldn't. Because...Sarah.

"Don't read anything into that," Felix said coolly. "You need to let it go. Sarah and I have. It's as if it never happened."

"Good."

"Why would it anger you so much anyway? Your parents wanted us to marry." Felix realized his error immediately and wished he could take the words back. "Forget I said that. I'd be angry too if my best friend was kissing my sister."

"My parents would have wanted Sarah to marry an oak tree. They hated that she wasn't wed already, and they hated that I wasn't ready to wed either. They were fucking obsessed." His lip curled. He was angry with them. Felix understood that—he'd been angry with his father for a long time.

Felix hadn't known they were that upset about Anthony not marrying yet. He knew they'd wanted him to and hoped it would be soon, but they'd seemed to direct all their efforts and desperation toward Sarah.

Silence reigned for a moment before Anthony exhaled in resignation. "Sarah wants to go?"

Felix had no idea and didn't care—they were going. "Yes. We're going to have a splendid time. You'll see. It's just what you both need."

Anthony looked up at him with the most honest—and painful—expression Felix had seen from him yet, and it pulled at his chest. "If anyone can bring us cheer—it's you."

That was precisely what Felix meant to do.

◆❧◆

THE AIR WAS fresher, the weather beautiful, the accommodations more than comfortable, but Sarah still felt hollow. *You just got here,* she reminded herself. *In time, you'll feel better.*

Her maid and the housekeeper and the butler in London had all been telling her this for weeks. As had Lavinia before she'd gone to Fanny's wedding. Time, however, had only made her feel more empty and disillusioned. She kept trying to make sense of what had happened to their parents, where there simply wasn't sense to be made.

Her maid finished dressing Sarah's hair, and after thanking her, Sarah made her way downstairs. The butler at Stag's Court, a middle-aged fellow by the name of Seales, with a balding pate and dark hair on the sides of his head, directed her to the breakfast room. With tall windows that overlooked the lawn sloping from the east side of the manor, it was a bright and cheerful place to start the day. Or it would be if she felt remotely bright or cheerful.

"May I prepare you a plate?" a footman offered.

"I'll just have toast," she said. "Not too dark, if you don't mind."

The footman nodded and then suggested a cup of chocolate.

"I can't refuse that," Sarah said, dredging up a small smile that was surprisingly not as difficult to summon as it had been of late. But then chocolate was worth a smile at least.

He poured a cup of chocolate and set it on the table, then left the room, presumably to have the toast made. Sarah walked to the windows and looked out over the lawn. She'd never been to Stag's Court before. When they'd arrived last night, Felix had said his grandfather had added a wing to the back of the Palladian-style house, but that the rest had been built in the late seventeenth century. It was larger and grander than Oaklands, her childhood home, which was a mere ten miles away.

It was about the same distance from London as Stag's Court, and yet it seemed much farther away. Or maybe that was just because Sarah wanted it to be. The thought of taking the road her parents had taken, of seeing where they'd died, filled her with dread.

The threat of tears pricked the back of her eyes and made her throat raw. She turned from the window and saw Anthony walking into the breakfast room. She blinked at him in surprise, unable to remember the last time she'd seen him before noon, yesterday's early departure notwithstanding. Granted, it was only a half hour before that time.

He was impeccably dressed and shaven, his hair neatly tamed. But he was a bit thin and pale, his eyes listless. He looked like she felt. And probably how she looked as well. In truth, she'd spent very little time contemplating her appearance over the past several weeks.

"Good morning," she said.

"Good morning." He went to the sideboard where the chocolate pot sat and picked it up.

"That's chocolate," Sarah said. "I think the other one is coffee, but I could be wrong." She knew Felix liked coffee.

"No tea?" Anthony asked.

"The footman will bring some." Or she'd get it herself. She was just pleased to see her brother drinking something other than ale. It seemed coming to the country had been precisely what he needed.

"Is there food?" Anthony asked.

"Somewhere." Sarah had noted it wasn't on the sideboard, but then they hadn't set a time to dine. "The footman offered me a plate."

Just then, the footman came in with a tray. He lifted the cover and set it on the sideboard, revealing Sarah's toast as well as butter and jam, which he situated on the table.

Sarah went to her seat, and the footman held her chair. "Thank you."

Anthony took the seat beside Sarah at the small rectangular table. "Is there more than toast?"

"Eggs, ham, kippers, and rolls, my lord," the footman said.

His use of "my lord" pulled at Sarah's chest. The first time their butler in London had called Anthony "my lord," Anthony had yelled at him to stop. He'd tried again last week, and Anthony had merely glowered. Today, Anthony's mouth twisted into a frown, but he said nothing.

"Shall I make you a plate?" the footman asked.

"Yes," Anthony murmured. He cleared his throat and said, "Thank you," with more volume and clarity.

"Please bring some tea for him as well," Sarah said.

The footman nodded and left again.

Sarah buttered her toast and wondered if she and Anthony would ever return to the way they'd been.

"Do you suppose we'll ever feel happy again?" Anthony asked, as if he'd read her mind.

"We must," Sarah said, moving to slather strawberry jam on her lightly toasted bread. "I can't imagine a lifetime of feeling like this." She wasn't even sure how she'd describe the way she felt. Sad, certainly. But also angry and…lost.

"You seemed tense on the journey yesterday," he said. "I should have said something. Or done something."

"You were tense too." She'd noticed but, like him, apparently, had been too wrapped up in her own emotions to help. "We're a pair, aren't we?"

He blew out a breath and leaned his head back to look at the ceiling for a moment. "Disaster," he said quietly. He lowered his head and looked at her. "I couldn't stop thinking of them on their way to Oaklands." His voice was low and dark. Ravaged.

"Me too," she whispered. Her mind had conjured all manner of horrific images, of her parents begging to be spared. Of the Oaklands staff finding them after they'd failed to arrive.

"I know I have to go there, but I just can't." His head drooped. "Not yet."

She understood. Reaching toward him, she offered him her hand. He took it and squeezed. She was remarkably dry-eyed and yet full of emotion.

He let go of her hand as the footman returned with a second tray bearing Anthony's covered plate and a tea service. He placed everything in front of Anthony and offered to pour the tea, which Anthony accepted.

When the footman made to stay, Anthony politely asked him to leave them alone, which he did with alacrity.

Anthony stared at his plate. "I'm a coward."

Sarah froze in chewing her toast and then had to take a sip of chocolate to wash it down. She turned to him. "Why would you say that?"

"Because I've been hiding. Because I couldn't go to Oaklands. Because I still don't want to. Because it should have been *me* who died."

"None of that makes you a coward," she said fiercely. "Father and Mother would have gladly gone in your place if they'd known what awaited them." Sarah might have grown frustrated with them in recent months, but she'd never doubted their love for her or Anthony.

"I want to kill them," he said softly, with a deadly menace that made Sarah's neck prickle. "The men who killed our parents."

Alarm sparked in her chest. "You aren't going to look for them? You'd be mad to do so—the magistrate hasn't found them yet."

"And probably won't," Anthony said.

"Well, I would prefer you were a coward and didn't look for them yourself," she said with heat. "I won't lose you too." That he would even put himself in danger fed her anger.

He exhaled. "I won't go looking for them." He didn't look at her, and she wasn't entirely sure she believed him.

He picked at his food, eating more of it than she'd seen him do since their parents' death, which wasn't hard to do. Meanwhile, Sarah nibbled at her toast and drank her chocolate.

Felix came in then, and it was as if the sun had shone directly into the room. He was a whirlwind of energy and light, she realized. Well, she'd always known that, really. But in her current state, she was perhaps aware of him in a way she'd never been.

Or maybe it was because of the kiss.

She averted her gaze to her plate. Where had *that* come from? She hadn't thought of that in weeks. And it would probably be best if she didn't think of it at all, ever.

"We're going for a ride this afternoon," Felix said, depositing himself in the chair at the head of the table next to Sarah.

Anthony inclined his head toward Felix. "Good."

Felix's eyes widened. "No argument? I was prepared to do battle." He picked up his napkin as the footman came in.

"Would you care for anything, my lord?"

Felix looked toward Sarah's plate and frowned. "Tell me you ate more than toast?"

"All right. I ate more than toast."

He rolled his eyes at her and looked up at the footman. "Bring a basket of Cook's rolls." He glanced at Anthony's food. "I see Anthony was smart enough to at least try one."

The footman left, and Felix continued, "You're both wasting away. We're having a massive feast this evening, and I won't let either of you leave until I'm satisfied your clothing is too tight."

"That sounds rather uncomfortable," Sarah murmured. She appreciated his concern. And his humor.

Felix turned toward them, his gaze turning more serious. "I'm so glad you're both here. We're going to have a marvelous time."

"I'm still a bit surprised you brought us here," Anthony said. "You never invite me here."

"Not *never*."

"*Seldom*, then," Anthony corrected.

The footman returned and deposited a basket on the table. Felix reached for a roll. "True."

"Why is that?" Sarah asked. She understood why Felix never would have invited her, but Anthony?

Felix shrugged. "No reason."

She studied him, wondering why she didn't believe that. "Thank you for inviting us now."

He gave her a warm smile. "I suppose I was just waiting for the right time."

Something inside her loosened. It was only for a moment, but she felt a brief sense of contentment and maybe even a spark of something she hadn't felt in weeks: hope.

Chapter Seven

WHAT HAD STARTED as a lovely ride across the estate had been utterly ruined when Felix had encountered his uncle. He knew he'd have to see the man, but on his first day in residence? And now Uncle Martin, his son, and—even more unfortunately—Felix's aunt were coming for dinner.

Felix wished he could have come down with an ague.

Instead, he found himself trudging to dinner as if he were heading to be drawn and quartered. Upon consideration, that might have been preferable. Spending time with his aunt and uncle was nothing short of torture. He could only hope they would be on their best behavior for Sarah and Anthony.

And if they weren't, well, then Sarah would have her answer as to why he rarely invited people to Stag's Court. The only reason he'd done it this time was because they'd *had* to leave London, and because taking them to Oaklands hadn't been an option.

Anthony arrived in the dining room first. "Is no one here yet?" he asked.

The question didn't require an answer, so Felix didn't give one. Instead, he said, "The faster we eat, the faster they'll leave."

"That's important to you, I gather." Anthony arched a brow in question and, at Felix's bare nod, continued, "Consider it done." He moved closer to Felix and spoke quietly. "You rarely speak of them. I never realized it was because you didn't like them."

"It's not that I don't like them," Felix whispered. However, before he could say more, Uncle Martin, Aunt

Bridget, and their son Michael arrived.

Uncle Martin was shorter than Felix with thick hair so overtaken by silver as to appear several shades lighter than the dark brown he'd sported even five years ago. His eyes were a bit too large for his face, which gave him the impression of intensity and made him look obsessively curious. Michael had inherited those eyes, along with his mother's coffee-colored hair. He was the same height as his father, but sported a more slender build. Felix just then realized that Uncle Martin had been putting on weight over the last few years and was now verging on plump. Aunt Bridget, however, seemed to be defying age. She had hardly any gray hair, and her form was that of a woman who had never had children instead of delivering three. Michael, who was just nineteen, had two older sisters who were already wed.

"Why, Felix, it's been an age," Aunt Bridget said, gliding into the room and offering her cheek to Felix.

He lightly kissed her cool flesh, trying to remember the last time he'd seen her. Last summer, at least. "Good evening, Aunt. I'm glad you could come for dinner." That was a bald lie. While he'd hoped to avoid Uncle Martin, who lived in the dower house, he hadn't expected to see her at all. She spent most of her time in Bath or York with one of her sisters, alternating between the two. Anything to stay away from the husband she despised.

"Yes, it was quite fortunate I was here. I'm only visiting for a few days on my way to York for the rest of the summer. Michael is coming with me."

Felix looked toward his sallow-faced cousin and thought he really ought to invite the poor boy to London. "Now that you're finished at Oxford, you'll come stay with me in London soon."

Michael's eyes lit. "I should love that above all things."

His mother made a clicking sound with her tongue, and Michael shot her an apologetic glance. "Except for going to York. I've been looking forward to this for some time."

Felix didn't believe him for a moment but didn't say anything. He couldn't have even if he'd wanted to because Sarah entered just then, dressed for the evening in a stunning gown of dark purple silk. She wore a cunning feather affixed to a jeweled brooch-type accessory that was pinned into her upswept hair. He'd no doubt she'd designed it. Since learning of her passion for hat making, he found he paid special attention to her headwear.

Or maybe since he'd kissed her, he paid special attention to *her*.

His heart pounded for a moment until he pushed the memory from his mind. He hadn't thought of it in weeks, and he was far better off forgetting about it entirely.

Uncle Martin and Michael had met Sarah and Anthony that afternoon when they'd come across Felix's relatives who had been visiting a tenant. Uncle Martin had managed the estate since Felix's father's death—a role Felix was content to have him continue to fulfill. Aunt Bridget, however, had not met them, so Felix conducted the introduction, hesitating before he referred to Anthony as Viscount Colton. Anthony gave him a subtle nod, and Felix went ahead.

"And this is Miss Sarah Colton," Felix said. "Sarah, this is my Aunt Bridget, Mrs. Martin Havers."

"Pleased to meet you," Aunt Bridget said as she cast a glance toward Felix. "He calls you Sarah?"

"We've known each other a very long time. Almost my entire life, actually."

Felix didn't remember their first meeting. He'd only been eight. He recalled the specific visit to Oaklands because there had been a tree house in which he and

Anthony had spent every possible moment. Other than that, it was a distant memory.

He tried to think of his first memory of Sarah. She was maybe five or six, and she carried a doll. No, two dolls. And they'd both had hats. He smiled to himself.

"That's right." Aunt Bridget looked between Sarah and Anthony. "I forgot you are the friends who live nearby. At Oaklands, is that right? How are your parents?"

"*Bridget.*" Uncle Martin took her by the arm and guided her toward the table. He lowered his head and whispered in her ear.

She sucked in a breath and then swatted him away before glaring at Michael, who rushed forward to help her take her seat.

Felix moved to help Sarah sit, offering the chair beside his. "I'm sorry," he murmured.

"It's fine." She looked at Anthony, whose expression was stoic. He took the seat next to Sarah after she sat down.

With Aunt Bridget across from Anthony and Uncle Martin at the other end of the table, Michael took the only remaining seat to Felix's right. Once they were all situated, a footman poured wine while another served the soup.

"How was your Season?" Aunt Bridget asked. "Full of splendid activities, I'm sure."

"Felix organized a tournament of races," Sarah said.

"What sort of races?" Uncle Martin asked before Aunt Bridget could do so. She'd opened her mouth, but Martin had rushed to speak first. It had always been thus. Felix groaned inwardly and took a long drink of wine.

"Phaetons, mostly," Sarah answered. "It was very exciting."

"I always wanted a phaeton," Aunt Bridget said with an

overly sweet smile. "But my husband says they're frivolous, despite the fact that we could well afford one."

"You've no idea what we can afford," Uncle Martin scoffed. "Besides, you spend more than your allowance as it is."

Were they not even going to try to be pleasant in front of guests?

Felix sought to rein in the conversation. "Uncle Martin, what is new on the estate?"

He blinked at Felix. "Haven't you been reading your monthly reports?"

Oh, for God's sake, of course he had. Just because he allowed his uncle to oversee an estate that Michael would one day inherit didn't mean Felix was oblivious. But since he wasn't Martin, he didn't say that out loud. Instead, he stretched a smile across his lips. "Promptly. I was merely trying to make *pleasant* conversation."

Aunt Bridget made that disapproving click with her tongue again. "Really, Martin. You're so quick to think the most negative thing you possibly can."

Uncle Martin sent her a fuming glower as he sipped his wine.

Felix chanced a look at Sarah and Anthony, who were both almost comically interested in their soup. If nothing else, this disaster of a meal would maybe at least push their own troubles to the recesses of their mind. For that reason alone, Felix would suffer through the evening. Lord knew he preferred to toss his aunt and uncle out. Not that he ever had. No, he always suffered through their sniping and mutual disgust. He looked toward Michael, who seemed as if he wasn't even aware of their behavior. He was, probably, immune.

"I would have liked to see the races," Michael said a bit wistfully.

"He may organize them again next year," Sarah said. "They were quite popular. He even had a tournament for women."

"How wonderful!" Aunt Bridget exclaimed at the precise moment Uncle Martin said, "How horrid!"

Aunt Bridget threw him an acidic stare. "Women racing is perfectly acceptable."

"If they're loose," Uncle Martin grumbled.

Felix resisted the urge to tell him that some of their women friends had raced. Sarah, however, did not. "My dear friend the Marchioness of Northam raced her new vehicle. And my friend the Countess of Dartford won. It was exhilarating."

"Do you race?" Aunt Bridget asked, her eyes sparkling before she briefly narrowed them toward her husband.

Felix downed the rest of his wine, and the footman quickly refilled his glass before moving to do the same for Anthony.

"I don't," Sarah said. "I like to ride, but driving fast is not something I aspire to do. I did wager on the races, though, and that was quite diverting."

"Oh, splendid!" Aunt Bridget said as she dipped her spoon into her soup. "I may want to attend these races too." She turned to Felix and suggested he organize a tournament in Bath.

Uncle Martin rolled his eyes at her. "You don't have enough money to wager."

"You've no idea what I have, dear." Again, her voice was sickly sweet.

"No, I suppose I don't, and I'm quite happy with it that way." He lifted his glass to her and offered a taunting smile that made his aunt glare at him as if she were tossing daggers in his direction.

She turned her attention to Sarah and Anthony, who

were still doing their best to ignore the hostility between Martin and Bridget. "You're both fortunate to be unwed. I recommend staying that way, if you can."

"I would second that," Uncle Martin said in a rare show of agreement with his wife. "Although, with your title, you have a duty. Unless you've got a relative to inherit like Felix has."

"Uncle Martin, Aunt Bridget, let us not burden the Coltons with our family...concerns. They have their own troubles at present."

"Oh yes, of course," Aunt Bridget said. "I must apologize for my comment earlier. I didn't realize your parents had been murdered."

Felix watched, helpless, as color leached from both Sarah's and Anthony's faces. He saw Anthony's hand tighten around his utensils, his knuckles turning white. And Felix noticed the slight tremor in Sarah's hand as she picked up her wine. Rather than draw attention to their discomfort, he turned toward Michael and asked him about his final term at Oxford. This led Felix to draw Anthony into reminiscing about their days at Oxford, and they were thankfully able to keep Aunt Bridget and Uncle Martin relatively quiet.

And so they managed to endure the meal and his aunt and uncle's company. Afterward, Sarah said she was tired and bid them good night. Aunt Bridget said she didn't want to go to the drawing room alone, and so she insisted Martin and Michael accompany her to the dower house, for which Felix was exceptionally grateful.

Not five minutes after they left, he and Anthony were in his study with their coats discarded, cravats untied, and a bottle of whisky on a small table between the chairs in which they sprawled.

"Good Christ, those are miserable people," Anthony

said. "I begin to understand why you never invited me here. Have they always been like that?"

"Mostly, yes."

"And you let him run the estate?" Anthony shook his head. "I knew you allowed him to live in the dower house and that he looked after things when you were in London, but I didn't realize he was your de facto steward."

"I have a steward."

"Then you don't need your uncle."

This was another reason he didn't invite people to Stag's Court. How he ran his estate—his life—was no one's business, not even his best friend's. "His son is going to inherit someday. Why not let him oversee things? I'm quite content with this arrangement." He gave Anthony a cool look before taking a long draw from his whisky glass.

Anthony pressed his lips together and lifted his glass. "My apologies. I know you don't plan to marry. I just assumed that would change and that you didn't really mean to have your cousin inherit. Clearly, I was wrong."

"Yes."

"I can see the benefit of not marrying—many of them, actually." Anthony sipped his whisky. "However, I do not have a male first cousin. I'll have to do some digging. Bound to be someone along the line."

"As my aunt said, marriage isn't for everyone." It certainly wasn't for them.

"Was their marriage arranged?" Anthony asked before shaking his head. "And they have *three* children?" At Felix's nod, he laughed. "I presume they didn't always hate each other."

"My father said they did. Since they had two daughters before Michael, I have to assume they fucked each other through their mutual hate just to have a son."

"Why does that sound vaguely arousing?" Anthony said, laughing. "Mutual hate fucking, I mean."

"Because you had four glasses of wine at dinner and are nearly finished with a first glass of whisky." Felix didn't want to encourage him to get drunk, not after he'd had such a good day, but the fact was that Felix was already more than halfway drunk himself, and going all the way sounded pretty damn good at present.

Almost as good as mutual hate fucking. Or just fucking. An image of a woman wrapped in dark purple silk vaulted into his mind. He drained his glass and poured another. Before he set the bottle down, Anthony held his glass out for a refill.

"Looks as though we're getting completely stewed," Felix said.

Anthony held up his glass in a toast. "No one I'd rather do it with."

Felix had no idea of the time when he helped Anthony up to his bedchamber. They were both stinking drunk, but Anthony was nearly unconscious. His arm around Anthony's waist, Felix tried to open Anthony's door without losing hold of him. He failed miserably. Anthony hit the floor with a thud, drawing his valet to rush to the door.

"I've got him," he said, helping a muttering Anthony to his feet.

"Sorry about that," Felix said, wincing. "Take good care of him." He pulled the door shut with more force than necessary, causing it to slam. "Shit."

He turned too fast and leaned back against the door to steady himself.

The door across the hall opened, and standing at the threshold was a goddess. Dark hair plaited over her shoulder, with curls that extended down over her breast,

Sarah tied the sash of her dressing gown as she stepped out of her chamber.

"Felix?"

"'Tis I." He stepped forward and swayed.

"My goodness. You're foxed."

"Felix is foxed. I think I shall say that three times fast. Felix is foxed. Felix is foxed. Fox is felixed." He grinned and took another, far steadier, step toward her.

"I assume my brother is in the same condition?"

"A bit worse, actually."

She frowned at him, and he took another step toward her until he was right in front of her.

"Don't do that. Frown, I mean," he whispered, lifting his hand to touch her lip.

The connection made her gasp, and she took a small step back.

"You looked beautiful tonight." He waved a hand over his hair. "Your feather was stunning. You made it, didn't you?"

"Yes. Thank you." Her gaze was hooded, wary. And a bit seductive.

God, he was growing hard standing there looking at her in a state of undress. He realized he was in the same state—his coat and cravat were downstairs, and his waistcoat was completely unbuttoned. He wanted to touch her again, to kiss her.

"You should sleep," she said. "Good night, Felix. Or Fox. Whatever your name is." Her voice was cool and her gaze even icier. She turned and stepped into her room, closing the door firmly behind her.

He'd completely cocked that up. What the hell was wrong with him?

You're drunk.

Yes, but not too drunk to realize he'd just flirted with a

woman he had no business flirting with. He stalked to his chamber and shut the door, this time careful not to slam it. He leaned back against the wood and closed his eyes.

He refused to be attracted to Sarah. He couldn't be. It was simply that he'd been too long without a woman. He'd terminated his arrangement with Meggie after the Coltons had died.

Yes, not being with a woman was the problem. Tomorrow night, he would take Anthony into the village of Ware and they would find female companionship. It would do them both good.

And what of tonight and the inconvenient erection straining against his smallclothes?

Tonight, he would pray for oblivion.

⁘⁘⁘

THE UPSTAIRS SITTING room at Stag's Court afforded a stunning view of the garden below. With a profusion of roses, pinks, and Sweet Williams, it was bright and beautiful, the perfect backdrop for Sarah to write letters to her friends who were at Fanny's new home near St. Ives.

However after telling them about her first day at Stag's Court—with probably too much information about Felix's horrid aunt and uncle—she didn't know what else to say. She didn't want to talk about how she was feeling. Mostly because she didn't know.

Rather, because she was feeling too much.

She was angry with Anthony for turning to the bottle yet again. And angry with Felix for joining him. No, she was angry with Felix for flirting with her, for reminding her of how he made her heart race and how she'd begun to think of their kisses and recall how much she'd enjoyed them.

She was also sad, of course, but there were moments of hope and brightness, that things wouldn't feel so dark forever. She just wasn't sure what she was supposed to *do*. Her maid, Dovey, had told her to take each day as a gift and to not think too much about it. That, Sarah had decided, was not as easy as it sounded. Perhaps that was the problem—she had too much time to think. She needed to do something but wasn't sure what.

As she tried to come up with how to convey all that in a letter, she wished her friends were there in person. It would be so much easier to talk to them, to hear their voices.

"Sarah?"

She recognized the voice without turning and realized if he'd spoken in the closet at Darent Hall, she would have known him immediately. He had spoken, she recalled, but a short, single word that had barely permeated the fog of her shocking arousal. She *had* to stop thinking about it. Especially since she was annoyed with him.

Turning in the chair, she gave him a frosty look. "I'm writing a letter."

"I see that. May I interrupt you? Please? I've come to beg your forgiveness."

Surprise—and delight—bloomed in her chest, but she didn't show him. She wanted him to suffer at least a little. "I see." She repositioned the chair so that she was facing him.

He walked slowly into the room. Garbed in a dark blue coat and gray breeches, he looked as fashionable as any gentleman strolling along Bond Street, but then Felix had always been well-dressed. Sarah noticed these things, of course. Just as she'd noticed his state of undress last night.

She'd seen him in shirtsleeves before but had never

been impacted by it. That had been before they'd kissed each other, however. Now she saw him—and his bare neck—in a wholly different light.

He stopped a few feet from her chair, his face pulled into a wince of embarrassment. "I'm afraid I was rather foxed last night."

"And felixed, apparently."

His eyes clouded with confusion for a moment, and then he laughed.

"You remember?" she asked.

"I wasn't as sotted as you probably thought. I was, however, heavily felixed. Unavoidable, I'm afraid." His lips curved up in a self-condemning smile. "I am who I am."

She almost smiled but schooled herself not to. "You let Anthony get drunk again."

He flinched and dipped his head in shame. "Yes, but I should like to blame my aunt and uncle, if I may."

She would agree with doing that, but again, she wasn't going to make this easy for him. Not when everything felt so difficult to her. "That's a bit cowardly of you, isn't it?"

He put his hand over his chest. "A direct hit. Your barbs have exceptional aim, Miss Colton."

He was so good at livening every single moment. Too good.

"You shouldn't have let him drink so much."

"No, I shouldn't have," he said soberly. "And we certainly didn't need to continue after dinner. Would it help to know that I think it was helpful for him? It wasn't like before. We were just being—"

While he searched for words, she offered, "Stupid men?"

"Yes, that. Precisely. And I was even more stupid to behave as I did with you."

"What way was that?" Had her voice risen?

He briefly narrowed one eye at her. "I think I tried—poorly—to flirt with you. But I stand by what I said. You did look beautiful last night."

Her heart picked up speed, and she hoped he couldn't see the tremor racing through her body. "You've never said things like that to me before."

He frowned. "Surely I've commented on your appearance over the years."

Surely he had. "Not in that way. And you told me not to frown. And you tried—" She looked away from him, from the unbearable pull she felt toward him.

"I tried to touch you," he said softly. "Sarah, I was not myself. My aunt and uncle... They bring out the worst in me."

She snapped her gaze back to his. "Touching me is the worst of you?"

He winced again, then wiped his hand across his brow. He tipped his head toward the floor. "That didn't come out right at all. *Hell.* None of this is right. Not since Darent Hall."

He lifted his eyes to hers, and they simply looked at each other for a long moment.

"We can say it," she whispered, her voice sounding ragged. "Since we kissed."

"I don't want things to be different. You're still my best friend's sister. You're family, now more than ever."

She didn't want things to be different either. She needed all the family she could keep. "We can forget the event ever happened."

The edge of his mouth ticked up. "I thought I had—for a while there. But I think *pretending* it never happened is probably the route I shall have to take."

He was telling her he couldn't forget it. Well, neither

could she. In fact, she feared they were to be the kisses by which she would measure all others. "I shall do the same." As best she could. She exhaled with relief and perhaps with a tiny bit of something else. Regret, she realized.

"I'm glad we discussed it," Felix said, straightening and smoothing his hand over the front of his coat. "I do hope you'll forgive me—for all of it. I intend to nurse you and Anthony back to your gleeful selves."

"Is that really possible?"

"Of course it is." He was so matter-of-fact that she couldn't help but believe him.

"I suppose it must be. You recovered after your father died."

"Yes." His tone was tentative. "But I suspect that was much different. I was very young, for one thing."

"And?"

"And…" He shrugged. "You find other things to think about. Like shopping. Come, I'm taking you into Ware. I'm having the gig brought round. Fetch your maid and meet me out front."

Her maid. It took her a moment to realize she ought to take her maid. Yes, it was an open vehicle and yes, she and Felix were as good as family, but for propriety's sake, she ought to bring Dovey.

"I'll just be a trice," she said.

"Good." He grinned at her and departed.

She picked up her half-finished letter and dashed to her chamber, where Dovey helped her change into a walking costume. Sarah hurried downstairs and out into the bright afternoon, the brim of her hat shading her eyes from the sun.

Felix stood next to the gig, his hat pulled low on his brow at a cocky angle. She'd never acknowledged how handsome he was before.

And she certainly didn't need to start doing so *now*.

He helped her into the front seat of the vehicle and then helped Dovey into the back. Ware was a short two-mile drive. With malthouses, coaching inns, and shopping aplenty, it was a busy town, particularly with the traffic on the River Lea, which ran straight through.

"We'll visit Scott's Grotto while you're here," Felix said.

"My parents took us there once," Sarah said softly, remembering a day she hadn't thought of in years. Or maybe she'd forgotten it altogether, but Felix's mention of the grotto had resurrected the memory. "It was summer, and the tunnels were cool. They were beautiful—the shells and rock."

"I spent many a summer day hiding in them," Felix said. "Thankfully, Maria Scott has continued to allow people to visit. Her father built the grotto, if you didn't know. People would come from London to see it—which was his intent."

Sarah slid a glance at him as they drove into town. "I'm surprised *you* don't build a grotto."

"At Stag's Court?" He shook his head. "I don't have a chalk hill."

"But if you had one, you would build a grotto?"

"Of course." He flashed her a grin, and she was once again grateful for his sense of humor.

He took them past a series of coaching inns and malthouses before parking the gig in front of a shop. Sarah looked at the sign and then toward Felix, who was already bounding from the vehicle.

He came around to her side and offered her his hand.

"You brought me to a millinery shop?"

"Why not? I happen to know you like them." He helped her down, then did the same for Dovey, but she waved him away. "I'll wait here."

"The gig will be fine," Felix said. "This isn't London."

"It's all right, my lord. My back is paining me a bit today."

Sarah hadn't known that. She looked up at her maid, who wasn't even old enough to be her mother. "Did something happen?" Sarah asked.

Dovey winked at her. "Not at all. Just an old pain." That Sarah had never heard of. Was Dovey trying to give her time alone with Felix? Sarah would need to tell her that wasn't necessary, though it might not do any good. Dovey was as keen to see Sarah wed as her parents had been.

A sharp prick of loss stabbed into Sarah, and she worked to push it away. It lingered a moment, reminding her for the thousandth time that her mother would never see her wed. Did it matter anymore, then? Sarah had thought it had never mattered. And now she'd marry in a second if it meant she could have her parents back.

She took Felix's arm as he guided her into the shop. It was small and cool after the heat of the early afternoon sun. Hats and ribbons and gloves filled the space, and Sarah looked about in mild interest.

Taking her hand from his arm, Sarah went to a display of poke bonnets. She fingered one, admiring the craftsmanship.

"Do you like that?" Felix asked, coming up beside her.

"It's nice."

"I'd be happy to buy it—or any other—for you."

She gave him a reproving look. "You can't buy me things. Anyway, I don't buy hats." Because she made them all herself. But she hadn't wanted to since her parents had died.

"And why would you?" he said with a smile. "Perhaps

you should purchase some supplies, then. Some ribbons? Some silk flowers?"

"I don't need anything, thank you." She went to look at gloves.

He followed her. "I was hoping you could show me how to make hats."

"You were?" She wasn't sure she believed that. "Why would you need to make a hat?"

He shrugged. "You never know. I might find myself somewhere with no headgear to speak of and find myself in desperate need."

She cocked her hip and stared at him. "So you'd be without a hat but have all the materials and implements required to make one. Seems like that could happen."

He snorted. "Your sarcasm is killing me."

She turned, notching up her chin. "I learned from the best. That would be you and Anthony, in case you didn't realize."

"Oh, I realized," he said, chuckling. "Let me get some supplies. The sooner you get back to making hats, the sooner you'll feel like yourself."

He could be right, but she wasn't going to do it. Instead of telling him so, she strode from the shop.

He trailed her outside and touched her elbow. "Why did you leave?"

She turned to face him, giving in to her irritation. "I don't want to make hats. And I don't need to 'get back' to anything. My life is different now."

He frowned, his brow creasing. "It doesn't have to be. You can still open your shop in Vigo Lane. In fact, it might even be easier—"

"Just stop," she snapped. "I am not opening a shop in Vigo Lane." Her parents would have hated it, and she wasn't going to dishonor their memory in that way.

He clasped her elbow and drew her to the side of the walkway. "Why deny that which would make you happy?"

"Making my parents proud will make me happy."

"So now you want to marry," he said flatly.

"I always wanted to marry." She couldn't help feeling—or sounding, apparently—defensive.

He didn't appear convinced. "I believe you wanted to fall in love. Is that still a requirement?"

"It is…important. I'll accept a husband with whom I can be happy. Love isn't always necessary." She was now completely parroting her mother. Her throat constricted.

"I want you to be sure you know what happiness is—for you." He pressed his mouth into a determined line. "Come on, I'm taking you somewhere."

She moved toward the gig. "Where?"

He helped her up. "It's a surprise."

She looked down at him from the seat. "I hope it's not another millinery shop." Maybe it was the Grotto.

"It's not. We're going back to the estate." He circled the vehicle and climbed onto the seat beside her.

Not the Grotto, then.

As Felix took the reins, she was aware of his annoyance. Rather than upset her, it made her more resolute. She couldn't live her life like he did—pursuing whatever he wanted whenever he wanted. He allowed someone else to run his estate and had no intention of providing an heir. He had no sense of duty whatsoever.

It was no wonder he couldn't understand that she needed to satisfy her parents' wishes. It was, to her, more important than she could have ever imagined.

Fielding had sent a lovely note and flowers after her parents had died. Perhaps he was still interested in courting her—he'd said as much at Darent Hall. Marrying him would mean traveling to India for an indeterminate amount of time, but there were worse things. And her parents would be so pleased to see her wed, even if he didn't have a title. They'd be especially thrilled if he was awarded a position with the government. Yes, Fielding might do nicely.

She'd write to him as soon as possible.

Chapter Eight

❧

FELIX DROVE BACK to Stag's Court perhaps a trifle faster than he ought, slowing as he reached a lane that would deliver them to their destination. The irritation he'd felt toward Sarah was still there, but it wasn't truly directed at her. She was grieving. She would come to her senses soon enough. He just hoped she didn't make any rash decisions before then.

How could she, when she was here in the country away from potential suitors?

He relaxed a bit as he directed the gig along the lane. The house he was looking for came into sight as he rounded a bend.

"Where are we going?" Sarah asked again.

"Still a surprise," Felix said.

"You *are* building a grotto."

He laughed in spite of his lingering annoyance. "No. But if you keep haranguing me about it, I might have to."

"I am not haranguing." When next she spoke, her pitch was elevated. "Felix, you *must* build a grotto. I should be devastated if you do not. Think of all the people who would come to see it, of all the parties and other events you could host inside." She turned her head and pouted at him, batting her lashes. "I shall never speak to you again if you don't build a grotto."

He arched a brow at her, barely able to contain his smile. "Are you finished?"

"*That* is haranguing."

"You are quite excellent at it. I thought you liked horrid novels, but perhaps you've been reading *The Taming of the*

Shrew."

She laughed, and he let the last of his irritation fade away.

Dovey leaned forward between them. "I did catch her reading that some time ago—perhaps in March."

"Aha!" Felix turned the gig into the drive of the cottage and parked the vehicle. He jumped down and came around to help Sarah out. "Are you coming this time, Dovey?" he asked the maid.

"I'm not sure. I can't imagine what we're doing here."

He held up his hand to her. "It's worth your effort, I promise."

"How can I refuse?" She allowed him to help her to the ground.

As they walked toward the house, a woman came out and quickly bobbed a curtsey to Felix. "Good afternoon, my lord. Did you tell Mr. Jenney you were coming?"

"I did not," Felix said. "I'm afraid this is a surprise visit. I've come to see the puppies."

Sarah snapped her head toward his. "Puppies?"

"Oh dear," Dovey murmured.

Mrs. Jenney smiled. "Well then, come and have a look. Are you interested in having one, sir?" she asked.

"Not me, no." He glanced toward Sarah. "But Miss Colton might be."

She reached over and squeezed his arm. It was the type of touch he'd expected from her—somewhat impersonal and fleeting—before they'd kissed. He told himself to feel relieved that things were now back to normal between them.

"They're in the barn." Mrs. Jenney led them to a shelter several yards from the cottage. The building had three full sides, with a half-wall along the fourth. They passed through an open doorway to a penned area filled with straw. And a litter of terrier puppies nursing on their mother.

The sides of the pen were only a foot high—easy enough for the mama to scale and impossible for her pups. One of them stood and stretched, then waddled over to the edge where they were standing.

Sarah immediately dropped down. "How old are they?"

"About five weeks now, miss," Mrs. Jenney answered.

"They will soon be able to leave the pen," Felix observed.

"Undoubtedly," Mrs. Jenney said.

Sarah pulled off one of her gloves and reached over into the pen to stroke the puppy's head. This one was the lightest of the bunch, a pale cream. "They are absolutely adorable."

"Go on and pick her up, then," Mrs. Jenney suggested, as if Sarah needed much urging.

Removing her other glove, Sarah handed them to Dovey. Then she scooped the puppy into her arms and stood, cuddling the animal to her chest.

Felix could see she was already in love. "What would you name her?"

Sarah nuzzled the dog's head. "Blossom. Because she's beautiful, and she smells so very sweet."

"Well then, it sounds as if she's yours already," Felix said.

"I can't take a dog." She squatted down and put the dog back into the pen. Another trotted toward her, this one darker with a reddish hue. The animal thrust its head into Sarah's hand, and she picked it up next.

"You're right," Felix said. "Clearly you must take two."

She put the dog back in the pen and stood, shaking her head at him. "What if my husband doesn't like dogs?"

"Then he shouldn't be your husband."

Mrs. Jenney looked confused, and Felix said, "He's hypothetical at this point—the husband."

She nodded. "They'll be fully weaned in a few weeks. You could take one—or two—then, if you like. Two of them are spoken for. The darkest one there." She pointed to one that was nearly red and to a second one that was lighter and by far the largest of the litter. "And that big one. My son calls him Hero."

"What a wonderful name," Sarah said. Her gaze was so wistful, so full of yearning, that Felix could hardly stand it.

"Sarah, you're taking a dog," he said. "I insist. Make your choice. Blossom or the other one."

"She's a girl too. My son's taken to calling her Poppy. She's the friendliest of the bunch."

Sarah frowned. "I would hate to take your son's dog."

"Oh, she isn't his. Their mother is his pup, and he wouldn't trade her for anything. And we'll keep whatever pup is left when the other five have been taken."

"It's settled, then," Felix said. "We'll pick up Blossom and Poppy in two weeks. Will that be sufficient time for them to wean?"

"Oh yes, sir. That would be just fine." Mrs. Jenney smiled widely, revealing a gap between her front teeth. "I'm so pleased they'll have such a loving home. It's obvious you love dogs," she said to Sarah.

"I do." Sarah positively beamed, and Felix was aware of a tightening in his chest. Blast it all.

"Would you like to play with them a bit?" Mrs. Jenney asked.

"I would, thank you."

Mrs. Jenney stepped away from the pen. "I've lemonade in the house if anyone would care for some."

"Would you mind if I went inside, Miss Colton?" Dovey asked.

"Not at all." Sarah didn't look up from the puppies. She bent down and scooped Blossom up, then moved to sit on a pile of hay nearby.

When Mrs. Jenney and Dovey had left, Felix picked up Poppy and joined Sarah. The puppies allowed a bit of coddling before they demanded to be put down so they could explore.

"This was lovely of you," Sarah said softly. "Thank you."

"I know how much you adore dogs."

"I do. My parents wouldn't let me have one in London."

He hadn't realized that was the case. "I didn't mean to provoke any unpleasantness."

"No, it's fine." Her gaze followed the puppies as they wrestled with one another.

He thought about what might be going through her head. She wanted to honor her parents by getting married, and yet here she was with a pair of puppies, something they'd denied her. If she could accept the dogs, perhaps she'd come back around to pursuing her hat making. He hoped that would be the case. She deserved happiness—a happiness of her own making and not anyone else's.

Such as you have?

He swatted the voice to the back of his mind.

She looked over at him. "Thank you. I shouldn't take them, but I will."

"Good."

She smiled, and while he'd provoked several the last few days, this was the truest, most brilliant one yet. Her blue eyes sparkled, and her skin glowed. "This is the happiest I've felt in a long time."

"I can tell."

"What you do…creating diversions and amusements.

It's more than that. You bring people genuine joy."

"I try."

"Is that what makes you happy?"

"Yes." He said it without thinking. Because avoiding thinking too deeply was part of what made him happy. No, not happy. It was something else.

She cocked her head. "Have you ever tried to make your aunt and uncle happy?"

The change in topic—sort of—made him laugh. "I'm not sure. I have arranged for them to avoid each other, so in that sense, yes, I suppose I have. They rarely spend any time together. She's always in Bath or York, and Uncle Martin is always here."

"How sad."

Felix shrugged. "I don't think they're sad. They're making the most of a bad situation."

"Their marriage is a 'bad situation.'"

"Now you see why I have no interest and why I caution you to be certain it's what you want."

"Is that the truth?" she asked. "Living with your aunt and uncle after your father died, that's why you refuse to marry?"

Felix's insides twisted. This was dangerous territory—the places in his heart and soul he didn't touch. He searched, desperately, for humor where there was little, or none, to be found. "I hope you aren't going to pity me. There's no need for that."

"No, I was merely trying to learn something new about you." One of the puppies nudged her skirt, and Sarah scooped her up, settling the animal in her lap. Then she reached down and picked up the second and deposited her beside her sister. They curled together so that it was hard to see where one ended and the other began.

"I'm beginning to realize there is a great deal I don't

know about you."

His discomfort with the conversation grew. "You know the same as Anthony. Or anyone else."

"I do? I would have thought Anthony would know you better. But if we all see the same Felix…" Her voice trailed off, and he didn't like the direction her thoughts were taking.

"I'm not a terribly exciting person," he said. "I am precisely the man you see—entertainment maker, laugh provoker, and puppy obtainer."

"Yes, but I think you're so much more." She gave him an enigmatic look and stood, cradling the puppies in her arms.

He watched her put them back in the pen with their mother and siblings, then she turned to him, wiping her hands against her skirt. "I should get back to check on Anthony."

"I asked Cook to make him a headache tonic. He'll be fit as a fiddle, I'm sure."

"You take care of everyone," she said softly. "Who takes care of you?"

"No one." He'd taken care of himself his entire life, and he expected that to never change.

ANTHONY FOUND SARAH in the library before dinner that night. "Are those your horrid novels from London?"

She sat at a table with a trio of books stacked before her and turned to look at her brother as he came toward her. "Yes. Felix told you he ordered them for me?"

"I wish I'd thought of it," Anthony said with a hint of regret. "I haven't been a very good brother of late."

"I haven't been that great a sister either, but I think

we've done what we must." She gestured for him to sit with her. "Is it better, being here instead of in town?"

"I think so. I enjoyed being out yesterday. And I went for a long walk today."

"You seem to be feeling all right." She studied his features, and he gave her a small smile.

"Please don't worry about me. I couldn't bear it." He looked away from her. "This has been a shock."

"Yes, it has." That was the very best way to describe it. One minute, they'd been enjoying themselves at Darent Hall, and the next, they'd been plunged into confusion and grief.

Anthony rested his elbow on the table. "I wanted to ask if you would mind if Felix and I missed dinner tonight."

"Oh?"

"Felix suggested we spend the evening in town."

"And you want to?" She reached forward with a smile and touched his arm. "That's wonderful. Of course I don't mind."

His shoulders dipped in relief. "Thank you."

"I've plenty to keep me busy." She patted the stack of books. "And soon I will have even more to occupy my time. Felix took me to meet terrier puppies today."

"Oh no, how many are you taking?" He let out a low laugh.

"Two. At his insistence." She snagged the inside of her lip with her teeth. "But it feels a bit…wrong."

"Why?"

"Mother and Father would never let me have them. Not in the house and definitely not in London."

He looked away again, nodding. "I understand." He found her gaze again. "And I think they would understand too. We must do what we can. If puppies will make you happy, you should have puppies."

"What about you?" she asked. "What will make you happy?"

He shrugged, letting out a deep exhalation. "Right now, spending the evening with my friend and pretending as if nothing has changed."

"Can you really do that?" Sarah wasn't sure she could.

"I'm going to try. Felix says it will help."

She wasn't surprised by this—he'd spent the day trying to distract her from melancholy. "Felix is a master at diversion."

"Of course he is. I can think of no one better to help us through this time."

"Should we—" She hated to ask the question, but she'd begun to start thinking about what to do next, and she liked having plans or at least ideas and strategies. When it looked like she might not marry, she'd concocted an alternate scheme. It was both comforting and inspiring. "When are we going to Oaklands?"

Anthony stood and stalked across the room, stopping in front of a bookshelf and running his fingertip along the spines. "I don't know. I'm not ready yet."

The pain in his voice cut right through her. She rose and went to stand beside him. "It doesn't have to be soon."

He nodded.

"I'm just trying to…think ahead. How soon do you think I can wed?"

He whipped his head about to stare at her. "*Wed?*"

"Yes."

"Do you have a suitor?"

"No, but I think I could have one." She thought of Fielding, whom she planned to write to after dinner.

"Who?" he asked.

"Mr. Fielding."

Anthony blinked. "I'm afraid I don't remember him."

"He was at Darent Hall. Stocky fellow, pale brown hair, most amiable."

Anthony seemed to think for a moment, then gave his head a slow, single shake. "Still can't place him, sorry."

"It doesn't matter."

"It *does* matter. I shall have to ensure any suitor is up to snuff. That is my responsibility now."

Irritation ground up her spine. She didn't want to have to seek his permission. "I hope you don't expect to choose a husband for me."

"Not at all. But I should at least ensure he's worthy."

Sarah relaxed. This was all so new to them. "He's up for a government appointment in India. Is that acceptable to you?"

"No title?" he asked. She shook her head. "Mother and Father really wanted you to have a title."

"Yes, but Mother had begun to say it didn't matter so long as I married."

Anthony winced slightly and returned his attention to the books for a moment. Without looking at her, he said, "India? That's acceptable to *you*?"

"I must marry, Anthony," she said softly. "It would have made Mother so happy."

He turned and pulled her into his arms. She hugged him around the middle and laid her head on his chest.

"I think you could marry by year's end. Presumably this Fielding fellow would wait."

"He has family matters to attend here. He doesn't have plans to return to India this year."

"I would miss you dreadfully."

"I would miss you too." Emotion clogged her throat, but she didn't want to cry all over his cravat.

"Good evening, friends!"

Sarah and Anthony separated as Felix strode into the room.

Felix stopped before them, looking from Sarah to Anthony and back again. "What familial bonding have I interrupted?"

"Sarah and I were just discussing her marriage," Anthony said.

"Ah, yes, she mentioned something about getting married earlier today." Felix gave her a benign look that told her nothing as to how he felt about the topic. But she knew from their conversation in Ware that afternoon that he had an opinion about whom she should wed—someone she loved, probably.

Anthony leaned against the bookshelf. "She's considering some gentleman from the party at Darent Hall. Fielding. But the bloke's going to India, and I'd rather not send my sister halfway around the world."

Sarah gave him a pointed look. "You don't get to decide." He lifted his arms in a gesture of surrender.

"There are other options. What of Sherington or Blakesley or a few of the other guests at Darent Hall? Baron Hardwick is purported to be looking for a bride."

"Hardwick has too many creditors, in my opinion," Anthony said. "And Blakesley isn't ready to settle down. Sherington could work, however."

Sarah cleared her throat. "I am still here."

Both men blinked at her. "Of course you are."

"Then perhaps you might ask me what I think of those men." She smiled prettily—perhaps too prettily, but she didn't appreciate their cavalier attitude.

"My apologies," Felix said, offering a slight bow. "I merely want to help facilitate your search. I am happy to continue my services when you are ready."

His services. Helping her find a husband. While she'd

eagerly accepted his offer before, that was…before. Now the thought of him finding her a suitor felt a bit wrong.

So far, she was doing a rather poor job of pretending they'd never kissed. It seemed he was having no trouble, however. He was more than ready to marry her off.

"I can't imagine reentering the social world any time soon. Perhaps in the fall. In the meantime, I shall consider my options." She was eager to abandon the topic.

"Sarah, I will support whatever you decide to do," Anthony said earnestly.

"Thank you." She smoothed her hand over her skirt. "And now I understand you are both off to Ware, which leaves me to read my horrid novels."

"Would you like to take dinner in here?" Felix asked. "Or somewhere else? I can let the staff know."

"I'll take care of that, thank you," she said. "What do you plan to do in Ware?"

"We'll have dinner at one of the coaching inns," Felix said. "The Golden Bear has a French chef, if you can imagine."

"How wonderful. I shall have to go sometime." Indeed, she wondered why they hadn't invited her to come. But then they exchanged a glance, and she knew. Dinner was just the start of their evening. She could well imagine what they'd be doing next.

Her insides twisted, and she had trouble making eye contact with Felix. So she didn't. Instead, she went to the table with her books and picked up the stack. "Have a nice evening. Don't drink too much." She looked at Anthony but not Felix.

"We'll be on our best behavior," Anthony said.

Nodding, she turned and left, all the while silently repeating: *pretend it never happened, pretend it never happened, pretend it never happened.*

Better still: *pretend he doesn't exist.*

THE DINING ROOM hardly resembled the dining room, what with the table covered in various items, but Felix could think of no better use for the space. He surveyed the collection of bizarre items and waited for his guest to arrive.

A moment later, Sarah entered. "Dovey told me I was needed in the dining room." She moved toward the table with a look of confusion. "Felix, what is all this?"

"We're making hats."

She blinked at him. "With books and baskets and moss and…is that a teacup?"

He clasped his hands behind his back and smiled at her. "It is."

"I told you I didn't want to make hats."

"*I'm* making hats. But I need a little direction."

"Felix, you can't make a hat out of a basket and a teacup."

He narrowed his eyes at her. "You are not very imaginative. What are hats but overdecorated baskets?"

She stared at him, and he feared his plan was going to fail. He went to pick up a basket and then grabbed a handful of moss, which he'd tasked a footman with collecting. "If you aren't going to help me, I shall do it on my own." He moved to the other end of the table and sat down to affix the moss on the basket.

He opened a jar of glue and picked up the brush that sat beside it. Dipping the brush into the adhesive, he used the implement to slather it on the basket. Then he stuck wads of the moss onto the wet glue.

"What on earth are you doing?" she asked, having

joined him at the end of the table.

He glanced up at her, encouraged that she'd followed him. "Making a hat."

"With glue?"

He blinked up at her. "Is there a better way? Perhaps you would like to show me?"

She pursed her lips and narrowed her eyes. "No."

"I shall continue, then." Determined to engage her, he got up and fetched a few more items for his basket hat: pigeon feathers, a small fan, and a rosebud.

"Wherever did you find that fan?" she asked as he considered where to attach it.

"No idea. I asked the staff to bring me a variety of things, and this was one of them. I think there's an old stocking somewhere in the pile." He set the fan on top of the hat to give it height, but it didn't look right. Next, he tried putting it on sideways so that it looked like a fin on the side of the hat. "Oh yes, this will do," he murmured, slapping a dollop of glue onto the basket and then pressing the fan on top of it.

"That looks ridiculous."

Felix looked up at her in faux innocence. "Does it? And here I was hoping to persuade you to wear it."

She rolled her eyes. "What is your true intent here?"

"The same as always: to have a good time. Would you rather scowl at my pathetic efforts or join me? I am confident you will create something far finer than I."

She arched a brow at him. "Is that a challenge?"

Oh yes, this was the Sarah he was hoping to provoke. "It is."

"I bet I can make something worse than yours."

That was not what he'd expected, but it was far, far better. He laughed. "Just you try."

She spun on her heel and walked around the table

picking up various items. Then she returned to his end and sat down as she began to quietly assemble her hat. The first thing she did was open her own jar of glue. Using a newspaper as the base, she attached a variety of ribbons to the sides.

"See how helpful the glue is?" he asked.

"For my project, yes. For your basket, no. I am confident the glue leaked through the weave. Aside from creating a mess, it may make the basket uncomfortable for the wearer."

He stared at her in mock surprise. "Comfort goes into your design?"

She ignored him as she finished gluing her ribbons. Felix picked up the basket and saw there were indeed dried dollops of glue on the tablecloth. Thankfully, the staff had possessed the foresight to cover the table. He peered into the basket and saw clumps of glue in a few places.

"You could sew the moss on," she suggested. "Unless you're done with that."

He had no desire to sew anything. Picking up the brush once more, he dabbed glue on the base of the open fan and carefully stuck the pigeon feathers on.

"You should sew those too," she said.

"I can't sew."

"You can't make hats either, but that doesn't seem to be stopping you."

He grinned, but she didn't look up from her work. She'd glued a teacup to the top of the newspaper.

He surveyed his hat. God, it was hideous. It needed ribbon, for function as much as form. If the objective was to make it as awful as possible, perhaps he should use the old stocking. He stood and went in search of it but couldn't find it. Glancing back toward Sarah, he saw her gently gluing the edge of it—she'd torn it in half—to another edge of the paper.

Blast.

He didn't want to use ribbons. They were too obvious. But what if he altered the ribbons? He found several that didn't match and then set to work gluing moss, small leaves, and rose petals on each of them. Rather than glue them to the hat, he wound them through the basket weave.

"Finished!" he declared.

"I am too," she said, sitting back to survey her handiwork. It didn't even really look like a hat. "How shall we determine the winner?"

"A panel of judges seems in order," Felix said.

"Who?"

"Let me see who I can find." He stood and went to fetch the first three members of the staff he could find. He returned with the butler, Seales, a maid, and a footman and arranged them to stand near the end of the table where she and Felix had assembled their ghastly headwear.

"Your job is to vote for the ugliest hat," Felix said. "Are you ready?"

"Where are the hats, my lord?" Seales asked, appearing to take his assignment very seriously.

"Right here." Felix picked up his hat and set the basket on his head. Then he attempted to tie the collection of ribbons beneath his chin. A clump of moss dropped to the floor, as did a rose petal.

He looked to the side as Sarah rounded the end of the table. She'd put on her hat, and he knew he was sunk.

She'd tied two of the ribbons beneath her chin and the rest dangled free, like some sort of wild, multi-colored hairstyle. Due to tying the ribbons, the newspaper curved around her head like an actual straw hat might have done, and the teacup sat in the place of prominence atop her crown. It almost invited one to pour tea into the vessel. Or perhaps she was collecting rainwater. Damn, her hat was both comfortable—if she was to be believed—and functional, if entirely ugly. Finally, the stocking covered her face like a veil, lending a somber appearance to the most absurd piece of headwear he'd ever seen.

"Whose hat is the most atrocious?" Felix asked, already knowing the answer.

All three retainers looked toward Sarah. "Miss Colton's," they each said.

Through the veil, she smiled beatifically and Felix had no choice but to howl with laughter. How he wished he were skilled at art, for he would have sketched a picture of her to remember the moment.

"I should let the lot of you go," Felix said, smiling. "Thank you, you're dismissed."

The maid's eyes grew wide. "From our employment?"

Felix shook his head in horror. "No! You're dismissed from here."

Her body relaxed, and she responded with a smile. "Shall I clean this up, my lord?"

"Later," he said.

The trio left the dining room, and Felix turned to Sarah as she removed her hat. "You're taking it off?" he asked.

"Should I wear it into town?" She laughed. "You look ridiculous."

"Thank you. I had no chance with you. Your hat was hideous, comfortable, and functional."

"Because it would keep the sun off my face? Yours would not," she noted.

"Doubly functional, then. I was thinking you could collect rainwater to drink."

She looked at the hat and giggled. The teacup promptly fell off, and Felix moved quickly to catch it. She gave him an apologetic smile, widening her eyes slightly, and he placed the cup on the table.

Felix then untied the ribbon beneath his chin and tried to pull the basket off, but pain shot through his scalp. "Ow!"

She set her hat on the table beside the teacup and stepped toward him. "What's wrong?"

"I think it's stuck. You were right about the glue."

Stifling a laugh, she moved closer. "Let me help you." She gently pushed at the hat, and he winced. "Sit down."

He sat in the chair he'd vacated earlier, and she turned the basket around on his head. He flinched again. "Just pull it off. I'll deal with the bald spot."

She tugged harder, and off it came. A sharp pain stabbed his scalp and he reached up to rub the area. His hand found hers as she smoothed at his hair.

The connection shot through him like a lightning bolt. He looked up at her to find her staring down at him. She was so close, standing just between his knees, and her breasts would be at eye level right in front of him if he lowered his head.

A powerful spell of awareness and desire wove between them. He skimmed his fingers along her hand atop his head and stared into the alluring blue of her eyes. This was what he'd missed when he'd kissed her—the anticipation of knowing it was her before their lips met.

Would he have even had anticipation before that night? He would never have considered kissing her, not without Fate stepping in and making it happen.

She drew her hand away and took a step back, breaking the spell. The air felt suddenly cooler, and Felix suppressed a shiver.

She put the basket on the table and wiped her hands against her skirt. "I still don't want to make hats. At least not as an enterprise. I shall always trim my own headwear."

He exhaled, struggling with the desire still pulsing through him and trying to focus on what she said. Today was a success, then—she at least wanted to trim her own hats. "That's a start. There are real hat-making supplies in the sitting room upstairs for when you change your mind." He stood. "Did you at least enjoy yourself?"

"I did." Her smile was small but infectious, sparking a heat inside him that banished the chill of the broken moment. "Thank you. But really, Felix, how long can you keep this up? Entertaining us, I mean."

"As long as necessary. It's what I do. In fact, I wondered if I should invite Beck and Lavinia to come visit."

"Oh yes, please!" Her eyes fairly glowed with excitement, and Felix grinned with pleasure.

"I'll send a messenger to them posthaste," he said.

"They're at Huntwell with Fanny and David, at least for a few more days."

"Shall I invite them too?"

"I don't know if they'll come. They are newlyweds, after all."

"I'll extend the offer," Felix said. "Are you sure you don't want to make another hat? We have plenty of supplies."

"No, thank you. I've a horrid novel to finish—thank you for those."

"It's my pleasure."

"Everything you do is for your pleasure," she said softly. "And everyone else's."

She was more right about the latter than the former.

"Pleasing others, seeing to their enjoyment is what gives me joy." He hadn't meant to sound seductive or provocative, but saying those words to her, he realized he would like to please her—in every way possible.

But that was never going to happen. She was on the hunt for a husband, and she was not a woman with whom he could dally.

She didn't break eye contact with him for a long moment, and the air between them seemed to heat once more. At last, she pivoted. But before she left, she picked up her abominable hat and took it with her.

Felix *had* given her joy, if only for a while, and that would have to be enough.

Chapter Nine

THE HORRID NOVELS held no appeal for Sarah that night. After dinner, Anthony and Felix had left again, but this time, they hadn't revealed their destination. She could well imagine where they'd gone, however.

It was late when she found herself in the sitting room adjacent to her bedchamber. Several crates full of hat-making supplies stood against the wall. Kneeling in front of them, she looked through the forms and ribbons and fabric. There were a few flowers, but nothing that inspired her. She'd begun to fashion her own blossoms and wondered if she might be able to use the glue to create something interesting.

She sat back on the floor and pulled out a length of ribbon. She twirled it around her finger to make the bud of a rose. Yes, glue could work nicely. She began to think of the things she could make, and then she began to think of Dolly and her expertise and how together, they could create the most beautiful hats in London.

"You can't do that!" Her mother's voice intruded on her fantasy.

"Why not?" Sarah said to the empty room. The shop *would* make her happy, just as it would have disappointed her parents. And now there was no one to stand in her way. Her parents' death had made it possible for her to pursue the life she wanted—her shop and marriage to a man she loved, *if* she loved one.

The realization stole her breath for a moment. She couldn't be *glad* they were gone. Of course, she wasn't. And she refused to benefit from them being gone.

Hot tears tracked down her cheeks as anger and frustration boiled inside her. She threw the ribbon back into the crate and wiped at her face.

"Sarah?"

The sound of Felix's voice cooled her emotions.

He came into the sitting room and sat down beside her. "Contemplating your next creation?"

He smelled a bit like whisky, but not overly so. His cravat looked as though it had been loosened and retied. She could imagine why that had been necessary.

She sniffed. "No."

He turned toward her. "Sarah, have you been crying?" The concern in his voice could have broken her, but she wouldn't allow it.

"No."

He frowned. "I can see you have." He reached for her hand, but she stood up and stalked away from him.

She turned her back to him. "Save your concern. I don't want it."

"Nevertheless, you shall have it." He'd come up behind her. She could hear his proximity—she could feel it too.

She spun about. "I said, I don't want it. You are not my brother, Felix. You are not my husband. You are nothing to me."

He moved closer. "Am I?" His voice was low, seductive, so tempting. This was not the way to pretend they'd never kissed.

She glanced at his rumpled cravat. "Don't you dare flirt with me. Save that for your women. And especially don't do that after you've just been with one."

He narrowed his eyes at her. "Where do you think I've been?"

She crossed her arms in front of her chest. "I'm not stupid."

"I have never for a moment thought you were. You think I was with a woman?"

"Where else would you and Anthony go?" She uncrossed her arms as emotion welled inside her. Tears threatened once more, and damn it, she was tired of crying. She wanted to leave, but the only way out was past him. "Never mind, I don't care."

She tried to walk by him, but he curled his arm around her and drew her into his arms.

"I know how it feels to be so overwhelmed by helplessness that you can hardly see straight."

She'd wanted to push him away, but his words froze her in place. He sounded small and young and so unlike the Felix she knew. She let herself relax against him. He stroked her back, his hand moving gently up and down her spine. Suddenly, she didn't want to cry anymore.

His lips grazed her temple, and she closed her eyes. She lifted one hand and placed it next to her face against his chest. His heart beat strong and sure beneath her palm, a song to ease the agitation inside her.

They stood together for what seemed forever, and Sarah thought she could go on like that for another eternity. She looked up at him, grateful for his presence. Standing on her toes, she kissed his cheek.

His hand stopped moving along her back, instead flattening against the middle of her spine. The movement kept her on her toes, and he returned her gesture, pressing a soft, fleeting kiss on her face.

It felt so nice, so…right. She moved her hand up to his collarbone, steadying herself to brush her mouth against his. She shouldn't, but he was right there. And he was…kissing her back.

He brought his other hand up and cupped her cheek, holding her tenderly as their mouths moved together. It was gentle and careful and not at all like their kiss at Darent Hall.

Until it was.

She was suddenly aware of the hardness of his body and his crisp, masculine scent. She remembered it from that dark closet, and the memory sparked a need she'd tried to forget.

His thumb traced from the corner of her mouth along her jaw to the sensitive spot just in front of her ear. His touch took the kiss from comfort to something far more dangerous. She should step away, but she couldn't. Nor did she want to.

She wanted more, not less. She wanted *him*.

Curling one arm around his back, she pushed the other up along his collar until she found his nape. She flattened her palm against the warmth of his flesh. She parted her lips as he did the same. Their tongues met, coming together with heat and passion. She gripped him tightly, never wanting to let go.

His hands moved over her, stroking her back, her neck, her cheek, awakening her senses. She mirrored his eagerness, touching him everywhere she could but never feeling a moment's satisfaction. She'd never experienced such a need, such a *hunger*.

Because she wore only her night rail and a dressing gown, she felt him more than she had in the closet. But it wasn't enough. She brought her hands down between them and pushed at the front of his coat.

He helped her cause, shrugging his shoulders from the garment as she shoved it down his arms. He tossed it away behind him and put his hands on her the moment he was free, caressing her shoulders, her side, her hip. It seemed he meant to explore every part of her. Good, she wanted to do the same.

She grasped his cravat, searching for the ends. But then she recalled its rumpled state, and finally had a moment's lucidity. She pulled back and looked up into his familiar face that suddenly appeared very different than she'd ever seen it. His eyes were impossibly dark, the lids drooping low with seductive promise. His lips were red, his cheeks flushed.

"Was there another woman tonight?" she asked softly, her voice a bare whisper between them.

"There hasn't been another woman since Darent Hall."

Her knees wobbled, and her insides melted. He held her fast as she found his cravat and plucked the knot apart.

She gripped the ends of the silk and pulled his head down to her. "Good." She closed her eyes and kissed him again, using every bit of skill he'd unwittingly taught her.

He groaned into her mouth and swept her against him, practically lifting her from the floor. Her pelvis pressed into his, and she could feel his erection. The hard length pushed into her sex, and pleasure radiated from where they touched. She rotated her hips, wanting more. She felt helpless and desperate.

He unsealed his mouth from hers and kissed along her throat, forcing her to cast her head back and open herself to his attention. It was glorious. His tongue and lips tantalizing her flesh as his hand came up and cupped her breast. He'd briefly done that in the closet, and the sensation of it crashed into her again. That was when they'd had to stop, when reality had rudely interrupted.

She wasn't going to let that happen again. Not tonight.

Opening her eyes, she tore the cravat from his neck and dropped it to the floor. Then she tucked her hands inside the collar of his shirt, allowing her palms to caress his warm flesh. The muscles of his neck and shoulders corded beneath her touch as he stroked his thumb over her breast.

She gasped, closing her eyes once more as she gave herself completely into his care. He untied the sash at her waist and opened her dressing gown, leaving just the thin cotton of her night rail between them.

When his hand touched her breast again, she felt him so much more keenly. She had to grip his shoulders and hold tightly lest she collapse into a heap. His mouth moved lower, kissing the flesh above the top of her night rail. He tugged at the fabric, making the garment rise up in the back and press against her neck.

But it was enough to expose her breast. He pushed her flesh up, and cool air bathed her nipple just before his fingers closed around it.

She thrust her hand into the hair at his nape, tangling her fingers in the soft strands and tugging with need. He pinched her gently, drawing a low moan from her throat. Then his mouth replaced his fingers, his lips and tongue suckling her flesh as a wave of desire pulsed to her core.

He wasn't against her down there anymore, and she missed the pressure of him. She needed to feel him, to savor the promise of whatever he would do to deliver her from this sweet torment.

"Felix, please."

He lifted his head, his eyes dark with passion, his features taut with need. "Please what?"

"I need… I don't know what I need."

"This is not a good idea." And yet he didn't move.

"No, but it's the only thing I've wanted in weeks." Was she asking him to fulfill her desires? That was what he did, wasn't it?

Oh God, she couldn't ask this of him. There were limits to what a person could give. And there were certainly boundaries, especially between them.

"Felix, I want… I want you."

"You want what I can give you."

She wasn't sure what he was trying to say. And she was afraid the obstacles between them were too great. "Is that so bad?"

He kissed her again, his mouth ravaging hers. Then he swept her into his arms, drawing a gasp from her lips, and carried her to the settee, where he laid her down.

He bent over her, and drew in a ragged breath. "If you want me to stop, I will stop. You have only to say so—at any time."

She reached up and unbuttoned his waistcoat. "I will expect you to do the same."

Felix dropped one shoulder and then the other as she pushed the garment from his body, tugging it down his arms and then casting it aside. He leaned forward again and kissed her, a now familiar and incredibly arousing sensation that Sarah doubted she could ever get enough of.

He put his knee between her thighs, pinning her clothing around her, as he dragged his mouth down her throat, his tongue trailing along her flesh. Fire blazed wherever he touched her, sending her into a feverish urgency. Her flesh tingled, her breasts felt full and sensitive, her sex pulsed with need. She found herself pushing against his thigh to ease the craving she didn't know how to satisfy.

His hand skimmed along her thigh, and he lifted his leg as he pushed the night rail up. As with her breast a few moments ago, cool air rushed over her sex. She felt utterly exposed and wanton. She *should* call a halt to this, but she could not.

When his fingers touched her there, she rose up off the settee, her body tensing with a combination of surprise and yearning. He rubbed her flesh, feeding the flames burning within her.

He teased one of her nipples with his other hand, stirring every part of her. Flooded with sensation, she cast her head back, desperate for wherever he was taking her.

He stroked the flesh between her legs, pushing her toward something she was eager to grasp. She arched up, her body tensing, and grabbed his upper sleeve, her hand fisting around the linen. His arm moved as he touched her, his fingertips moving with deft precision, finding every spot that would elicit sensation more arousing than the last.

Just when she wondered how this could possibly end, he slipped a finger inside her. She knew the fundamentals of sexual intercourse and that he would put a body part into her, but she hadn't expected that one. She hadn't expected any of this. She fought to hold on to rational thought, but it began to slip away beneath the onslaught of his attentions. In and out he slid, creating a delicious friction. She moved her hips, seeking, wanting, needing more.

He'd managed to move her night rail to suckle her breast again, and the draw of his mouth coupled with the stroke of his finger and the push of his thumb sent her over the edge of the precipice she hadn't even realized she'd reached.

Her body tensed as rapture spun through her. She was lost in a dark, sweet oblivion. His mouth crashed over hers, and she realized she'd cried out. But now he swallowed the sound, kissing her with deep abandon.

Gradually, her body relaxed, and her limbs felt as though they would melt into puddles. He'd gentled the kiss, and now pulled back, moving his lips across her jaw before leaving a final kiss just beneath her ear. He eased away from her, drawing her night rail down over her thighs.

Sarah opened her eyes. "You're finished?"

His eyes narrowed slightly, and there was a flash of uncertainty in his gaze. "You enjoyed that, didn't you? I was sure you did."

"More than I can say. More than I ever imagined. But you… What about you?"

He smiled and pressed a kiss to her forehead. "This was never about me." He took her hand and drew her up to a sitting position.

She shifted her legs to the floor but kept her body angled toward him. "I didn't realize that." If it was about her, then she really didn't understand. "I didn't ask you to stop."

He sat facing her, his leg bent so that his knee was on the settee. "This is all we can—or should—do," he said. "Mostly."

"Mostly?" She couldn't stop looking at the V of his chest exposed by the opening of his shirt. Dark hair peeked through the opening, and her fingers itched to touch him.

"There are other things."

"Such as you putting your…cock inside me." She used the word Lavinia had told her.

He sucked in a breath. "Sarah, could you not use…that word?"

She flinched. "You find it offensive?"

"No, I find it arousing."

Heat swelled inside her. "Oh. Will you show me more?"

"Not tonight. And I probably shouldn't ever." His face creased, making him look pained. "This was rather ill-advised."

"I don't regret it, and I never will. Please don't tell me

you do." She looked at him intently. "I'm quite serious—don't tell me."

He took her hand and lifted it to his mouth, pressing a kiss into her palm. "I could never regret anything with you." His words were as heady as the things he'd done to her, as the promise of the things he would do.

"I would like you to show me more. And next time, it won't be entirely about me." She leaned forward and kissed him, her lips lingering against his for a moment before she pulled back and looked into his eyes. "It can't always be about pleasing others, Felix. You must let someone please you."

"And that someone is you?"

She gave him a saucy smile in response and stood from the settee. She pulled her dressing gown closed and tied the sash as she made her way from the sitting room.

Once inside her chamber, her heart began to pound as the enormity of what had just occurred slammed into her. Things had changed forever when they'd kissed at Darent Hall, and they'd changed yet again tonight.

One thing was certain: her relationship with Felix would never be the same.

◆E•3◆

THE WIND WHIPPED over Felix's face as he rode across his estate at a breakneck pace. The exercise felt good, both in his body and his mind. He'd spent most of the night tossing and turning—and staring at the ceiling—contemplating what in the hell he'd done.

But not regretting it.

He slowed his horse to a walk and patted his neck as they picked their way along the edge of the forested part of his land. After days of fine weather, today was overcast and cool, but it felt good. Probably because he was still overheated from last night.

He hadn't meant for any of it to happen. She'd been upset. He'd wanted to comfort her. Somehow, he'd kissed her temple. He hadn't even thought about it. His body had simply reacted to what she needed and provided what he thought would help.

And then she'd kissed him back.

He didn't think they could pretend this event hadn't happened, but then they hadn't been able to pretend the one at Darent Hall hadn't either. What the hell was going on? How had he become so desperately attracted to *Sarah Colton*?

Was it more than physical attraction? He couldn't seem to stop thinking about her in ways he never had before. Ways he'd never thought of any woman.

Felix wiped his hand over his face as if he could physically banish the thoughts and memories, but they were forever emblazoned on his mind. Forever?

He couldn't say, but he was certainly tormented by them. All night, he'd thought of her, even after frigging himself the moment he'd returned to his chamber. Images of her doing what she'd all but promised—pleasuring him—claimed his thoughts, both waking and sleeping. Even now, he was growing hard thinking of the provocative smile she'd given him.

"You must let someone please you."

"And that someone is you?"

God yes, he wanted it to be her. But how could he allow that? He had no intention of marrying her, and her brother was his best friend. Plus, their parents had *just died*. She was vulnerable, and he was a prick for taking advantage.

Maybe they could pretend it hadn't happened. Like

they'd been able to pretend Darent Hall hadn't happened? He scoffed at himself.

He could only hope that she'd awakened today and recalled last night in horror. He inwardly flinched at that, but it would be for the best. What he really ought to do is stay clear of her. But how did he do that when he was committed to helping her—and Anthony—work through their grief?

He didn't have an answer, but what he did have was a plan to stay away from the house all day. Which was how he found himself at the dower house to meet his uncle.

Martin was already on horseback awaiting Felix as he rode up. "It looks as though you've already been for a ride," Martin said.

"Yes. Shall we go?" Felix had sent a note earlier requesting Martin tour the estate with him.

"Of course." Martin urged his horse forward and joined Felix along the track. "I was a bit surprised to receive your note."

"Why? I always take a tour in the summer," Felix said, continuing to walk his horse.

"True, but with guests in residence, I assumed you would be busy."

"I don't know why you would assume that. I never have guests."

"That's true." Martin cocked his head. "Why is that? I hope it's not because of me."

It was—in a way. Stag's Court didn't feel as much of a home to Felix as his town house in London. Probably because he spent very little time here—a handful of weeks in the summer and maybe a few in the winter before the Season started. The rest of the time he spent in London or at a house or hunting party with friends.

"Your reputation is one as a host," Martin continued.

"You could host a house party here. Just because Michael will inherit one day doesn't mean you can't still enjoy your time as earl."

His "time." As if it were a fleeting thing. But Felix supposed it was. If he'd learned anything, it was that life was short, and it was up to each person to make the most of it. Or not.

Felix tried to make the most of it—for himself and for those around him.

This belief had never felt more important than since the Coltons' death. Death had snatched them away, robbing them and their children of their "time." Just as it had done with Felix's mother. He gave himself an internal shake. Why was he thinking of *her*?

Martin exhaled. "I was merely trying to make a suggestion."

Felix realized he'd never responded to his uncle. "I was considering it," he said. "I did invite more guests, but I wouldn't call it a party." Though with him, Anthony, and Beck together, it would certainly be entertaining. Provided he kept Anthony from falling back into his guilt.

And kept himself from dreaming of Sarah.

It was good that Beck and Lavinia were coming. Lavinia would keep Sarah busy, and then Felix could stop paying so much attention to her.

They rode in silence for a moment before Martin said, "Thank you for inviting Michael to town. I was going to suggest it. He'll need some exposure at the clubs and in Society."

Because he would be earl one day. "Pardon my morbidity, but what if he dies before me?" Felix asked.

Martin sent him a surprised look. Or maybe not. With his overly large eyes, it was hard to tell. "I shall pray that doesn't happen. The other reason I'm pleased you're taking him to town is so he can join the Marriage Mart. I suppose I should go with him to support his search for a wife. Or his mother, at least." Martin's lip curled as he mentioned her.

"Does Michael wish to marry so soon?" Felix felt sorry for the boy.

"He knows his duty," Martin said with a careless air. "He understands how important the earldom is, and his role within it."

Felix's insides churned with malcontent. Martin hadn't been trying to slight Felix—of that Felix was certain. Martin *wanted* his son to inherit and so accepted Felix's desire to remain unwed. Felix tried to recall when they had first discussed this arrangement, but no memory came to mind.

"Still, he needn't hurry." Felix didn't want his choice to remain a bachelor to push Michael into a marriage he might not want.

Martin gave him a smile that didn't seem to reach his bulbous eyes, but then they rarely did. His eyes were like those of a fish—all-seeing, emotionless, and rather unnerving. "You needn't worry about it, Felix."

No, he supposed he didn't. He kicked his horse into a trot and turned his attention to the estate.

By the time Felix returned to the house, it was midafternoon. He'd done a good job staying away— rather, avoiding Sarah—and now he would take a bath to continue that evasion.

However, as he passed the upstairs sitting room, he slowed at the sound of loud voices.

"I can't believe you would do this," Anthony said. "Mother and Father would be horrified."

Felix's heart stopped and then beat a rapid staccato, the sound resonating in his ears. He couldn't move.

"They wouldn't care so long as the end result was my happiness."

God, she hadn't told him about—? Felix removed his hand and combed his fingers through his hair. Anthony was going to be furious. Hell, he sounded halfway there already.

"What does Felix say?" Anthony asked, his voice climbing. "Or was this his idea?"

Oh, fuck, this wasn't good. Felix was torn between inserting himself into the conversation and hiding in his bedchamber until tomorrow. Or maybe next year.

"It was his idea to bring me these things, and he does support my plan. But the shop is entirely my design."

The shop.

Felix exhaled, and his body nearly sagged into the floor. He should insert himself, then—to convince Anthony it wasn't a terrible idea.

"Did I hear my name?" he asked as he stepped into the sitting room.

Sarah stood in front of a table upon which sat a half-made hat. The form was covered in a pale yellow fabric she was clearly in the process of stitching to the straw. She turned to look at Felix, as did Anthony.

"What the hell are you doing supporting this ridiculous notion of a millinery shop?" Anthony asked.

"It's not ridiculous," he and Sarah said in unison. Their gazes connected, and an undeniable warmth passed between them.

"Our parents wouldn't approve." Anthony frowned. "This is no way to honor their memory." He glowered at Sarah. "I thought you were going to marry."

"I plan to. In the meantime, I will start a millinery shop. I have it all sorted, Anthony. I have an assistant who will manage the store in Vigo Lane. It will be called Farewell's and have no outward connection to me at all. No one will know I own it or that the designs are mine."

"In Vigo Lane." Anthony blinked at her in disbelief. "You already have the store?"

"Not yet, but Felix was working on it."

Felix winced as Anthony turned his ire toward him. "You've been in on this for some time."

"Just since I offered to help her find a husband. Anthony, she doesn't want to marry just anyone. She wants to marry for love. If that doesn't happen, she has a plan to support herself and live happily in the pursuit of something she *does* love. What could be wrong with that?"

"Just because you're content to lead an unmarried life, doesn't mean she should. Christ, Felix, you can't force your unorthodox behavior on her."

"Why is Felix unorthodox?" Sarah said, springing to his defense. "Plenty of men—and women—don't marry."

Anthony looked at her with condescension. "Plenty of women, yes. There are more of them due to the wars. Men, particularly men in Felix's and my positions, must wed. It's our duty. That Felix chooses to shirk his is unorthodox."

Felix stared at his oldest friend and wondered who the hell he was. He knew how hard Anthony had taken his parents' death. "I think your grief is driving you to the brink of insanity," Felix said quietly, hoping to calm Anthony's anger.

"Or at least foolishness," Sarah said, exchanging a hopeful glance with Felix.

Anthony snorted. He looked toward Felix. "So you think I'm a lunatic." He transferred his gaze to Sarah. "And you think I'm a fool."

Sarah stepped around the table toward her brother. "No, I think you're sad and angry. I am too. I gave up on making hats after Mother and Father died. Felix has been trying to encourage me to start again. Today, I finally wanted to. Anthony, we can't spend the rest of our lives wallowing, nor can we live under the pressure of making Mother and Father proud. We did that before, and I, for one, wasn't happy."

"So you don't care what they think?" Anthony sounded beaten, his eyes glazed with defeat. "You'd dishonor their memory and take advantage of their death?"

Sarah paled, and she drew in a sharp breath.

Felix moved forward, instinctively wanting to protect her. "Of course Sarah cares what they think. Ensuring her own future happiness is something they would want."

"Through marriage," Anthony grumbled.

"And what if that isn't possible?" Felix said, allowing his voice to rise. "We can't force someone to marry her, and we shouldn't force her to marry."

Anthony glowered at him. "You said 'we.' Do you think you're somehow involved in what happens with Sarah?"

Hell and the devil. Did he? He *had* been involved when he'd played matchmaker for her. He inwardly winced at that word—now even *he* was using it. "I offered to help her," he said evenly. "And I still will, if she wants it."

"Anthony, I do still want to marry." Sarah took another step toward him, her gaze and tone compassionate. "But I'm also going to make hats and open a shop in Vigo Lane, and that's final."

Anthony stared at her for a moment, the tension in his shoulders lessening. He massaged his forehead. "I don't know…" He let out a soft growl, then spun on his heel and quit the room.

Sarah watched him go, her face creased with worry. "I thought he was feeling better being here, but perhaps I was wrong."

"His guilt is immeasurable," Felix said. "He thinks *he* should be dead, not your parents. Absent that, he thinks he has to take over where they left off, particularly with you."

"He's just not the Anthony we know." Her voice was soft, anguished.

Felix moved toward her, but was careful not to get too close. He knew what happened when he tried to comfort her physically, and he needed to keep his distance—for her as much as for him. "He will be again." Felix didn't know when, but it would happen. It had to. He wasn't going to let death and grief crush his friend the way it had done his father.

Sarah stepped toward him, and Felix's body came alive with awareness. She was close enough that he could reach for her, but he didn't. Instead, she reached for him, touching his sleeve.

He stepped back, and her eyes widened for a brief flash. He glanced toward the open door, worried that Anthony could return at any moment even though he was unlikely to do so. "Sarah, we should keep our distance."

She nodded in agreement. "We should be more discreet."

"That's not what I meant," he said, resisting the urge to smile. "What happened last night... It can't happen again."

"All right."

He'd expected her to argue and was surprised when she didn't. He was also a bit disappointed.

"Good. I'm glad we're agreed."

"As you said, there are other things, and we should move on to explore them. I meant what I said." She gave him that seductive look of promise again, and his body reacted. His muscles grew taut, and his cock began to lengthen.

"Sarah." The word was a low growl. "I'm going now."

"Yes, leave me to my hat for now," she said, moving to retake her seat.

The fact that she wasn't pressing the issue made him want to do so. His body was practically screaming for her.

In the end, he turned and left. As he made his way to his chamber, he prayed Beck and Lavinia would arrive soon to distract them all. If not, Felix feared he would give in to temptation. Again.

Chapter Ten

❦

SARAH HESITATED OUTSIDE Anthony's bedchamber. What if he didn't want to see her? He probably didn't, but she couldn't let him suffer alone. And she absolutely believed he was suffering.

Why else would he treat her the way he had earlier?

Gathering her courage, she lifted her hand to knock on the door. It suddenly opened, surprising her and making her take a step back.

Anthony stood on the other side of the threshold, his hair tidy, his clothing immaculate. He smelled as if he'd just bathed. His face was nearly impassive. There was just the faintest crinkle around his mouth and eyes to indicate he even registered her presence.

She clasped her hands in front of her waist and offered him a sunny smile. "Good evening. I wondered if you might want to dine with me? Alone. Without Felix, I mean."

"I had meant to dine alone, in fact. But I was going to drive into Ware."

"To The Golden Bear?" Sarah asked hopefully. "I could go with you. Is the chef really French?"

Anthony's brow furrowed. "Is the chef—?" He shook his head. "I have no idea."

"But didn't you and Felix go there the other night?"

"Yes, I suppose we did. But I scarcely remember the food." His skin turned pink just above the top of his collar. "Er, never mind. Perhaps tomorrow we can go for a ride," he suggested. "Alone."

"Anthony, I'm not letting you leave after what

happened earlier. I understand this is a challenging time, but I don't want us to fight. I don't have enough emotion to be upset with you in addition to everything else."

His gaze softened, and he took her hand. "I'm sorry, Sarah. I don't know why I reacted like that. Even so, you must agree that you opening a millinery shop is rather outrageous."

"Perhaps." She wasn't sure she would say *outrageous.* "It's definitely unusual."

The corner of his mouth ticked up. "You are nothing if not unusual—and I mean that in the most complimentary way possible."

"Thank you." She exhaled. "Who knows if I'll actually open the shop? Right now, I'm just trying to get back to something I enjoy, which is making hats." Doing so also distracted her from Felix—the other thing she apparently enjoyed. And wasn't *that* revelation perhaps the most confounding thing about her emotions right now?

Not that she was working terribly hard to distract herself from him. No, she was actually looking for ways in which they might find themselves alone together. But he was right—they shouldn't. And so her brain had driven her here, to her brother. To safety.

"I'm glad you enjoy it," Anthony said. "That doesn't mean you need to profit from it. I will ensure you are always taken care of." His gaze was sober and intent. "Even if you're a spinster." He cracked a small smile then, and she laughed softly.

"Well, that's a relief. I do think you should apologize to Felix."

He winced. "Yes, I probably should."

"Ahem, *yes.*"

Sarah turned as her heart skipped over itself. Just the sound of his voice was apparently enough to provoke a response from her. Felix stood a few feet away. He was also perfectly groomed, as if he too had just completed an intensive toilet. She could smell the soap he'd used, and the scent did scandalous things to her body.

"You can't seem to help but eavesdrop today," Anthony said.

"You two can't seem to stop talking about me today," he said jovially. "Should I be concerned?"

Anthony shook his head, smiling. "You've saved me the trouble of finding you. I'm sorry about earlier. However, I must ask that you cease anything to do with this millinery shop."

Sarah snapped her attention back toward him and opened her mouth to protest, but he held up his hand. "Only because if anyone is to help Sarah, it will be me," he said.

"Then I should tell you I already leased the shop in Vigo Lane," Felix said, drawing Sarah to whip her attention back to him.

"What?" She hadn't known he'd done that.

Felix shrugged, his expression just a bit sheepish. "I did so a fortnight ago—just in case."

Sarah was thrilled but also annoyed at his presumption. "I didn't ask you to do that."

"No, but I wanted to do so as a precaution on the chance that you would choose to open the shop. If the property was gone and you wanted to open the shop, you might have been disappointed. I didn't want you to have to deal with another..." He glanced away. "Well, you know what I mean."

Sadness. Devastation. Defeat.

"Thank you," she said softly. "That was incredibly thoughtful." Her chest expanded with warmth, and she couldn't think of anything else to say.

Felix cleared his throat. "I came this direction to see you, Anthony. I was going to apologize as well. I didn't mean to overstep into your family business."

"It's all right," Anthony said. "In a way, you are family. Like our brother."

Felix's gaze drifted to Sarah, and a flash of heat broke over her. He was nothing like a brother to her. Not anymore.

"I thought we could go to dinner at The Golden Bear," Sarah said, eager to change the topic and to plan for an evening in which she wasn't alone with Felix. Which she would be if Anthony went into Ware alone.

And being alone with Felix was both exciting and terrifying. Mostly exciting. Actually, it was only exciting. She ought to be terrified, but she just couldn't muster that particular emotion. Not where Felix was concerned.

"An excellent idea," Felix said. "I'll have the coach brought round."

"Then I'd best get dressed," Sarah said, taking herself off. She vaguely heard Anthony saying something about how that would be fine with him and wondered if she detected a note of sarcasm.

All sense of sarcasm had been forgotten by the time they'd reached the final course of their elaborate dinner at The Golden Bear. The inn *did* have a French chef, and the food was absolutely divine. Sarah hadn't eaten so much in weeks. Since…well, *since*.

"Would you excuse me for a few minutes?" Anthony said, excusing himself from the semiprivate dining room they shared with two other parties.

Sarah watched her brother go and realized she was now alone with Felix. But not alone-alone, so she could rest easily. Perhaps not *easily*, since she couldn't seem to be in his presence anymore without feeling a seductive pull in his direction. She looked at him, and all she could see was his head bent at her breast. He spoke, and all she could hear was him telling her that her use of the word *cock* was arousing.

"Anthony seems in much better spirits this evening," Felix said, apparently immune to the desperate attraction she was suffering.

"He does. But I understand how that happens. One moment, I feel fine, and the next, I am awash with sadness."

"In time, the sadness will fade."

She turned to Felix, who sat on her right. "Will it? Is that what happened with your father?"

"As I've told you, it was different. Honestly, I don't really remember."

"That is both a blessing and a sorrow. You said you don't miss your mother, which I understand since you never knew her. Do you miss your father?" He'd evaded that question before. Maybe he would answer it now.

"Not particularly. He's been gone more than half my life, so in some ways, it's the same as my mother. My memories have faded."

Sarah looked at the half-eaten syllabub in front of her and suddenly felt a bit sick. She was more than eager for the sadness to dissipate, but to think her memories of her parents would go with it was painful. Perhaps she'd cling to the sadness a bit longer.

Felix reached for her but stopped short of touching her, perhaps deciding it was best if he didn't. He dropped his hand in his lap. "Sarah, you knew your parents as an adult. I have to think your memories will last a lifetime, unlike mine. You shouldn't worry about losing them."

Her mouth lifted in a half smile. "You discerned that's what I was thinking?"

"It wasn't hard. I know you quite well."

Yes, he did. And he knew her now better than ever before. He was perhaps realizing that too, for he directed his attention to his wineglass.

A serving maid—a different one than they'd had for dinner—came forward to refill Felix's wine. He looked up at her with a smile and thanked her.

"My *pleasure*, Lord Ware." Her answering smile was warm and plainly seductive as her gaze dipped over Felix.

A flash of possession flared through Sarah, and she leaned toward him, picking up her own glass for a refill. Which was a bit silly because it wasn't empty. She quickly drank the contents, then held it up for the maid with a toxic smile. "If you please?"

The maid refilled Sarah's glass and turned her attention back to Felix. "Will you be staying tonight?"

"No, my home isn't far."

"Pity, we had such fun the other night." She laughed, then took herself off, her hips swaying.

Sarah pursed her lips and glowered at Felix. "I thought you said you didn't come to Ware for women."

"I didn't. At least not with Anthony the other night." He took another drink of wine, looking distinctly uncomfortable. "When she said the other night, she meant several months ago."

"So you *have* come into Ware for women? In the past." She was torturing herself with this question, but the jealousy tearing at her insides was a ravenous beast.

"Sarah, I've done many things in the past. As you yourself have noted, I'm a bit of a rake."

Of course he was. Who else but a rake would kiss her as he'd done in the closet at Darent Hall? Or pleasure her as he'd done last night? Her body flushed with desire, banishing the jealousy.

"Except since Darent Hall," she said, vaguely aware that her voice carried a rather sensual quality.

"We shouldn't discuss that." He kept his voice low and drank more wine.

For whatever reason, she enjoyed provoking him about it. He was always so self-assured, so commanding. And talking about whatever was happening between them set him completely out of kilter.

"Pity. We had such fun the other night." She parroted the maid's coquettish statement, which earned her a sharp stare and an intake of breath from Felix.

Before she could continue the flirtation, Anthony returned and ruined the entire thing. Burying her scowl, Sarah sipped her wine.

"Shall we return to Stag's Court?" Anthony asked.

Felix practically leapt from the table. "Yes, let's."

Sarah sat beside her brother on the ride home. She'd hoped Felix might take the front-facing seat with her, but should have known better. He spent the short journey evading eye contact and just looking generally uncomfortable.

When they arrived, Seales informed Felix that George and Vane had arrived. Sarah knew that George was his secretary but had no idea as to the identity of Vane. "Who is Vane?"

"My valet."

"Felix?" A strong, feminine voice came from the room just off the entrance hall, and Felix strode in that direction.

Sarah, curious as to who else might have arrived, followed him along with Anthony.

"George!" Anthony exclaimed as he stepped forward and took her hand. "It's good to see you."

Wait, George was Felix's secretary. And she was a

woman? Not just a woman, but a beautiful one at that. She was tall—taller than Sarah by several inches—with pale blonde hair and light blue eyes. She looked as though she belonged at Almack's or in the middle of a grand ball at Clare House in London, not in a sturdy dark blue traveling costume, bearing the title of secretary.

Sarah recalled what Felix had said at The Golden Bear: *I've done many things in the past.*

Did any of those things involve an exquisitely handsome woman who was now in his employ?

That terrible beast—jealousy—reared inside Sarah once more, and she realized she was in real danger if she didn't rein in her emotions. It was one thing to flirt with Felix and to delight in the pleasures he offered, especially now, when the diversion was most welcome. She could not—*must* not—expect more than he would ever offer. Jealousy had no place in her relationship with Felix.

"George, allow me to present Miss Sarah Colton," Felix said. "Sarah, Mrs. Georgiana Vane, my secretary."

Mrs. Vane. "Is Felix's valet your husband?" Sarah blurted.

"Why, yes, he is," she said, her eyes sparkling.

"Is that how you came to be Felix's secretary?" Still, it was odd that Felix would have hired a woman. Sarah didn't know any gentlemen with female secretaries. Now that she'd pushed her jealousy aside, she found the idea rather wonderful and wasn't the least surprised Felix had done it.

The others in the room were looking at Sarah, and she realized she was being rude with her questions. "My apologies," she rushed to say. "I've never met a woman secretary before. It's fairly fabulous."

Felix chuckled. "George is my steward's daughter. I've known her my entire life. When I hired Vane, the two of them fell madly in love."

George smiled. "It's true."

"So you're the person behind all of Felix's elaborate plans," Sarah said with a bit of awe. "I should have known you would be a woman. It makes perfect sense now."

George laughed. "They are his ideas. I simply execute them."

"Better than I ever could," Felix said. "Now if you'll excuse me, George and I have some business to discuss. I shall see you on the morrow."

And with that, Sarah felt dismissed. She supposed she could barge into his bedchamber later, but she wouldn't. Having set her jealousy aside, she decided it was past time to be cautious. And probably past time to let her…flirtation, for that was the only word she was willing to acknowledge, with Felix go.

If she could.

No, she *must*.

She didn't need him to distract her from her grief. She had her hats, and she'd decided long ago that they would be enough.

⋆ε•3⋆

THE BRIGHT BEAUTY of summer returned the following day with a lush blue sky and warm, sparkling sunlight. It was far too fine to remain indoors, so Felix had suggested an excursion to Scott's Grotto since Sarah had seemed keen to go.

"You say we should spend the day outside, and yet the grotto is a series of tunnels, are they not?" Sarah asked with more than a little sarcasm. But then she'd winked and said she was joking and that she'd love to see the grotto.

Since taking just her was not the wisest idea, Felix invited Anthony, but he'd declined in favor of fishing. And so Felix found himself waiting outside for Sarah, wondering how he could cancel the outing without disappointing her.

She emerged from the house in a particularly fetching costume of lavender trimmed with dark blue. Her hat was, of course, the best part of her ensemble. Styled as a cavalier, a bright red feather jutted up from the side.

"Your hat is stunning, as usual," he said.

"Thank you. I was a bit nervous about wearing the red feather with my mourning clothes, but I'm afraid I can't resist a jaunty feather." Her gaze flashed with self-reprobation as she moved toward the open gig.

"Sarah, we can't go," he said without preamble and with immediate regret as her eyes clouded. "Anthony's not coming."

"I'll send for Dovey."

"I'm not sure that's wise." Felix didn't want to draw attention to why. After she'd flirted with him at dinner last night, he'd worried she might seek him out after returning to Stag's Court. Worried? No, he'd hoped. But she hadn't, and that was as it should be. Temptation, it seemed, was always before him where she was concerned.

"But I really want to see the grotto." She exhaled. "I suppose I could just go with Dovey. You don't need to come."

Wise or not, he hated seeing the disappointment in her gaze. To hell with it. "I'm coming. I'll have Seales fetch Dovey."

Sarah's face brightened to the shade of the sun. "Brilliant."

Yes, she was.

A short while later, they were on their way to Scott's Grotto. Set into a chalk hillside on the grounds of Amwell House, which was currently owned by Maria Scott, the grotto had been built by her father, John Scott. It was quite large, extending dozens of feet into the hillside and going perhaps thirty feet beneath it.

The crowd today wasn't excessive, but there were maybe five or six vehicles parked outside. Felix stepped down from the gig and helped Sarah to descend. Then he offered his hand to Dovey.

The maid smiled and said, "I'll wait here. My back is troubling me again."

Felix didn't believe her for a moment. It was clear Sarah's maid was trying to facilitate a courtship. He just wondered if Sarah was behind it.

Sarah linked her arm through Felix's. "Did you know John Scott was a poet?"

Felix sent her a sideways glance. "Are you trying to distract me from your maid playing matchmaker?"

"Not at all. You noticed that too? She hasn't said anything, but when she stayed in the gig in Ware the other day, I assumed that's what she was trying to do." She looked at him as they walked toward the porch in front of the entrance. "You think I put her up to it?"

He shrugged. "I admit I wondered."

She gave him a prim stare. "I did not. Now, back to John Scott. He was also a gardener."

"Did you happen to know all this?"

"No, I spoke to Seales about it. He's quite knowledgeable about local people and events."

She'd been speaking to his staff? "What else has my staff told you? Do I need to be concerned?" He couldn't imagine why he would, but he was an intensely private person. Not that any of his staff saw who he truly was.

No one did.

Was that true? He shook the notion away.

"What a suspicious question," she said with a laugh. "Yes, they've told me how I may steal all of Stag's Court's valuables."

He laughed too, marveling at how he never failed to enjoy her company. How had he never noticed that before? They went into the main entrance chamber and found the guest book. Felix signed his name and handed the pen to Sarah.

She hesitated to sign and looked up at him. "Do we really want to make a record of our being here? Alone. Together." She gave him an audacious stare followed by a cheeky smile.

Damn, she had a point. But it was too late, for she signed her name.

Moving into the center of the chamber, she looked up at the ceiling, her eyes wide. "This is spectacular."

The walls were completely inset with shells and colored glass and all manner of rocks, including fossils. Felix realized Lavinia might find it of interest.

"Lavinia must see this," Sarah said, echoing what he'd just thought. They did that often, he realized—finishing each other's sentences or seeming to read each other's minds.

He joined her in the center of the large chamber. "I was just thinking that. When she and Beck arrive, we'll arrange another excursion."

Sarah looked at him, her lips curved into a winsome smile. "She could help you when you build one."

"You like to plan things for me to do, I've noticed. Apparently, I'm hosting races next year as well as building a grotto. What else should I do?"

"Let me think." She put her arm in his again as they

made their way to the right into the passageway. "If you turn out to be adept at matchmaking, you should definitely broaden your services."

"Good God, *no*. I only agreed to help you because I like you. I couldn't tolerate any other unmarried chits."

"We're 'chits,' are we?"

"Not you." No, she was unlike any other woman he knew and certainly not a chit.

The passage led to a large, round chamber. The walls were as studded with shells, glass, and stunning rock as the entrance hall and passageway, and there were also seats inset into the walls.

Sarah's indrawn breath filled the empty space. "I can't imagine how long this took to make."

Though Felix had seen the grotto before, it had been a few years. And it was as if he'd never seen it at all. He felt as though he were viewing it for the first time with her. He found himself staring at her upturned face instead of the grotto.

"It's so beautiful," she breathed.

"Astonishing," he said.

A group of four people entered from the other doorway. Felix was glad for their arrival because he'd begun to consider how he might best use their time alone in a dark tunnel.

They continued on, moving from the chamber to the passageway the other party had just left. This one was long and narrow and very poorly lit. In fact, it was so narrow that he had to walk in front of Sarah.

"It's rather dark, isn't it?" Sarah clasped his hand.

Though they wore gloves, her touch lit through him like a spark catching flame. "There are light wells, but none along this passageway. We have to rely on the light from behind and in front of us."

"It reminds me a bit of Darent Hall and the dark closet."

Why had she mentioned that? His body was already in a state of half arousal and needed no encouragement. The passage turned to the left where there was more illumination due to a light well above them. Carved through the hillside, these wells provided sunlight to the grotto. Felix could imagine how much darker it would be if the day were overcast or raining.

The passage opened into another round chamber, this one maybe half the size of the one they'd left a few moments ago. There were no seats in this one and, so far, no other people.

Felix went to the wall to study a particularly bright rock. It was a gemstone. "I'm surprised no one has pried this off."

"Who would be so terrible?" Sarah had come up beside him, and he was too aware of her proximity. "Did you hear what I said about this feeling like Darent Hall?"

"Yes. I thought it best if we didn't discuss it." It was bad enough they were here alone. The word temptation, which he'd grown to loathe, hummed through his mind and body.

She exhaled. "Probably. Do you ever think about what might have happened if the footman hadn't interrupted us?" Apparently, she wasn't going to heed his suggestion. He should protest, but he simply couldn't. Whether it was the breathy, seductive timbre of her voice or the delicious nearness of her parted lips, he was quickly losing the battle of staying away from her. But then if he'd really meant to do that, he would have abandoned this outing the moment Anthony had declined to go.

And yet here he was. Staring into her lush blue eyes, his cock hardening with every passing moment.

Her hand moved forward and grazed against the front of his breeches. It was the same way she'd touched him in the closet, which he'd assumed had been accidental. Now he wasn't so sure.

"Did you do that on purpose?"

Her eyes narrowed. "Yes."

"At Darent Hall, I mean." He was entirely certain she'd done it purposely just now.

"No. That was unintentional, and I was horrified. But also titillated." She let out a soft giggle. "And that was before I knew who you were."

"This is a very dangerous situation, Sarah."

She blinked and tipped her head to the side. "How so?"

"Don't pretend to be naïve. You can see where this might lead."

"In a grotto? I must admit, I'm intrigued." She moved closer until their chests barely touched. "Tell me."

He would do better than that. God, he was a fool. Or an idiot. Or both.

Taking her hand, he pulled her from the chamber into the next passageway. If he remembered correctly, there was a small alcove that nearly everyone missed. He hadn't, of course, because he'd been looking for a place to steal a kiss.

Where the passageways turned, there tended to be an alcove of sorts at the juncture—it was like two passages intersecting. At this intersection, the alcove was slightly larger than the others, and there was far less light at the back. Because of that, it was easy to miss the smaller alcove tucked behind the wall of the passage.

Felix pulled her into that tiny alcove. It was just large enough for the two of them—and only if they touched.

"*Felix,*" she breathed.

He could hear the excitement and anticipation in her

voice, and it fed his desire. He pressed her against the wall and kissed her, his mouth eagerly devouring hers.

She returned the kiss with sweet and sultry abandon, her hands curling around his neck. Her fingers tangled in the hair at his nape, tugging the locks and scraping his flesh through the thin cotton of her gloves.

He dragged his mouth over her chin and down her throat until he reached the prohibitive top of her gown. This wasn't the place to disrobe her, so he did his best to fondle her through the layers of her clothes.

The gloves were a bloody nuisance. He removed the right one and handed it to her. "Hold this."

He couldn't see her face in the dark—and God, this was so like the closet at Darent Hall and that only made the occasion more arousing—but sensed her curiosity.

"I can't wear my glove, and I need my hands free." He started to lift her skirt.

She sucked in a breath. "Felix, this is very naughty."

He paused. "Do you want me to stop?"

"Don't you dare."

"Good." He would, of course, but he'd much prefer not to. When her dress was at her waist, he took her free hand and moved it to grasp the fabric of her garments. "Hold this here. And if you need to put the glove in your mouth to keep from screaming, please do so."

She drew in another sharp breath, and he kissed her once more, using his teeth and tongue to tease and worship her. When he finished, she was breathless.

He dropped to his knees—damn, the floor was hard—and smoothed his bare fingers over her sex. Though it was pitch-dark, he found her easily. "Part your legs, my love."

She did as he bade, widening her stance. Her scent washed over him—roses and something indefinable but wholly Sarah—and he nearly shook with want. But like the other night, this wasn't about him. It would never be. It was only about her and giving her all the pleasure she deserved.

He braced his gloved hand around her hip, holding her steady, and then he licked along her sweet folds. She cried out, and then the sound became muffled. She'd stuck the glove in her mouth.

"Good girl," he said, smiling against her heated flesh.

He used his bare fingers to stroke her clitoris, pushing and teasing her until she began to move against him. Then he used his mouth, his lips and tongue ravaging her sex with sucks and licks. He was vaguely aware of her muted sounds of ecstasy, but it was difficult to hear over the roar of his own thundering heartbeat in his ears.

Slipping his tongue inside her, he pushed at her thigh. Her legs began to quiver around him, and her muscles tensed. She was so responsive, so wonderfully sensual that he could hardly keep a thought in his head. Except for one: how badly he wanted to bury himself inside her.

And so he did. With fingers and tongue, he filled her. She rotated her hips against him, pressing herself into his mouth. He sucked her clitoris and thrust his fingers into her core, curling until he found that spot that would send her over the edge.

He was certain she would have screamed if not for the glove in her teeth. He held her hip tightly as she came in his mouth, never ceasing his attentions for even a moment as she crested the wave of rapture.

She stiffened one last time, and the shaking in her legs increased. He slowed, stroking her outer flesh until her body began to quiet. Then he stood and took the skirts from her tightly clenched fist, letting them fall to the floor.

He pulled the glove from her mouth and kissed her again, driving his tongue deep into her mouth as he curled his arm around her back and pressed her tightly against him. Gradually, he lightened the kiss until he broke it completely, his breath coming hard and fast.

"My God, Felix. I had no idea."

"None?"

"Not really. I knew there were…things beyond sexual intercourse, but nothing like that." She clasped the back of his neck and kissed his earlobe. "Thank you," she whispered. "Now what about you?"

He stepped back, turning his body to reenter the larger alcove, pulling on his glove as he went. It was damp from her mouth, and when he thought of her with it clenched between her teeth, he wanted to frig himself until he came in spectacular abandon.

Alas, that would have to wait until he got home. He hoped he could make it that long. He'd never had an orgasm without someone touching his cock, but right now, he feared that was possible.

He took deep breaths, seeking to return his body to a less frantic state. But then she joined him in the alcove, moving behind him so that her breasts pressed against his back as she reached her hands around to stroke his chest.

He moaned softly. "Sarah, we need to go."

"Where?" she asked hopefully. "Is there another alcove where I can do for you what you did for me?"

He turned and dropped a kiss on her forehead. "No. There is no other alcove. Not like that one."

"Then let's go back—"

Felix was saved when a party of three ladies emerged from the dim light as they made their way along the passageway. They bid Felix and Sarah good afternoon and asked if they knew the way out. They'd somehow become turned around.

"I do, in fact," Felix said. "Follow us." He led them in single file, making a few slight turns before taking a sharp turn to the left to return them to the entrance chamber.

"Oh, thank you," the older of the women said. Now that they had more light, Felix thought she must be mother to the other two. "I worried we would be lost in there for some time!" She laughed with an edge of nervousness, then they bid farewell and left the grotto.

"Come, it's getting late," Felix said, guiding Sarah out into the sunlight.

She turned to him with a slightly puzzled expression. "Why won't you let me give you the same pleasure you've given me?"

"Because it's not about me."

She scowled and cast a look toward the sky. "Stop saying that. You deserve to have someone do something for you. Or maybe you're incapable of allowing that." She arched a brow at him.

He suppressed his own scowl. "Let's get back to Stag's Court. Dovey is staring at us in open interest. Please tell her to stop trying to push us together."

"Do we really need her help?" Sarah murmured as they walked to the gig.

No, what they needed was for her to act like a bloody chaperone and keep them apart.

Dovey asked about the grotto as they drove back, and Sarah told her all about the shells and glass and rocks, as well as the darkness and cool temperature. Felix hadn't even noticed the latter because whenever he was around Sarah, his body felt as if it were on fire.

When they arrived at Stag's Court, a coach was just being driven toward the stables.

"I think that's Beck and Lavinia's coach!" Sarah

exclaimed. She barely waited for Felix to help her down from the gig, and as soon as she hit the ground, she hurried toward the house.

Seales opened the door, and she rushed inside. Felix helped Dovey down, and they followed at a more sedate pace.

"The Marquess and Marchioness of Northam are in the drawing room, my lord," Seales said. "Miss Colton has already started in that direction."

"Thank you, Seales." Felix was glad to see her so excited. He was also relieved to have their friends here as a necessary buffer between him and Sarah, because he couldn't keep surrendering to temptation.

Chapter Eleven

◆E◆3◆

AFTER DINNER THAT night, Sarah was delighted to remove to the drawing room with Lavinia while the men remained in the dining room to drink port.

"It seems you are very excited to have me alone," Lavinia said, laughing, as soon as they sat down together on the settee.

A footman brought a tray with two glasses of sherry, which Sarah and Lavinia each took, then departed.

Sarah didn't take a sip before saying, "I'm glad you're here. I have so much to tell you."

Lavinia *did* take a sip of her sherry. "You seemed to be brimming with news when I saw you briefly after we arrived earlier. I own I am surprised to see how improved you are. Improved and, dare I say, happy." She took Sarah's hand and gave it a brief squeeze.

Was she improved? Definitely. Was she happy? She certainly wasn't as weighed down with sadness as she'd been. And that was due to Felix. "It's Felix."

"Of course it is," Lavinia said. "He's the master of cheer and diversion. If anyone could help you navigate this time, it's him. What has he been doing to distract you and Anthony?"

Sarah blinked at her. "Kissing me. Touching me. Doing unspeakable things to me."

Lavinia's eyes widened, and she squeezed Sarah's hand again but this time didn't let go. "What is happening?" She leaned forward, her lips parted in anticipation. "Are you in love?"

The question stopped Sarah cold. She hadn't thought

about emotion. Because she'd purposely shoved all emotion to the recesses of her mind. "I don't know," she said quietly. "And I don't think I want to contemplate it." When Lavinia opened her mouth to speak, Sarah spoke over her. "What would be the use in loving Felix? The emotion would never be reciprocated."

Lavinia pursed her lips and let go of Sarah, easing back. "True." She swore softly. "Why do some men have to be so terrible?"

"He's not *terrible*," Sarah said with a hint of a smile. "But he can be rather stubborn. Twice now he's…given me pleasure—"

"Have you had sex?"

"Not that specifically, no." Sarah now took the opportunity to take a long drink of sherry. She felt as though she needed fortification. "He used his hand and his…mouth."

Lavinia's brows arched, and the corner of her mouth ticked up. "Well done, Felix," she murmured. "And how was it?"

"Should we really be discussing this?"

"Of course. All women do."

"You don't discuss it with me—not like this." She'd satisfied Sarah's questions about what happened between men and women, husbands and wives, but she hadn't elaborated as to how it had *felt*.

Lavinia's cheeks heated to a dull pink. "I didn't want to get into specifics since you weren't wed."

"I'm not wed now."

"Don't be obtuse. You know what I'm getting at. Why tell you how wonderful it is to be with a man when you aren't with a man? It seems unkind."

Sarah could understand that. "It was lovely."

"Lovely?"

"And wild." It was Sarah's turn to blush. "And I am desperate to do it again."

"Then I would say Felix is definitely doing it right. Though I wouldn't have doubted it, given his reputation."

As a rake.

"You said he was stubborn," Lavinia prompted. "Before I interrupted." She gave Sarah a sheepish smile.

Sarah was used to Lavinia's…conversational exuberance. "He hasn't let me reciprocate."

"Ah, I see. Have you offered?"

"Of course I have. But he always says it's about me, not him." She rolled her eyes. "He's long been too focused on pleasing everyone around him. I'm not sure he knows how to allow others to do the same for him."

"You mean to ensure he does."

Sarah nodded, then winced. "However, I have no idea what to do."

Lavinia's lips spread in a wicked, conspiratorial smile. "Well, I can help you with that."

Sarah relaxed back against the settee. "Thank goodness." She sipped her sherry and awaited Lavinia's advice.

"Do you want to marry him?" Lavinia asked.

"No." She hadn't thought about it because it wasn't even an option—not with Felix. "Felix won't ever marry."

"Do you still plan to?"

"Yes." She narrowed her eyes at Lavinia. "Why does any of this matter?"

"You can't very well have sex with Felix if you plan to marry."

Sarah snorted. "I should remain a virgin for my husband while it is all but likely he has not?"

Lavinia's nose wrinkled as if she'd smelled something noxious. "That is the generally accepted norm."

"Do women really do that?" Sarah asked. "Were you a virgin when you wed Beck?"

"Er, no. But I was when we lay together the first time. And that was the day we became betrothed. Fanny and I discussed this the other day. She admitted she had sexual intercourse with David before they were betrothed." Lavinia shook her head. "But our circumstances are very different. You *know* Felix won't marry you, so why risk your future marriage?"

Sarah stuck her tongue between her lips and blew to make a noise of disgust. "Whether I have sex with him or not isn't something I want to debate. I merely wanted advice on how to give him pleasure. However, if you'd rather counsel me on morality, I shall manage on my own."

Lavinia exhaled. "My apologies. You are my dearest friend. I am only looking out for your future—and your feelings. It doesn't seem as though you are allowing emotion into this liaison."

"Love. I'm not allowing love. I do care for Felix." Sarah set her sherry glass on the table beside the settee. "I never imagined something like this could have happened between us," she said softly, trying to think of how they'd arrived at this place. It was because of her parents' dying, because of her grief. Uneasiness crept over Sarah.

"We never really talked about Guess the Kisser at Darent Hall," Lavinia said slowly, her gaze probing.

"No, because my parents were murdered and such conversation seemed rather trivial." It still was. The melancholy that had ruled Sarah's mind for so many weeks tried to take command once more.

Lavinia nodded solemnly, and they were quiet a moment. At length, she said, "I take it Guess the Kisser changed everything between you and Felix?"

More than she ever could have imagined. Not that she'd even imagined. Kissing Felix had never entered her mind. "Yes."

"I assumed it would. Unless the kiss was terrible." Lavinia laughed softly, giving Sarah some much-needed levity. "Although that would have changed things too. Can you imagine if he'd had terrible breath? Or if he hadn't known how to kiss?"

Sarah grinned. "Or if he'd smelled bad, like rotting fish, perhaps."

They giggled, and Sarah felt much better. She was so glad to have her friend here.

Lavinia sipped her sherry once more. "But the kiss was exceptional, of course."

"Of course."

"But then… Well, never mind. Did anything happen in London?"

Sarah shook her head. "Not until we came here. It seemed to be this…thing between us. So we talked about it and tried to pretend it never happened."

Lavinia's brown eyes sparkled. "I can see how well that worked."

"Yes, quite. We did try. It's difficult when you're in a dark grotto that reminds you of a dark closet where you kissed for the first time." When Sarah had greeted Lavinia and Beck that afternoon, she'd told them that she and Felix had just come from Scott's Grotto. She and Felix had told Lavinia all about the wonderful rocks and fossils embedded in the tunnels.

"I completely understand." Her gaze took on a determined glint. "I can see there are other reasons I must visit this marvel."

Sarah laughed softly. "Then perhaps we won't accompany you. I'll be sure to tell you where to go."

"I would appreciate that, thank you." Lavinia straightened and took a deep breath. "Well, if I'm to educate you on pleasing Felix, we should get to it before they barge in."

Sarah stiffened her spine and turned her full attention to Lavinia, eager to hear what she had to say. "Yes, do tell."

⚜

CASTING HIS LINE back into the pond, Felix shifted his weight to his other foot. The movement was punctuated with an odd sound.

"Is Anthony snoring?" Beck asked, glancing back toward the blanket spread beneath the large oak tree.

"Seems to be." Felix tilted his head back and squinted up at the bright late-morning sky.

Beck stifled a yawn. "We *were* up late playing cards."

"It wasn't *that* late." Felix suspected Anthony wasn't sleeping well. His eyes looked a bit haggard, and Felix often caught him yawning.

"True. I was up later, however." His gaze was focused on his line in the pond, but his mouth curled into a satisfied smile.

"I do not want to hear about your bedroom activities."

"Who said they took place in a bedroom?"

Felix chuckled, looking toward Beck, who was now grinning. "I'm glad to know Stag's Court is so accommodating. Or arousing."

"Or both." A moment later, Beck sent him a quick glance. "Sounds as though it's been the same for you."

Bloody fucking hell. Felix snapped his head around to make sure Anthony was still asleep. How did Beck know about his *activities* with Sarah? Maybe he didn't and was just making an assumption. Felix decided to pretend he was ignorant. "What are you talking about?"

"I wondered if you'd prefer to act as though there was nothing going on. I can understand given the circumstances."

He knew. Felix exhaled. "How did you find out? And keep your voice down in case Anthony wakes up."

"Sarah told Lavinia, and Lavinia told me. We don't keep secrets in our marriage."

Yes, their union was disgustingly perfect. It was astonishing to Felix, who had grown up with the absolute worst example of marriage one could witness. That one of his closest friends had married so well pleased Felix, but, if he were honest, he wasn't sure he expected their harmony to last.

He suddenly thought of the Dartfords, who'd been married for a couple of years and still seemed quite happy and in love. Felix decided they were an aberration too. Plus, the relationship was young and would likely cool.

His mind returned to Sarah and her loose tongue. "Sarah and I are *not* married. I shall speak to her about the importance of secrecy."

"Don't be angry with her," Beck said. "Her mother is gone. She was looking for feminine advice."

She was? Felix could only imagine about what, and he wasn't going to ask. This conversation was uncomfortable enough. "Of course I won't be angry with her."

No, the only person with whom he was angry was himself. He'd been an imbecile to allow their...*activities* to continue. But damn, when he thought of yesterday in the Grotto... He'd best not, unless he wanted to make an embarrassing display in his breeches.

"Secrecy is still important," Felix said, glancing back at Anthony once more. "What if he found out?"

Beck blew out a breath. "He wouldn't like it, which is why this is a dangerous situation. I would never dream of intruding in your private affairs, but this is Anthony's sister. This is Sarah."

He bloody well knew it was Sarah. Yet he'd been powerless to resist her flirtation, her charm, and the devastating attraction he felt toward her. She'd occupied his mind and body for weeks. Since Darent Hall.

"I've already resolved that it won't happen again," Felix said.

"Does Sarah know this?" Beck didn't sound convinced.

Felix realized he hadn't actually told her they couldn't continue. He'd only told her it had all been for her. Because if he allowed her anywhere near his bare cock, he was going to be completely and utterly lost.

He had to talk to her. "I'll make sure she understands."

"I think that's best. Unless you've changed your mind about marriage." There was no hope in Beck's tone or even a question.

"This is why I count you among one of my closest friends," Felix said. "You understand me, and you accept me."

"I also recognize a bit of a similar soul, although you are much better at hiding it."

Felix froze for a moment, shocked by Beck's insightful words. Beck was prone to bouts of darkness and even melancholy. He poured his emotions into his poetry and music. Felix walled off his emotions so they could never be accessed—or seen. Did that make them similar?

That Felix even acknowledged that wall to himself was terrifying, and Felix suddenly wanted to take back what he'd said. "If you could understand me in silence, I'd appreciate that," Felix said.

Beck laughed. "Whatever you prefer."

Beck's line went taut, and he worked to bring the fish in. He grasped the trout and removed it from the hook, then tossed it into the basket on the bank between them. As he reworked his line to cast again, he said, "Is there any occasion in which you would reconsider your anti-marriage vow?"

Felix suppressed a scowl. "It isn't a vow. I don't see the point in marriage. I don't want a wife, and I don't want children. And I don't need either."

"What if you fell in love?"

Irritation roiled inside Felix. "Beck, you're beginning to test the limits of this friendship, and after I just thanked you for your *silent* understanding of my nature."

"Forgive me. I am, which I don't expect you to understand, completely enamored of my wife, and will do anything she asks. Including question you about the possibility of marriage."

Hell. Had Sarah put Lavinia up to this? They hadn't discussed marriage at all, and he didn't have the impression she wanted anything other than what they'd been doing. But then they hadn't discussed that either. Talking, it seemed, was not their priority.

"Have you caught anything?"

Felix breathed a deep sigh of relief at the welcome sound of a feminine voice—Lavinia's, to be exact. Turning his head just enough to see the path from the house, he caught sight of her and Sarah approaching the bank, arm in arm.

Sarah stopped at the blanket and stared down at her brother. "Are you sleeping?"

Anthony bolted upright. "What? What happened?"

Sarah and Lavinia laughed, and Beck smiled. Felix was still too unsettled to do either.

"May we fish?" Lavinia asked.

"There are only three poles, but clearly Anthony isn't using his," Beck said with a sardonic edge. "You're welcome to it."

"Brilliant." Lavinia picked up the pole and prepared the line.

Anthony rose from the blanket. "What if I want to fish?"

Arching her shoulder, Lavinia gave him a saucy look. "You can wait your turn." She turned to Beck and asked for help with casting. Given how well she hooked her line, Felix wasn't sure she needed it. But watching Beck put his arms around her and the way she smiled at him explained why she'd asked.

Sarah took a step closer to Felix, having taken over Beck's line while he helped Lavinia. "You didn't answer the question about whether you caught anything," she said, peering down into the basket where there were three fish. "And there is the answer. Did you catch them all?"

He shook his head. "Anthony caught one, and Beck the other two."

At that moment, Felix's line tugged.

"I've brought you good fortune," Sarah said.

Beck took his line from her and looked over at Felix pulling in his fish. "About damn time you caught something. It's your pond!"

"But he scarcely spends time here," Sarah said. "Seales says he hasn't fished at the pond in years."

Felix removed the fish from his hook and deposited it in the basket. "Does Seales even function as my butler anymore, or does he just talk to you all day?" He turned toward Anthony. "You can have my pole, if you like."

Anthony came forward and took the pole. "Sarah has always bothered the staff."

"To excess, I'm afraid." Sarah laughed. "Father used to

banish me to my room because I'd keep our butler or the housekeeper from their work."

Her eyes widened slightly, and she glanced toward Anthony. Then she sealed her mouth closed and turned her head to stare at the pond. It seemed as though the casual mention of her father had upset her. It was the first time he'd heard her speak of her parents anecdotally. He saw it as a good sign. In fact, he found it a bit relieving because he didn't relish telling her there would be no more *encounters* between them. He suspected their liaison was helping her to work through her grief, and he didn't want to upset her progress. But neither did he want to exploit her vulnerability.

Liaison? He couldn't call it that. A liaison was planned. Intentional. This was spontaneous. *Reckless.*

"Beck," Lavinia said, breaking into the silence and diverting the conversation as a good friend would do. "I think we must go to Scott's Grotto tomorrow. I am desperate to see the rocks and fossils." She leaned closer and whispered something in his ear.

Beck grinned and pressed a fast kiss to her neck, just below her jaw.

A shock of envy stabbed through Felix, surprising him. "It's rude to whisper." The comment fell from his lips without thought.

"Too bad, because she's not repeating it," Beck said. "Some things are meant to stay between a man and his wife."

"A woman and her husband," Lavinia corrected, earning her an appreciative chuckle from Beck.

Watching them, it was easy to see how one might fall in love and marry and be blissfully happy. But Felix knew the truth of it. He was suddenly anxious to distance himself from their marital joy.

"If you'll all excuse me, there are things that require my attention in my study."

"We'll have to send George back to London," Anthony said. "Then you won't be interrupted." He chuckled as he cast his line into the water.

Normally, Felix would have laughed along with him. Wasn't his primary goal to create amusement and enjoy himself?

Inwardly grumbling, he stalked back to the house, where he did indeed meet with George for a short while. After she departed his study, he loosened his cravat and removed his coat, draping it over the back of his chair. He stalked to the windows that looked out toward the drive and stared at a hunting bird perched high in a tree, his head bowed as he searched for prey.

"Felix?"

He suddenly felt as though he were prey.

That was silly. Sarah wasn't hunting him. And yet here she was, standing inside his study with the door closed.

Closed?

Perhaps she *was* hunting him.

"Sarah, you shouldn't be here."

"Why not?" She sauntered forward and removed her wide-brimmed hat, tossing it atop his desk.

"We need to talk about what's been happening."

"You aren't going to tell me we have to stop again, are you?" She kept moving toward him and then beyond. She loosened the ties on the drapes and drew them over the window. The room was plunged into near darkness with just strips of light filtering past the edges of the curtains.

"Sarah," he rasped. The mere action of closing the curtains had sent his body into a state of anticipation.

She turned from the window to face him and put her hands on his waistcoat, her fingers opening each button.

"Yes?"

He had to put a stop to this. "It occurs to me that you're using me to avoid your grief."

Her hands stilled, and she blinked, her dark lashes fluttering for a bare moment before she looked up at him. "Is that what you think?"

"Am I wrong?"

"I'm not sure how I can use you when you won't allow me to do anything *to* you." She resumed unbuttoning his waistcoat, flicking the last one open and then pushing her hands beneath the garment to stroke her hands across his rib cage.

His breath vacated his lungs, and his cock jerked in response.

"Let's say I am using you," she said, her fingertips caressing him through the lawn of his shirt. "Would you mind?"

God, no. "That isn't the point."

"I would argue that you are Felixing me."

Confusion crowded up against his lust—for which he was grateful. "Felixing? Are you referring to being foxed?"

"No, *Felixing*." She scraped her nails across his chest and pressed her thumbs against his nipples. He tried to suppress a groan, but it erupted low in his throat. "You're diverting me. You are the Duke of Distraction, I've decided."

"Christ, I have one of those bloody nicknames now?" He fought to retain some semblance of rational thought and feared he was failing beneath the onslaught of her seduction.

"Only between us."

"Sarah, we must stop."

She pushed his waistcoat over his shoulders and

dragged it down his arms, then let it fall to the floor. "I wanted to see your bare chest, but I can see I must get right to the matter." She skimmed one hand down his abdomen and found the buttons of his fall.

His cock stretched, hardening at her touch. "This is a very bad idea."

"This can be the conclusion of our…distraction. But I insist on giving you the same pleasure you gave me. Twice. Or at least trying to. I may not be very good at it." She gave him a sheepish look as she unbuttoned the front of his breeches.

"If you do nothing further, I will already declare you are quite excellent."

She gave him a saucy, seductive grin. "You are too generous, but then I knew that already."

The fall of his breeches fell open, and she reached into his smallclothes. Her fingers found the tip of his cock.

"You are already wet," she murmured.

"You know about that?" A mix of jealousy and wonder shot through him.

"Don't ask questions. And don't think I've done this before. I just told you I haven't."

She hadn't said that—she'd said she might not be good at it—but he wouldn't correct her. He was far too eager for her to try and convinced himself that to make her stop would be cruel.

Later, he would realize what an asinine thought that was.

She closed her hand around his shaft and slid it to the base. Her fingertips grazed his balls, and he groaned again, more loudly this time.

She whispered, "Shhh," before kissing him, her free hand moving up to cup his nape while her other hand continued to stroke his cock.

Closing his eyes, Felix swept his tongue along hers, ravenous for her kiss. His hips moved forward as she worked his shaft, urging her faster.

And then her mouth was gone from his as she dropped down before him. He opened his eyes and saw her on her knees. Then her mouth was in—or on—an altogether different place, and he had to bite his lip to keep from crying out.

This was the moment he'd both dreamed of and dreaded. She drew his cock along her tongue, her hand holding him at the base. She moved slowly, but with such heat and precision that he had to work to rein in his body lest he pump himself down her throat.

She took him deep and then eased back, still going slowly. Stroke after stroke, she maintained a sedate but sensual pace. He was glad because it stopped him from coming. And oh, how he wanted to.

What was he thinking? He couldn't come in her mouth. She'd never done this before, and he'd shock the hell out of her. And yet there was no way he wasn't coming. This wasn't like the other times when he'd kept himself in check until he was alone and frigged himself until he couldn't see straight.

There was no escaping completion. She was going to get what she wanted. And so was he.

Suddenly, she began to move faster, her mouth moving over and around him, up and down, her tongue licking along his greedy shaft. She tightened her grip and braced her other hand on his thigh.

He clasped her head, unable to stop himself from moving now. He thrust into her mouth as pleasure built and blood rushed to his cock. His head fell back, and he closed his eyes, certain his orgasm was just a moment away.

But then her mouth was gone. Cold air shocked his bare flesh, and he opened his eyes to see her standing before him. Her blue eyes were wide and luminous, her cheeks flushed, her lips red and glistening from what she'd been doing to him. She was the most beautiful thing he'd ever seen.

She lifted her hand and touched his face. "I want to have sex."

Chapter Twelve

LUST GLAZED FELIX'S green eyes as he stared at her. His lips parted, and she traced her thumb across the lower one.

"Sarah—"

She rotated her thumb to a vertical position and covered both lips. "Shhh. Don't tell me we shouldn't. I have no idea what my future holds—beyond a millinery shop—and I don't want to regret not experiencing this."

His brow creased, and he did not appear convinced. "May I speak now?"

"Only if you plan to agree."

The hint of a smile tugged at his mouth. "Against my better judgment," he said. "You are incredibly hard to refuse. Impossible, it appears. Since you had the forethought to close the drapes, dare I hope you locked the door?" He cringed slightly, and she suspected he was thinking how he should have asked that question earlier.

"Of course I did." She stroked her hand along his erection, which hadn't flagged in the slightest as they'd stood there. She was amazed at how she enjoyed touching him there, everywhere. "I suppose it's too much to hope to be naked."

He moaned before claiming her mouth in a swift but thorough kiss. "It is, I'm afraid. But we'll make the most of what we have." His eyes locked on hers. "You're certain?"

She clasped the side of his neck, drawing his head down. "Kiss me, Felix."

His mouth opened over hers, and his tongue drove

deep inside, stirring her already white-hot desire to even greater heights. She kissed him back, moving one of her hands beneath the hem of his shirt to feel the smooth plane of his back. He was warm and hard, his muscles taut against her palm.

He tipped his head up. "There is no good place to lie down in here."

"The carpet?" she suggested.

"It wouldn't be comfortable." He looked down at her with a hint of mischief in his eyes. "How adventurous are you feeling?"

"With you, I want to explore everything."

His gaze darkened, and he took her hand, leading her to the small settee angled near the fireplace. Turning, he sat down. "Lift your skirts and put your knees on either side of me."

Sarah's sex pulsed as she looked down at his jutting erection. Reaching down, she raised her skirts and situated herself as he'd directed. She immediately felt the heat of him against her and inhaled sharply.

He burrowed his hand beneath her skirts, and his fingers found her sex, stroking along the sensitive folds and stoking her arousal. His eyes met hers again. "You're certain?"

"*Yes.* Stop asking me that." His finger pressed inside, and she closed her eyes in ecstasy. She put her hands on his shoulders, letting her skirts pool around them.

Sliding in and out of her, he used his thumb to tease that spot that seemed to be the point of release. Whenever he touched her there, her body tensed with pleasure and she wanted to shout with rapture. Shouting, however, would be bad, so she only allowed a soft whimper.

"Kiss me, Sarah," he urged.

She dipped her head and held him tightly as she put her mouth on his. He continued his campaign on her sex, and she was helpless against the sensations. Her hips moved, almost of their own volition, as he propelled her toward her climax.

Just as the waves of pleasure broke over her, his hand moved, and she felt his cock against her opening. He pushed inside, his other hand outside her skirts clasping her waist and holding her steady.

She cried out into his mouth as her body spasmed, and his shaft filled her. There was discomfort but also an intensifying of the shocks streaming through her body.

Taking her mouth from his, she fought to breathe, her heart pounding. He kissed her neck, the edge of her collarbone, the base of her throat. "Move, if you want," he said against her, his tongue teasing her flesh. "In this position, you can control everything."

She was working to become accustomed to having him inside her. It was an incredibly different and exciting sensation. She rotated her hips against his pelvis, a hesitant inquiry to determine what she wanted.

She realized she liked the feel of him against her on the outside as well as having him on the inside. His hand splayed on her outer thigh, massaging her and urging her on.

"It's a bit like riding," she said.

"Exactly."

"But far more pleasurable."

"I should hope so. I am beginning to wish we were naked. This position is ideal for giving me access to your breasts."

She glanced down and saw that he was indeed perfectly placed to take them in his mouth. "Well, that's a shame." She wanted to say they would be naked next time, but she was fairly certain there would be no next time. He'd tried to behave as a gentleman ought, and she'd already pushed him past the limit. She wouldn't do so again.

This would have to be enough.

Sarah cupped the sides of his head and kissed him again, sweeping her tongue along the inside of his mouth as she increased her pace, rising and falling as if she were indeed taking her horse from a trot to a canter.

His fingertips dug into her thigh, and she moved even faster. It was such an incredible feeling as she drove them toward release. Her muscles tensed, and she knew she was so very close. Was he? She had no idea.

But then his hands tightened on her waist and her thigh, and he thrust up into her, his body meeting hers with ever-greater need. Another climax rushed over her, and she broke the kiss, trying hard not to scream his name.

And still he moved, his cock driving into her again and again. Then he tensed, and she knew he was there. Satisfaction poured through her and then broke when he left her body.

She opened her eyes to see his head cast back against the top of the settee. His eyes were closed, his face drawn, his lips parted in ecstasy as he drew and expelled air from his lungs in rapid succession.

"Why did you stop?"

"I didn't." His voice was strained, and his eyes remained closed.

She felt a sticky wetness between them and understood. Lavinia had told her about a man withdrawing his sex before he spilled his seed in order to prevent making a child. She appreciated his forethought, because she certainly hadn't thought of it.

At last he opened his eyes, and she'd never seen them a

more pure green or more incandescent.

"Thank you," he said simply and leaned up to kiss her again, his lips moving softly and deliciously over hers.

"Felix, I have news!" The door crashed open.

Sarah turned her head, and her entire body froze.

Anthony stood at the threshold and stared at them together on the settee, his jaw dropping nearly to the floor. "What the *hell* are you doing?"

⚬❦❧⚬

SARAH SCRAMBLED TO Felix's right side, using her body to shield him while he put himself back together. Not that it mattered. The damage was done. There was no way to interpret what Anthony had walked in on other than the truth.

Once his fall was rebuttoned, Felix stood and faced his best friend. "I know you're angry, but this really isn't any of your concern."

Anthony stalked toward him and, before Felix saw it coming, had planted his fist against Felix's cheek. Felix's head snapped back, and pain exploded across his face.

Sarah leapt up from the settee and clasped Anthony's arm. "Stop!"

"I demand satisfaction," Anthony growled. "Name your second."

Felix rubbed his hand over his cheek. "A duel? You're mad."

Anthony ripped his arm from Sarah's grip and advanced on Felix once more. "You're the one who's mad if you think you can ruin my sister and go unpunished."

Sarah dodged between them, putting her back against Felix's chest. "Anthony, stop. There isn't going to be a duel. I am not *ruined*."

Anthony shifted his wild gaze to Sarah. "I know what I saw."

"And I'm sorry you saw it. But that will teach you to barge in on a closed door." She turned her head to look at Felix. "I was certain I'd locked it."

"This is *my* fault?" Anthony thundered.

"No, it's mine," Felix said calmly, hating the pain creasing Anthony's face.

"It isn't either," Sarah said, narrowing her eyes at Felix before she returned her attention to Anthony. "It's mine. I seduced him. If you want to punish someone, it should be me. But I don't think you ought to punish anyone. Felix and I are able to make our own decisions and are prepared to live with any consequences."

Felix inwardly winced. Did she have to use that word? Hopefully there would be no child—he'd certainly tried to avoid it, hard as that had been.

"You bloody well will live with them," Anthony said with considerable venom. "You're getting married."

"We're not doing that either," Sarah said firmly. "Really, Anthony, this is between Felix and me."

While Felix appreciated what Sarah was trying to do, there was no point. However, before he could say so, Anthony continued on, his eyes raging with fury and a dozen other gut-wrenching emotions. "I am the viscount now, Sarah, head of our family. It is my responsibility to ensure you aren't ruined and to see you safely, if not happily, wed. I can't allow Felix—or any other man—to take advantage of you and walk away without concern."

Felix saw the guilt, already a daily challenge for Anthony, rise to the surface and knew there was nothing he wouldn't do to ease his friend's suffering. "We'll marry."

Anthony's body relaxed the slightest bit, but not as

much as Felix had hoped. He was still furious, and he had every right to be. Felix was the worst sort—he had taken advantage of Sarah. Whether he wanted to acknowledge it or not, she was incredibly vulnerable right now, and he never should have allowed her to persuade him.

As if he'd required much persuasion at all.

Sarah moved to the side and turned her head to frown at first Felix and then at Anthony. "We will not marry. Felix doesn't want to—"

"It doesn't matter what he wants." Anthony kept his gaze pinned on Felix, and Felix worried their friendship was forever damaged.

"No, it doesn't." Felix bowed his head briefly before looking Anthony in the eye. "I humbly beg your forgiveness."

"You're a cad and a reprobate. I never imagined you could take advantage of a woman in Sarah's position, let alone my sister."

"He didn't," Sarah said, her voice rising. "Stop talking about me as if I'm not here." She looked at Anthony. "You don't speak for me." Then she turned her attention to Felix, her eyes blazing. "And if you want to marry me, *ask*."

"Will you marry me, Sarah?" Felix didn't even recognize his own voice.

"No."

"It's what our parents wanted!" Anthony shouted. "If they were here—" He didn't finish, but he didn't have to. The damage was quite done.

Sarah paled, her lips parting in horror. Then she turned and fled the room.

"I know you're angry," Felix said, his own ire now pricked. Sarah hadn't deserved that. "But trying to make her feel as guilty as you do is cruel."

"Fuck you, Felix." Anthony stalked from the room next, leaving Felix alone.

Emotion swirled in his chest. He took several deep breaths and briefly closed his eyes. Then he went around and picked up the discarded items of his clothing, slowly putting everything back on. When he was finished, he sat back down at his desk and began to read the correspondence George had given him.

Distraction was the key to harmony and peace. Distraction was all he knew.

THANKFULLY, SARAH HAD managed to keep the tears from flowing until she'd left the house. She didn't cry for long—angry tears never lasted as long as sad ones.

It was her own fault. She never should have pressed Felix. The look on Anthony's face... Angry as she was at him, she felt awful. She was a wanton and selfish, and her parents would be horrified.

No, she wasn't going to think about them right now, because then the tears *would* turn sad and she would dissolve into a puddle and likely never find her way back to the house. As it was, she was striding purposefully along the path toward the pond without actual purpose. And she didn't want to return to the pond.

She cut across the lawn instead and mentally chided herself for not bringing a hat, for it was both warm and bright. Indeed, she'd begun to perspire, so she slowed her pace. She ought to return to the house for a bath, particularly to clean herself up from earlier.

She stopped and closed her eyes, allowing the enormity of what she'd done to settle on her shoulders. Guilt and shame threatened, but why should she surrender to those emotions?

Because that was what her mother would want her to feel. Her throat began to clog.

"Miss Colton?"

The feminine voice rescued Sarah from falling into a well of despair. She opened her eyes and blinked against the bright afternoon. "Mrs. Vane?"

"Please, call me George." The woman's warm smile gave Sarah a dose of much-needed comfort. "You forgot your hat." She was still smiling, which made it feel like they were sharing a joke.

"I did, which is rather ironic."

George cocked her head. "Is it?"

"I design hats. It's bizarre to be out without one, but for me, it's almost a crime."

"I am terrible at fashion," George said, gesturing to her dull brown dress. "I rarely have need of it, of course, in my profession."

Profession. George was a woman with employment. "How is it to work?" Sarah asked.

George shrugged. "I enjoy what I do, if that's what you mean."

"I'd like to open a millinery shop."

"Oh!" George's eyes widened with surprise. "The shop in Vigo Lane? Felix had me organize his inspection of the property, and I communicated with his solicitor about the lease. I didn't realize the shop was for you. He didn't say."

Sarah marveled at the woman's capability and felt a stab of envy. It sounded as though Felix relied on her. That had to feel…good. "You call him Felix."

"We've known each other since we were children, and though he was Lord Bramfield then, he always made me call him Felix. We used to fish in the pond together and swing from the willow tree. I tried calling him Lord Ware after he became the earl, but he forbade me from doing that too. In truth, at thirteen, no boy should be called 'lord' anything unless it's Lord Idiot."

Sarah laughed. "I'm very glad I ran into you. Do you mind if I accompany you on your walk?"

"Are you sure you don't want to return for a hat?"

"No, I'm rather enjoying the warm sun." She'd probably have a few freckles for her trouble tomorrow, but who would care?

"I'm just on my way to visit my mother," George said. "You're welcome to join me."

"I'd like that, thank you." Sarah moved forward, and George joined her. "Where is the steward's house?" She hadn't been there.

"Pardon me for the confusion," George said with a hint of apology. "My mother passed away two years ago. She's buried in the Ware plot, and I'm going to pay my respects."

And just like that, the sadness Sarah had worked to keep at bay came rushing back, tightening her throat.

George lightly touched her arm. "I didn't mean to upset you. This must be a difficult time."

That Sarah had only seemed to complicate. "I thought it was getting better, but…" She let her voice trail off before it broke.

"My mother was ill," George said as they walked up a gentle slope. "I knew she was going to die, but that didn't make it any easier."

"My parents were murdered." Sarah's voice was soft but firm, for which she was grateful. "But you probably know that. We were completely unprepared for…this."

"I did know, and I'm so sorry for your loss. I'm sure Felix has done his best to ease your suffering. He's exceptionally good at that."

"Yes," Sarah murmured. She knew George couldn't possibly realize the *extent* to which Felix had eased her, and she certainly didn't plan to tell her. Unless they married. Sarah couldn't hide that.

Was she considering his proposal? If one could call that a proposal.

As they crested the hill, the graveyard came into sight. There was, in fact, a small stone building. "Is that a church?"

"Yes," George said. "Though the family hasn't it used it as one as long as I've lived here. It houses the Ware family crypt. My mother is buried outside."

Sarah's heart twisted. She hadn't yet visited her mother's tomb at Oaklands. She hadn't attended the burial, of course, and she hadn't wanted to see it. She should. Perhaps soon.

"Are Felix's parents in there?" Sarah asked as they descended the hill.

"Yes, but he never visits."

"Why?" It was a beautiful place nestled at the base of a hill, with a pair of large oak trees standing sentinel and patches of wildflowers dotting the landscape.

"I think because he never knew his mother. He just doesn't feel a connection with her."

"But surely he did with his father?" She recalled what he'd said about forgetting and wondered if maybe George remembered.

"Not really. The earl drank to excess—pardon, to me, Felix's father is the earl." She moved toward one of the groupings of cowslips, daisies, and cranesbill. "I'm just going to pick some flowers for my mother."

Sarah trailed along after her, though she was intensely curious about Felix's father and wanted to go into the church to see his tomb, as well as Felix's mother's. She couldn't keep from asking about the former earl. "So Felix wasn't close to his father?" Had his passion for drink prevented a familial relationship? And was it that Felix didn't want to remember as opposed to not being able to?

"Not really. The earl was nearly always melancholy. My mother said he never got over losing his wife." She bent to pluck a handful of stems. "It's sad when you think about it. I'm not sure how I would carry on without Mr. Vane. I would, because I must, but it would be difficult. Far more difficult than losing my mother, I think, whom I miss every day."

There was no mistaking the love in George's tone, both for her husband and her mother. "To have so much love in one's life is truly a gift. You're very lucky," Sarah said softly.

George gave her a warm smile. "I am fortunate. And grateful. I've been fortunate to have Felix too. Aside from giving me an opportunity no other man would give a woman, he's been an incredible support and friend. When my mother died, he was always there with kindness and laughter for me and my father. But that's his nature."

It was indeed, but Sarah began to think there was a reason for it. "I imagine you did the same for him when his father died."

George gathered the flowers she'd picked and led Sarah toward the churchyard. "Of course, though it wasn't that necessary. Honestly, the earl's death was a relief to us all."

"He wasn't sad?" Sarah struggled to understand how that could be. She didn't always agree with her parents, and Lord knew their relationship had been strained of late, but she couldn't imagine feeling relieved or not being sad.

"Not that he showed, but you know how he is."

George stepped through the gate into the churchyard, and Sarah reached to hold it open.

Yes, she knew how he was, and now she was beginning to understand. She tried to think of a time when he'd expressed any strong emotion—anger, disappointment, sadness…love.

Sarah stood back while George went to her mother's grave. After laying the flowers in front of the headstone, she spoke softly—words Sarah couldn't hear and didn't try to. Then she put her hand to her lips and pressed her fingertips against the headstone. Sarah's throat closed, and tears stung her eyes.

She turned and made her way to the church. Circling around to the front of the building, she pushed open the door and stepped into the dim interior. One large window over the door provided most of the light, but smaller windows were set at intervals along the sides. There were two rows of pews on either side facing the aisle, and the altar stood at the opposite end.

George came in behind her. "The Ware tomb is behind the altar. Do you want to see it?"

Though she felt a bit like she was intruding, Sarah decided it wasn't strange to want to pay respect to one's future in-laws.

Was she truly considering marriage? She'd already refused him. Surely he was basking in relief, and she had no expectation he'd ask again.

"If you think it's all right," Sarah answered.

"Of course."

Sarah followed George down the aisle and behind the altar. The tombs were stacked within the wall with the names and dates etched on the face of each one.

George moved to the right and gestured toward the floor. "Here are Felix's parents."

Sarah squatted down to read their names—his father on the bottom and his mother above him. Mary Havers, the Countess of Ware, had died on July first. "The day after tomorrow will be the anniversary of her death."

George nodded. "Felix's birthday, of course."

Blinking, Sarah rose. "I hadn't put the two together, but of course it is." Because she'd died giving birth to him. "I just realized I've never known when Felix's birthday is."

The only reason it stuck out to her was because Felix never failed to remember her birthday or Anthony's. Or anyone else he considered a close friend. In fact, she recalled the birthday celebration he orchestrated when Anthony turned twenty-one. She'd only heard about it because she certainly hadn't been invited.

She suddenly wanted to do something nice for him, as he'd always done for everyone else. "We should have a party to celebrate since we're here—and Lavinia and Beck."

George shook her head. "I don't think he'd care for that." Then she shrugged, seeming to change her mind. "Maybe ask him about it."

"I will." Sarah was more curious about him than ever. She looked at the names on the stone another moment and then told George she was ready to go.

"Are you going back to the house?" George asked as they made their way from the church.

She probably should, but she wasn't particularly looking forward to seeing Felix or Anthony. She did, however, want to talk with Lavinia.

Had she and Beck heard Anthony yelling? Or hitting Felix? Sarah flinched as she recalled the punch and hoped Felix was all right. She hadn't even asked before she'd fled the house.

House... George had asked her if she was going back

there. "Eventually," Sarah said with a vague smile. "It's such a lovely day."

"I'm on my way to see my father. You're welcome to come along—I'm enjoying your company." She flashed another warm smile, and Sarah thanked her for the invitation.

It was a ten-minute walk to the steward's cottage, a charming two-story home with a thatched roof. Set back behind the stables, it was no wonder Sarah hadn't seen or been to it. Nor did she have reason to seek it out, of course. "This is where you grew up?" Sarah asked.

"Yes. Close enough to the stables that I made myself a nuisance so that when Felix learned to ride, I did too."

"Are you the same age?" Sarah had thought George to be younger than Felix's twenty-eight years.

"Nearly. I'll be twenty-eight early next year."

"You and Felix really did grow up together."

"I suppose we did. Until Felix went off to Eton. Your brother went there too, didn't he?"

Sarah nodded. Her mind drifted to Anthony. She couldn't avoid seeing him. She needed to make him understand why she shouldn't marry Felix just because of what happened.

Sarah stopped on the path. "I should get back to the house. Thank you so much for allowing me to accompany you."

George paused and turned to face her. "It was my pleasure. I hope we can do it again. If you decide to talk to Felix about his birthday, please let me know what he says—and if I can help with anything. I'd love to do something nice for him for once."

"I would too." Sarah smiled, then turned and headed back to the house, grateful for the shade on this part of the path.

As she rounded the corner of the stables to turn toward the house, she nearly ran into Martin Havers, Felix's uncle. She stopped short before they could collide.

"Goodness, I'm afraid I was walking rather quickly there," he said jovially. "I beg your pardon."

"It's quite all right," Sarah said, returning his smile and intending to carry on.

He frowned at her bare head. "Whatever happened to your hat?"

"It blew away."

He appeared confounded. "But there's hardly a breeze."

"I was joking."

"Ah." He didn't crack a smile, nor did he move out of her way. "It's been so different to have you and your brother here, and now there are more of you."

Sarah found his observation strange. It wasn't as if Martin spent time at the house. Aside from the dinner when they'd first arrived, she hadn't seen him. Why would he find their presence "different" or otherwise? She couldn't think of how to respond.

"I imagine you'll be staying as long as you can." His forehead creased. "I hope you don't have any unrealistic expectations where Felix is concerned."

What the devil was he talking about? Sarah blinked. "I don't believe I do," she said hesitantly.

"That's comforting to hear. I did wonder, given the way you look at him. You must know he'll never marry."

"Everyone knows that." She couldn't quite keep all the derision from her tone.

Martin exhaled, then smiled in a thoroughly condescending fashion. "That's good to hear. Just looking out for my nephew, you understand."

No, she didn't understand. "I don't think you are. I think you're looking out for your son. If Felix marries, and presumably sires an heir, your son won't inherit as you intend." Sarah wondered if Martin had planted the idea of not marrying into Felix's mind years ago, maybe even as soon as his father had died.

Martin's eyes widened, and his lips moved, but the only sound that came out was a series of gasps. Finally, he managed, "You forget yourself!"

"I think *you* do. As it happens, Felix has proposed marriage, and I've accepted." The words flew from her mouth before she could think better of it.

His eyes, already wide and large to begin with, practically fell out of his head. "You just said everyone knows he will never marry!"

"I was being polite in the face of your presumption and rudeness. I'd planned to let Felix tell you our news, but I find I can't contain myself."

"It's never going to happen. I don't know what spell you've woven to bring this about, but he's absolutely committed to remaining unwed."

"Not anymore." She gave him a final glare, then stepped around him as she hurried toward the house.

Heart pounding, she wondered what the hell she'd just done. Had she changed her mind about marrying him? Apparently so. But what if he didn't want to marry her?

Of course he didn't want to marry her—he'd only proposed because Anthony had caught them together. She'd refused *because* she knew he didn't want to.

Only *she* did.

The realization slowed her gait as she neared the rear door that led into the saloon. When she thought of the rest of her life alone, specifically without Felix, well, she didn't want to think about that. What she *did* want was to marry him. Because she was in love with him.

Chapter Thirteen

❦

IT WAS AN uncomfortable sensation, the feeling that he'd done something wrong—which he had—and that he couldn't fix it. Which he likely could not. His friendship with Anthony was ruined and his... What did he have with Sarah? Friendship? Yes, they'd had that. But it had all changed after that kiss at Darent Hall.

Goddammit.

He hated feeling like this. He'd spent his youth in a constant state of upset, his insides in knots, worrying about his father's next outburst and knowing he was powerless to stop it. Then he'd spent his entire life since his father's death doing everything possible to ensure he never experienced that feeling of helplessness again. And here he was, fraught and frayed, all because of his cock.

No, it was more than that. *Sarah* was more than that. But God, he didn't want her to be.

Think, Felix, think.

He paced his dressing chamber. There had to be a way to divert the situation, to persuade Anthony that all would be well. He didn't have to worry about Sarah. She'd declined his proposal.

He stopped. He didn't have to worry about her? Hell, he'd stolen her innocence.

Did he really think that? He'd behaved like a blackguard, but he wasn't entirely to blame. He scrubbed his hand over his face, wishing he could erase the entire day.

Vane stuck his head into the dressing room. "Miss Colton is asking to see you. What should I tell her?"

Felix looked down at himself as if he couldn't recall his state of dress. And maybe he couldn't. He was nearly ready for dinner as it turned out.

"Your coat is there," Vane said, helpfully gesturing toward the garment hanging on the door of the armoire.

Felix took it from the hook and thrust his arm into one sleeve. Vane came forward to provide assistance.

"Where is she?" Felix asked.

"Just outside."

"I'll meet her," Felix said, pressing his lips together in a grim frown.

"You may not wish to look as if you're marching off to your doom," Vane suggested.

"I'll try," Felix muttered. He made his face impassive before he stepped out of his chamber into the outer reception area that led to the end of the long gallery that spanned the first floor.

Sarah looked every bit as tormented as he felt, her face pinched into lines, her hands clasped together. Christ, what had they done to each other?

He went to her and took her hand, unable to stop himself from trying to ease her pain. "What's wrong?"

"Everything?" Her lips curved into a small smile, and miraculously, he felt himself relax just a bit. She touched his cheek, causing him to wince. "I was going to ask if it hurts, but I think you just answered that question."

It had turned purple over the last hour. "It's probably less than I deserve. I'm so sorry about earlier," he said. "It was entirely my fault."

"No, it wasn't, and don't argue with me. If anything, it was entirely *my* fault. I should regret it, but I…don't." She removed her hand from his and turned, walking away from him before pivoting back, her hands clasped together and her shoulders tense.

She took a deep breath. "I told your uncle we're getting married."

For a moment, Felix couldn't find the right response. *Was* there a right response? "But you refused me."

"Yes, but then he was so smug about you and your birthright, and I just couldn't stand there and let him steal it from you." Her brows slashed low over her eyes, and there was a defiant tilt to her chin.

"Steal it from me? Why would you think that?"

She unclasped her hands and stepped toward him. "Because he is! He thought I had designs on you and felt it his duty to inform me you will never marry. Even after I told him we were betrothed, he said you wouldn't go through with it."

"But we aren't betrothed." He wasn't entirely certain what she was about. "Unless you're telling me you've changed your mind."

She took another deep breath and lifted her chin. "Yes, I've changed my mind."

Goddammit.

His insides twisted anew, and he fought against the roil of emotion. "You weren't wrong before. I don't wish to marry. Nothing has changed."

"I should hope *something* has changed." She blanched. "That's not fair of me. You didn't ask for this."

"I didn't mean it like that," he said, trying to put his thoughts into words. "Of course things have changed. They changed at Darent Hall, and clearly we can't go back to the way they were." He moved toward her, leaving just a few feet between them. "I meant that my feelings about marriage haven't changed. *But*, if I am to marry anyone, I would prefer it were you."

She stared at him a moment, and he had no idea what she was thinking. At last, she said, "Thank you?"

He smiled, the tension inside him easing again—not entirely, but a little, at least. "People marry for all sorts of reasons, and many of them don't even end up liking each other. Just look at my aunt and uncle. We at least like each other. I should hope we will always be friends, and I would think that would make for a rather successful marriage."

She didn't look convinced. "As just friends?"

Friendship couldn't begin to describe what he and Sarah shared. And right now, he had no idea *how* to describe it, or if he even could. "Well, a bit more than that. It seems as though we're rather attracted to each other."

She blushed, and he wondered if he'd ever grow tired of seeing her do that. "So it seems," she murmured.

"Then we'll wed." As he said the words, his body felt as if it were detaching from his brain and floating away.

"Yes." She gave him a tentative look. "If that's acceptable to you."

"It is." *Barely.* How was he going to do this?

Just like you do everything, as if you haven't a care in the world. Get a hold of yourself.

"You're uncle isn't going to be happy," she said.

"Probably not, but that isn't my concern. And anyway, maybe we won't have a son."

Her brows ticked up, acknowledging what he said, but she didn't say anything in response. Instead, she said, "We should tell Anthony."

Felix's discomfort elevated once more. Anthony would be satisfied, but Felix still worried their friendship was irrevocably damaged. No matter what he said, Anthony would never be able to forget what he'd seen or change what he believed—that Felix had exploited his sister in a time of extreme vulnerability. Did she believe that too?

"Sarah, I want you to know that I never meant to take advantage of you."

"Of course I know that. You tried to talk me out of my foolishness. I just…" She looked away. "Perhaps I surrendered to my own feelings of loneliness." When she returned her gaze to his, her eyes were bright with tears. "I'm sorry for putting you in this position. If you truly don't want to marry, Anthony will come to understand."

He wouldn't either. Felix closed the distance between them and put his arms around her, drawing her against his chest. She rested her cheek against his coat and hugged him in return. "I'm not marrying you to save my friendship with Anthony. Though I will be honest and tell you I hope it *can* be saved. Right now, I'm not optimistic."

She looked up at him. "Have faith. Anthony is just having a difficult time."

Yes, he was, and Felix wished he could take his friend's pain away. "Let's go find him."

Felix took her arm, and they went to Anthony's chamber. After knocking twice, the door finally opened. Anthony held an empty tumbler and scowled at them.

"We're getting married," Sarah said.

"Good." It was more a grunt than a word. Anthony lifted the glass to his lips and drank. Upon realizing it was empty, he frowned and lowered it. "When?"

Sarah looked at Felix. They hadn't discussed that. "As soon as you say so," Felix said, hoping Sarah would find that acceptable.

Anthony exhaled, and it was clear he'd been drinking for some time. Probably all afternoon. "Any time soon isn't ideal." He looked at them both as if they were naughty children. "A month from now should suffice."

Felix turned to Sarah. "Do you want to wed in Ware or Harlow? Or London?"

"Ware," Anthony said, drawing Sarah to snap her attention toward him. She nodded in agreement, and Felix was curious as to why they both seemed to prefer that. "I'm leaving for Epping in the morning." Anthony's lip curled. "I received word earlier that the highwaymen attacked another coach. One of them was shot and taken to the magistrate. I will see he hangs for murder."

That had been his news, why he'd stormed into Felix's study when the door was shut. Felix had no doubt Anthony had gone to his study to ask him to accompany him to Epping.

"I could go with you," Felix offered, hoping their friendship wasn't completely destroyed. He looked at Sarah. "Are you certain you wouldn't prefer your parish? I could stop in Harlow and obtain the license."

"I don't need you to come," Anthony said.

That was all the answer Felix needed—to Anthony, their friendship was dead. And Felix wasn't sure he blamed him.

Loss stabbed through him and stole his breath. *No,* he wouldn't give in to it. "Perhaps you'd consider taking Beck," Felix suggested. "If you don't wish to go alone."

Anthony gave Felix a cool stare, leading Felix to believe he wasn't as sotted as he'd assumed. "Alone doesn't bother me. Not anymore."

The three of them stood there in silence for a moment until Anthony finally said, "Is there anything else?"

"No, I don't believe so." Felix worked to make his voice sound normal despite the tightness in his throat. "Should we expect you for dinner?"

"I should think not." Anthony let out a soft snort, then closed the door in their faces.

Felix felt Sarah tense beside him. "He just needs time to get over being angry."

"And sad," she said, sounding sad herself. "If he can." She slid him a curious, almost probing look that made him a bit uncomfortable.

He turned from Anthony's door, fighting against the sense of loss he didn't want to feel, and desperately tried to focus on something else. Something he could manage. Something he could control.

He suggested they go down to dinner and offered her his arm. "So next month, we'll marry in Ware?" he asked. "I can obtain the license tomorrow."

She put her hand on his sleeve, and they started toward the stairs. "What about your family church?" Her question surprised him. "Perhaps the vicar could perform the ceremony here."

Felix's heart pounded so hard, he feared she would hear it. "You know of the church?"

"I visited it today with George." They turned and began to descend to the ground floor. "It's such a beautiful location."

"I'd, ah, prefer to marry in Ware." He never went to the church. His father had dragged him there every year until he died. Felix hadn't gone back.

Halfway down the stairs, she nearly sent him tumbling to the base. "Your birthday is day after tomorrow. How about we have a celebration? Anthony won't be here, but Lavinia and Beck will be. I believe they plan to stay a week more at least."

"I don't need a celebration. We should focus on planning for a wedding celebration." Yes, focus on *anything* else.

Her forehead pleated as they reached the bottom of the staircase. "We shouldn't really have a celebration. It's too soon after my parents."

He seized on the excuse, aware that it perhaps didn't fit

and not caring. "Then we definitely shouldn't have a birthday celebration for me."

She took her hand from his arm and turned to look at him, her brow still creased with concern. "There's no reason we shouldn't. Unless you'd prefer not to."

Cornered, he took the evasion she provided. "I'd prefer not to." It was also the truth.

"Why not? You work so hard to entertain everyone. Can't we entertain you for once?"

Flatter. Flirt. Fend. Do whatever you must to deflect and distract. "Sarah, I should think it would be obvious that you entertain me greatly."

Her eyes narrowed slightly. "You could do with a little self-indulgence."

He wanted to argue with her, to shout that self-indulgence was what had thrust him into this marriage disaster. But he didn't. Instead, he summoned a smile and took her arm once more. "Then I'll leave it to you to tutor me." He gave her a flirtatious smile and guided her to the dining room.

"I'll look forward to it." She sent him a sidelong glance. "And you will too."

Of that, he had no doubt.

※·3·

ONCE MORE, SARAH and Lavinia sat together on the settee in the drawing room following dinner. Anthony had never joined them, nor had he offered an excuse for his absence. Felix had told Beck and Lavinia about the highwayman being shot.

After that distastefulness, Sarah and Felix had shared the news of their upcoming marriage but without giving the details that had prompted it. It should have been fairly obvious—at least to Lavinia given what Sarah had told her and the ways in which Lavinia had advised her.

"Now that we're alone, you can tell me everything," Lavinia said as soon as they sat down and the footman left after depositing their glasses of sherry on a table. "Why on earth are you marrying Felix?"

"Isn't the better question why on earth is Felix marrying me?" Sarah chuckled softly. It wasn't really humorous, but what else could she do in this situation? She'd forced marriage upon a man who didn't want it.

"Probably, but I wasn't going to ask like that." Lavinia scooted closer to Sarah. "You had sex, didn't you?"

"Yes, but that alone wouldn't have prompted a wedding. Anthony walked in."

Lavinia's jaw dropped. "How horrifying. For everyone."

"*We'd finished.*" Sarah felt it was important to clarify that part. "Still, it was obvious what we'd been doing."

"So Felix didn't have an accident in the stables today?" Lavinia referred to the excuse he'd given for the bruise at dinner.

Sarah shook her head.

Lavinia snorted softly. "I don't know why he lied. It's not as if Beck and I wouldn't have found out. I suspect he's telling Beck the truth of it now. And if he doesn't, I will. On that note, I should inform you that I told Beck about you and Felix." She winced. "We don't keep secrets, and I was just so happy for the both of you. I truly hoped you would find a way to marry."

Sarah opened her mouth to speak, but Lavinia continued. "And Beck said something to Felix this morning at the pond. He wasn't overly pleased that you'd disclosed your relationship to me."

"I see." But he hadn't said anything. Then again, when would he have? "Thank you for telling me. Perhaps I should stop talking to you."

She winced again. "I'm so sorry. If you need to tell me something in strict confidence, I promise I won't tell Beck."

Sarah could see that would be hard for her. "I think it's nice that you're both so honest with each other. That's how a marriage should be, I think." That was how she wanted her marriage to be with Felix. But how did you have an honest marriage when one person loved the other and didn't tell them?

Isn't it better to keep something from someone that they don't want to hear?

She thought he didn't want to hear that she loved him? Maybe.

Sarah let the confusion and worry flow out of her. "Lavinia, I don't know what to do about this."

"About Felix?"

"His feelings about marriage haven't changed. He's marrying me to please Anthony."

"And you, I hope."

"I said no initially. I didn't want to force him, not when I know he doesn't want it." She swallowed against the pain rising in her throat. "But then I realized *I* want it. I want him." She picked at a bead sewn into the skirt of her gown. "I ran into his uncle, and he was so smug about Felix and the estate, as if he were the earl and not Felix. He had the gall to tell me I shouldn't have designs on Felix. Why would he even think that?"

"I don't know."

"He said it was the way I look at Felix. Do I look at him a certain way?"

"You do now, yes." Lavinia offered her a weak smile. "Sorry. It is rather plain to me you are besotted."

"Besotted?" Sarah jumped up and paced away from the

settee before turning back and staring at Lavinia as emotion rumbled through her. "I'm not besotted."

Oh, yes you are. You think of him constantly. You dream of him. You can't wait until you see him next. You already know you love him, so why hide it from your best friend?

Sarah put her palm over her eyes and exhaled. Then she felt Lavinia touch her shoulder. Dropping her hand, Sarah gave her best friend a look of utter despair. "I love him."

"I know." Lavinia pulled her into a hug. They stood there like that for a moment before she asked, "Is there a chance he loves you too?"

"How would I possibly know? Have you ever seen him display an emotion beyond amusement or mild disgust? And even the latter is from something like manure blocking a path."

"No, I have not. It's interesting that you mention this because Beck said something to me earlier about the same thing. He commented that he and Felix both feel very deeply. I admit I scoffed."

Sarah stepped back and briefly pressed her hands to her flushed cheeks. "I would have too. In fact, I'm scoffing now."

"Beck explained, and I think he might be right. The difference between them is that Beck puts all his emotions into his music and his poetry. Where does Felix put his?"

After a minute, Sarah said, "Into his entertainments?"

Lavinia gave a single nod. "Or nowhere at all."

Sarah let that seep into her brain. "His birthday is the day after tomorrow, but he doesn't want a celebration." She focused on Lavinia. "After everything he does for everyone else, he refuses to celebrate himself."

"Why do you think that is?"

Sarah had her suspicions, but she wasn't going to share

them. Not with Lavinia anyway.

Thankfully, she didn't have to respond because the gentlemen came into the drawing room. "That's it, Felix has completely convinced me we must go to Scott's Grotto," Beck said.

"You don't have to convince me," Lavinia said, smiling and returning to the settee. "Shall we go tomorrow?"

Beck sat down beside her, and Sarah took a chair situated nearby while Felix occupied another chair. "I don't know," Beck said. "Felix and I were just talking about Anthony and wondered if we should follow him to Epping. Just in case he needs…something."

"I don't think that's wise," Sarah said. "But maybe I should go. You're right that he shouldn't be alone."

"We could all go," Lavinia suggested.

Felix nodded slowly. "I suppose we could."

"I still don't know." Sarah thought of Anthony's current state. He was still so upset about their parents, but, unlike Sarah, he hadn't fallen in love amidst his sadness. Furthermore, he was furious with his best friend and only slightly less angry with her. Despite all that, she really did think he shouldn't be alone. "We'd have to follow at a distance."

"I recommend we give him an hour lead," Beck said.

Felix stood. "I'll arrange it. See you all in the morning." His gaze lingered on Sarah, and then he turned and left.

A short time later, Sarah stood in her chamber ready for bed. She wasn't the least bit tired. She was consumed with a desperate need to see and touch and talk to Felix. Why shouldn't she go to his room? They were betrothed now.

Tightening the sash of her dressing gown, she left her chamber and strode to his room. She stopped before going in—bad things happened when people entered rooms unannounced.

She knocked and waited anxiously for a response. When none came, she lifted her hand to knock again. But the door opened.

"Sarah." Felix looked surprised to see her. He also looked...undressed.

He wore a silk banyan and perhaps nothing else. She couldn't tell for certain unless she stripped it off. Suddenly, her mouth was dry, and her flesh was hot all over.

She lowered her gaze to his feet. They were bare.

Snapping her attention back to his face, she had to work to remember why she'd come. "May I come in?"

He held the door open and moved aside as she crossed over the threshold.

She turned to face him. "Aren't you going to close the door?"

He arched a brow but said nothing as he did as she asked. Once it was closed, he put his back to the door. Still, he said nothing.

"I thought you might refuse to let me in. Or at least to close the door."

"Why should I? We're to be married."

"Yes." Hearing him say it—or maybe it was his state of undress or the fact that they were standing in his bedchamber—flushed her with desire.

"Am I correct in assuming you came here to seduce me again?" He moved forward, taking two steps to stand just in front of her.

"No." She shook her head, feeling flustered. "Yes. And to talk."

His brow climbed his forehead once more as he reached for the sash of her dressing gown and pulled it loose. The front of the garment opened, and her breasts tingled with anticipation. "What did you want to talk about?"

He pushed the dressing gown over her shoulders and walked behind her to pull it from her arms. He draped it over a chair near the fireplace and returned to her.

Sarah couldn't seem to find any of the words she'd wanted to say. About his parents. His birthday. His emotions.

How much she loved him.

He picked up the braid of her hair where it lay against her shoulder and began to unwind the curls. "I haven't seen you with your hair down in years."

All she could hear was the steady thrum of her heart, its speed increasing as he worked, and the quickening of her breath. When her hair was loose, he ran his fingers through the locks and let it fall over her shoulders and down her back.

"Beautiful. How did I never see that before?" He looked at her in wonder, as if he'd never seen anything like her. She'd imagined a man looking at her like that, but never dreamed it would be Felix. It was both confounding and…right.

"The same way I never saw that you were unbearably handsome." She reached for one of two frogs that held the banyan closed at his front. "Are you…naked under this?"

He nodded. "Do you want to see? Please say yes, because I am *desperate* to see you."

Heat flooded her core, and she unfastened the garment, holding her breath as it separated to reveal his chest. She put her palms flat against his warm flesh. Dark hair tickled her as she moved her fingertips over his muscles. Her pinky met a small bump, his nipple, she realized. She pushed the garment aside and looked her fill.

"My turn." He bent slightly and with both hands

grasped the skirt of her night rail. Gently, he whisked the garment over her head, and the cool air of the room heightened her awareness. Her breasts, already heavy, tightened, especially as his gaze dropped to look at them.

"My God, Sarah. You are absolutely exquisite." He lifted his hands to her collarbones and gently ran his fingers along her flesh, moving outward to her shoulders and then down her biceps. Then his hands came inward to stroke the outer globes of her breasts.

Desire pulsed through her, and she worked to contain her need lest she cast herself forward against him. He circled his hands up to the top of her breasts, then brought his palms down so that they dragged softly across the ends of her nipples. She gasped softly, eager for him to do so much more.

Using his palms, he rotated them in circles over her flesh, drawing her forward as she sought more contact. Then he gave it to her, closing his hands over her and lifting the sensitive weight. She gasped again and closed her eyes, reveling in the new sensation.

Her breathing became even faster while his caresses remained slow and steady. He stroked her, sliding his fingertips around her breasts and pulling them down over the nipple. After several passes, he used a firmer touch, squeezing her flesh and tugging the nipples, then repeating the action over and over until she was fairly panting with need.

Then he pinched them both, but it didn't hurt. She opened her eyes as she sucked in a breath in surprise. He bent his head and cupped one breast as he suckled, then he moved to the other, using his thumb to tease the one he'd just left. Back and forth he went, tormenting her, and sparking a sweet craving between her legs.

She closed her eyes again, giving herself completely to

the delicious sensations he aroused. The more he worked, the more her pleasure built, and she wondered if he could bring her to release just like this.

Suddenly, something changed. His dedicated, methodical attention shifted. He nipped her flesh and sucked at her, then dragged his hand down her abdomen. His fingers stroked along her sex, and her knees wavered.

"*Sarah*. You are so damn wet."

She opened her eyes to see him straighten. He looked at her as he pushed a finger inside her. A growl started low in his throat just before he kissed her. His mouth was open and wet and incredibly wild. She clutched at his shoulders as he held one breast and stroked into her.

Then she was flying. Or so it seemed, because he swept her into his arms and carried her to the bed. He laid her down and kissed her again, sweeping his tongue deep into her mouth. She curled her hand around his neck and pressed her fingers into his scalp as she kissed him back. The desire she felt for him was both wonderful and terrifying.

All while he kissed her, his hands and fingers caressed her flesh, teasing her nipple and tantalizing her sex. She opened her legs wider, soundlessly begging him to give her release.

His mouth left hers and moved down her neck, his teeth and tongue ravaging her flesh. He drew on one nipple, closing his lips around her and sucking before moving to the other and doing the same. She grasped his hair and cast her head back in abandon. His fingers pumped into her, and then his mouth was on her there. He did to her sex what he'd done to her breasts, licking and sucking until she thrust herself up into him, mindless with need.

At last her release came, breaking her into a thousand

little pieces. She dug her nails into his shoulder and with her other hand grasped the coverlet. Before she recovered, he was between her legs, his cock against her sex.

She opened her eyes and looked up at him, a sense of peace and fulfillment spreading through her. He was so handsome, his familiar features so beloved. There was nowhere in the world she'd rather be—now or forever.

He clasped her hip and with his other hand guided himself into her sex. It was different from before and yet the same. She tilted her pelvis as he slid inside. Then he positioned her legs, curling them around his hips. He leaned forward, and she rose up to kiss him, brushing her lips against his.

"I love you," she whispered.

He stilled, but only for the briefest moment—so brief, she wondered if she'd imagined it. And then she stopped thinking, for he stole every rational piece of her mind.

His body moved over and into hers, claiming and worshipping her with each thrust and every caress. He kissed her mouth, her neck, her breast, and she was completely lost in his embrace. He drove deeper, then stroked her clitoris, pushing her to that place where darkness and passion collided. She cried out just as he did, and then he was gone. Mostly. He continued to touch her, seeing her through the climax until she tumbled to the earth.

She was vaguely aware that he'd collapsed beside her. Opening her eyes, she turned her head to see his arm flung across his forehead as he fought to regain his breath. His eyes were closed, his lips parted.

"You left me again. Why?"

He didn't open his eyes. "To prevent a child."

"But we're getting married. Why does it matter?"

"We aren't married yet."

Sarah rolled toward him onto her side. "Should I be concerned that we won't marry?"

He cracked his eye open then and looked at her, but only briefly. "No."

"Is it because of what I said?" She tensed, her breath catching as she waited for his response. She hadn't been able to contain herself. She loved him, and she wanted him to know.

"I'm not sure what you mean." He rolled over and kissed her.

Was he being purposely obtuse or was it possible he hadn't heard her? She wanted to make sure. Cupping his face, she stroked his cheek until he looked into her eyes. "I love you, Felix."

His expression didn't change. Until it did. He smiled, then kissed her again. "I'll see you back to your room."

She knew he'd heard her that time. He had to. What had she expected, a response of the same?

She sat up, afraid to ask what she needed to know, but realizing she must. "Felix, when you swore to never marry, did you also swear to never love?"

He sat up with her, then climbed from the other side of the bed. "I did not." His response was halting—whether from effort or uncertainty she couldn't tell. He picked up her night rail, then came around to her side of the bed and gave it to her.

She drew the garment over her head and settled it around her body, feeling cold. He went to fetch her dressing gown and brought that too.

Sarah slid from the bed and took the gown, pulling it on while he donned his banyan. After she tied her sash, she went toward him, moving slowly. "Does it bother you that I love you?"

"No." He finished fastening his banyan. "Ready?"

"No." She shook her head, feeling a myriad of emotions—bewilderment, frustration, disappointment. She hadn't really expected him to say he loved her back, but there was something more here. What did he feel? "I realize you don't love me now. At least I don't think you do, otherwise you would have said so. Am I a fool to think you ever will?"

He took a breath, but it was shallow, and the pulse in his neck seemed to pick up speed. "You aren't a fool, Sarah. Not now and not ever. Let me be honest."

"Yes, please. I deserve that."

"You do." He bowed his head a moment before fixing her with a steady stare. "I don't love anyone. I never have. And no one has ever said those words to me."

No one had *ever* said those words? Sarah's heart broke. She stepped toward him, her throat constricting. "Oh, Felix."

His gaze hardened. "Please don't. I don't want your pity. I *can't* have it." There was a plea in his tone and a haunting desperation in his eyes that she'd never seen before. It was the closest he'd come to displaying a deep emotion.

But then it was gone. He blinked, and it was as if the sun had pushed the clouds away and now shone brightly through the vivid green of his eyes. "It's late, and we need to rise early."

That much was true. She nodded, and he opened the door. She stepped over the threshold and realized he meant to come with her. He'd offered to escort her to her room.

She pivoted toward him. "I don't need you to come. Good night, Felix." She left before he could respond. Or maybe she simply couldn't hear him over the deafening roar of emotion in her ears.

Back in her room, she leaned against the door, her knees buckling. She slid to the floor and landed on her rump. What hell had Felix been consigned to without anyone to love him? How had he become the jovial Duke of Distraction whom everyone admired? How was it possible that he didn't feel loved?

She wiped at the tears stealing down her cheeks. He was *so* loved, and she was going to do everything she could to make sure he knew he deserved it.

Chapter Fourteen

◆❦◆

FELIX WAS GLAD Sarah and Lavinia were seated together on the forward-facing seat of his coach, leaving him to sit beside Beck. Because if he'd had to spend the twelve-mile journey to Epping nestled against Sarah, he might go entirely mad. Not just because he wanted her, but because of what she'd said last night.

He refused to even *think* the words.

He directed his gaze out the window as he had almost the entire trip. They'd reached the edge of Epping and would soon be at their destination.

A few minutes later, the coach drove up to large house situated atop a hill. With pale stone and elaborate brickwork, particularly on the chimney decoration, the manse was a beautiful depiction of architecture from the last century. It was strange to think a murderer was housed somewhere on the grounds, but this was where they'd brought the wounded highwayman.

Felix's footman opened the door to the coach and put down the step. Felix descended first, followed by Beck, who helped both ladies to descend.

Beck took his wife's arm, of course, which left Felix to take Sarah's. The moment she touched him, the anxiety inside him intensified, tying him into even tighter knots. This was torture, this knowledge of how she felt. He'd been a fool to think he could marry her.

They made their way to the door, which stood open. The butler greeted them.

"Good morning," Felix said. "We're here to see Lord Colton."

"He has already departed, I'm afraid."

Felix exchanged a look of confusion with Beck before looking back to the butler. "Do you know where he went?"

"I do not, but perhaps Mr. Allencourt can be of assistance. They met for a short period. Do you mind waiting here for a moment?"

The butler excused himself and left them in the entry hall.

"What do you suppose happened?" Sarah asked. Her hand on Felix's sleeve had curled around him with tension, and her face was creased with worry.

"Perhaps the prisoner was already transported to Chelmsford," Felix said. That was where the assize would be held soon, and the highwayman would be tried for his crimes.

Sarah frowned. "Then Anthony is surely on his way there." She withdrew from him and paced a few steps, clearly upset.

A man, maybe fifty years in age, swept into the hall. His dark hair was lightly tinged with silver, including the sideburns that encroached along the upper portion of his jaw. He smiled widely as his gaze settled on Sarah. "Miss Colton, what a delight to see you." He came toward her, and the smile fell from his face as quickly as it had appeared. Taking her hand in his, he bowed. "May I offer my deepest condolences? Your father was a splendid man and a dear friend." He released her hand, and Felix found he'd been holding his breath.

"Thank you." Sarah angled herself toward Beck, Lavinia, and Felix. "Allow me to present the Marquess and Marchioness of Northam, and the Earl of Ware."

Allencourt offered bows to all of them. "Welcome, welcome. I do wish you were visiting under better circumstances. Shall we adjourn to a more comfortable setting?"

"I do appreciate your hospitality," Sarah said. "However, we are looking for my brother. He was here earlier?"

"Yes, to see the prisoner." Allencourt's mouth pulled into a deep frown. "I'm sorry to report that he passed away in the night, the rotter. Too good an end for him, if you ask me."

Felix could only imagine how Anthony had reacted to the news. He'd been anxious to hold the man accountable.

"I see," Sarah murmured. Felix noted how her hand clenched and opened and clenched again. "Do you know where Anthony has gone?"

"Oaklands, I believe. Will you be returning there?" he asked.

"Yes. Thank you for your time, Mr. Allencourt." She offered him a weak smile.

He took her hand again. "I would offer any support you require, especially now. I believe your father would want me to look after you. When you are ready to accept callers, I shall be the first."

Allencourt looked at her with a fervent, almost sexual intensity that made Felix want to hit him. And then he recalled the man's name—Allencourt. This was the gentleman who'd expressed interest in marrying Sarah. Of course he wanted to call on her. Only she was already betrothed.

But you don't want that.

He mentally batted away the reminder. Just because he didn't want to marry didn't mean he was going to allow this man to prey upon Sarah. Felix stepped toward her and offered his arm. "Thank you again, Mr. Allencourt.

Good day." He escorted Sarah from the hall, preceded by Beck and Lavinia.

They stepped outside into the overcast morning, which was already showing signs of improving as the clouds began to thin.

"Shall we go to Oaklands, then?" Lavinia asked as they made their way back to the coach.

Felix imagined Anthony's anger and disappointment. He'd lost his parents, his best friend had ruined his sister, and now the man who'd killed his parents had escaped Anthony's vengeance. "He may prefer to be alone." Hadn't he said he wanted to be?

"I'm sure he does, but our following him clearly establishes that we don't agree with that sentiment." Sarah let go of Felix's arm. "We're going to Oaklands." She climbed into the coach, leaving no room for further dispute.

Once they were inside the coach, Sarah sent him an odd look. It was a mixture of curiosity and doubt. Whatever she was thinking, it only added to his discomfort.

It took nearly an hour to arrive at Oaklands, the Colton family's estate. Smaller than Stag's Court, it provoked a much stronger sense of nostalgia than Felix's own home. He recalled times spent here in his youth where other people had provided a buffer between him and his father. Happy times.

Maybe the happiest.

Sarah didn't take Felix's arm this time. She hastened to the door and embraced the butler, who hugged her warmly.

"He's in your father's study." The butler cleared his throat. "I mean, his study."

Sarah nodded and moved into the house. Felix inclined his head to the man, a sturdy fellow in his middle fifties.

"It's good to see you, Inman."

"And you, my lord."

Felix introduced Beck and Lavinia, but the butler greeted Lavinia as if they'd already met, and she did the same. "I've visited a few times," she explained.

Inman suggested they go to the drawing room. As they went, Felix felt as if he were walking on a field of broken glass. He was racked with inner turmoil about Sarah and Anthony, and fuck, everything it seemed.

"It must be difficult for them being back here," Beck said.

"I know it is for Sarah," Lavinia said. "She was torn between wanting to be here because it's home and needing to stay away." She gave Beck a sad look. He took her hand and pressed a kiss to her wrist.

Felix turned away. For the first time in years, he thought of his first visit here. He'd come with his father, invited by the Coltons. Aside from George, Anthony had been the only child Felix had met. To befriend a boy with whom he could run and fish and climb trees had filled him with a joy he hadn't realized he'd been missing. Oh, he'd tried to do those things with George, but she wasn't always allowed—either by her parents who thought she should behave more like a girl, whatever that meant, or especially by Felix's father who told him he shouldn't play with girls, particularly the steward's daughter. But that was only when his father was paying attention, when he wasn't submerged in a bottle.

After some time, Felix began to pace while Beck and Lavinia sat together on a small settee. They looked perfectly fine, content even, to sit quietly and wait. Felix felt as if he were going to explode. God, he hated this. How could he make it stop?

He needed to find something else to do. Something that

would take him away from this agony.

He turned to face Beck and Lavinia. "I think I should go. My being here will probably upset Anthony. He's still rather angry with me." And likely always would be.

"Yes, I am," Anthony said, coming into the room with Sarah trailing behind him. Her face was pale, her features tense. "You shouldn't have come." It wasn't clear if he meant Felix or everyone. "You should all go back to Stag's Court."

Beck and Lavinia stood. "We were sorry to hear about the highwayman, but at least he's gone," Beck said.

Anthony's mouth tightened. "I should have left yesterday as soon as I heard. But I was distracted by—" He sent a dark glare at Felix and then Sarah.

Felix, already wound up tight as a clock, could no longer keep himself in check. "Stop it. Stop shaming Sarah. You don't own the right to feel sad and angry and seek comfort where you may. That your sister chose me instead of a bloody bottle isn't your concern."

Anthony stepped forward, his eyes blazing. "You aren't really going to try that argument again, are you?"

"There is no argument." Felix felt as if his blood were boiling, but he managed to rein himself in. "Sarah and I are getting married. There is no damage done here."

"Not yet, but you don't want to marry her. You don't want to marry anyone. How long will it be until you turn from her? Until you devastate her?"

Yes, their friendship was over, and Felix was glad for it. "Go to hell, Anthony." He stormed from the room and wove his way back to the entry hall, where he brushed past Inman without saying a word.

Outside, he paused. He couldn't just abandon Beck and Lavinia here. And Sarah. Hell, it was her house. He couldn't abandon her where she lived.

Soon, your house will be her house.

"Felix!"

The sound of her voice hit him like an arrow. He slowly turned to see her standing several feet away. She'd removed her hat, which he took as a sign that she meant to stay.

She took a step forward. "You're upset. I've never seen you upset."

"I don't get upset." He worked to keep his voice even, as he hadn't done inside.

"I know. And you should."

"What good does it do? Look at Anthony. He's a mess of emotion, and it bleeds all over everyone else."

"Am I a mess?" she asked softly.

"Of course not."

"But I'm overflowing with emotion." She took another step.

Felix pivoted so that he presented her with his profile. "I can't." He shook his head. "I can't help you with that."

"But you have. You help everyone. That's what you do."

Yes, that was what he did. But he couldn't do that for her. Not knowing what he knew. That she *loved* him. When he'd realized everything had changed between them, he never imagined it would be this drastic. That being with her would rob him of his breath and tie him up so tightly that he felt as though he couldn't move.

He focused his gaze on a distant tree. "Anthony doesn't want me here, and I understand that. I'll be at Stag's Court. Stay here as long as you like, and we'll set the wedding whenever you decide."

She moved into his line of sight, her face a mass of concern and a dozen other emotions he didn't want to see. "You assume I'm staying here."

"Aren't you?" He lifted his gaze to her hair, dark and upswept, the curls a memory against his fingertips. "You didn't bring your hat."

"You also assume we're still getting married."

"Have you changed your mind again?" He kept his tone perfectly even. He wouldn't persuade her—either way. It was entirely her choice.

"When you didn't say anything to Allencourt this morning, I wondered if *you'd* changed *your* mind. Have you?" She blinked at him, her facing clearing into a stoic mask. Her voice held none of the emotion it had.

She was, he realized, behaving exactly like him.

"I'll just return to Stag's Court. Advise me of what you want to do about the wedding." He inclined his head toward his footman and climbed into the coach.

She moved to the doorway and looked inside. "I'll make sure Beck and Lavinia find their way back." Now her tone carried emotion—sarcasm.

He nodded, and she stepped away, allowing the footman to close the door.

As he departed the place he'd long thought of as a home, he wondered if he'd ever return. He wondered if the past had finally caught up with him and would steal the meager happiness he'd managed to grasp.

SARAH STARED AFTER the coach until long after it had disappeared, then turned and walked woodenly back to the house. Inside, she found Lavinia waiting for her in the entry hall.

"What can I do?" she asked.

Sarah shrugged, feeling numb. "I don't know. He's gone, of course."

Lavinia nodded. "Shall I send for tea? Or would you like to go to your room and rest?"

Hit with a sudden burst of anger, she strode away from Lavinia and went back to the drawing room. Beck stood near the fireplace, his head bent. He glanced up as she came in, but her gaze shot directly to Anthony. He held a glass of whisky or some other spirit and stared at the window toward the back garden their mother had loved.

Sarah stopped a few feet from her brother. "Anthony, you will cease behaving like a jackass."

He turned and glowered at her. "Did he leave?"

"Yes, thanks to you. You can't be angry with him."

"I'll be angry with whomever I like."

"Fine, then I'll be angry at you until you stop. Felix is going to be my husband, and even if he wasn't, he's your oldest and dearest friend. I seduced him, and he's trying to do the right thing, even though it's killing him." Her voice broke, and she felt Lavinia's hand on her shoulder.

Sarah took a deep breath to regain her equilibrium. "He needs me, Anthony. He needs *us*. Surely we've learned how important family is and how tightly we must hold and cherish it. Felix, even if we didn't marry, is our family."

"But you just said doing the right thing was killing him. Why should I—or you—want that for Felix if he's family?"

She didn't want that. And it *was* killing him. She could see it in the fleeting looks of terror in his eyes, in the way he'd revealed a depth of emotion today that he never had before. "He shouldn't be hurting. Which is why I have to save him." If she could. God, she prayed she could.

Anthony pressed his lips together and stared at the glass in his hand. "Go after him, then. I won't stop you."

"No, you wouldn't even if you tried. But will you

support me? Will you support *him*?" She moved toward Anthony, desperate to reach the brother buried beneath the fury and the sorrow. She had to save him too, she realized. "Mother and Father tried to include Felix after his father died, as much as his uncle would allow. They would want us to stand together. As much as he needs us, we need him too. Please, Anthony."

At the mention of their parents, his gaze had snapped up, locking onto hers. His eyes were full of sadness but also love. "When do you want to leave?"

Sarah exhaled. "After we visit Mother and Father. I'm going to fetch my hat, and I'll meet you in the garden."

She turned and gave Lavinia a brief hug. "Thank you."

"Do you want us to stay here?" Lavinia asked.

Sarah shook her head firmly. "No, you're coming too. Tomorrow is Felix's birthday, and we're having a party."

She only hoped he would come.

Chapter Fifteen

•€•3•

IT'S YOUR BIRTHDAY.

The words had always been spoken with disdain and sadness, never in joy. The day of Felix's birth had always been a cause for despair and sorrow. And blame.

There wasn't a day that went by in which Felix hadn't been acutely aware of the role he'd played in his mother's death and in his father's subsequent agony.

"This should be a joyous day. Your mother would have been so happy. But now look at her."

He could feel his father's hand on the back of his neck, forcing him to look at the cold letters and numbers etched into the stone that separated them from the woman his father had loved. The woman Felix had hated.

Felix looked down at the tomb that bore her name and the date of her death. Today. His birthday.

But he didn't hate her anymore. He hadn't even known her. She had been, by all accounts, a warm and lovely person, the kind of woman who'd loved children and adored animals. The kind of woman who lit the room with her presence and cheered everyone around her.

It was, he suddenly realized, the kind of man he'd become. But not because she'd made him that way.

Felix raised his eyes to his father's tomb. "You did that."

The stone stared back at him, frustratingly silent.

"Do you see that in spite of you, I am the man she would have wanted me to be?"

Still nothing.

Emotion unfurled inside him, and he dropped down,

squatting so that he could look at his father at eye level. "Almost the man she would have wanted. I don't think she would have wanted me to feel unloved. I don't think she would have wanted you to drink yourself to an early grave and wholly abdicate the duties of fatherhood."

The rock was nearly as stoic as his father when Felix had used to cry. Until the day his father had beat him until he stopped. Then he'd never cried again. Nor had his father raised a hand to him again.

"You didn't have to hit me after that, did you?" he asked softly. "Everything changed when you whipped the emotion right out of me. I knew I wasn't to show it, and so I never did." Even now, as rage poured through him, he couldn't yell or shout or even cry.

"Thank you for that. At least partly," he added. "I am glad to feel nothing for you, but you've left me incapable of feeling anything for anyone. You see, there's a woman who loves me. *Loves* me." His voice broke, and the wave of emotion completely stole his breath.

Felix leaned forward and braced his hand on the stone, careful to touch the tomb beside his father that belonged to a great-uncle. Closing his eyes, Felix fought to inhale.

At length, he raised his head and sat back, balancing on his feet once more. "I want to love her, but I don't know how."

"I think you already do."

Her voice was a balm to the blistering agony in his soul. He stood and turned, the blood rushing to his legs and making them wobbly. Or maybe it was just seeing her. Though he'd only left her yesterday, it had felt like an eternity.

"How—" He cleared his throat. "How can you know?"

"That you love me?" She came toward him. Garbed in soft, dove gray, she appeared fragile except for her hat. It sported a wide brim and was topped with a jaunty purple feather, and in it, she was quintessentially Sarah, full of charm and energy, of beauty and light.

He couldn't speak for the lump lodged in his throat, so he nodded.

She took his hand between hers, a gentle smile curving her lips. "Because when we're together, everything is better. That's what love is. Whether romantic or familial or friendship."

She was trying to tell him there were different kinds of love, that he'd experienced them all his life. At least that was what he thought she was saying.

"What kind of love do you feel?" His body went rigid. If she said she loved him as a brother or a friend, he thought he might crumple.

Her eyes crinkled at the edges as she smiled. "Do you even have to ask? I love you as, hopefully, my husband. As my lover. As my friend. As the first person I want to see when I wake up every morning and the last one I want to see when I close my eyes to go to sleep." Her thumb stroked the back of his hand as wave after wave of emotion crashed over him. "Tell me what you feel."

Words jammed in his throat. "I—I can't describe it. No, I can. I'm terrified. Of loving you. Of losing you." His voice cracked again, and this time, he looked away. He thought of his mother lying behind the stone, the woman he never knew. "I left your body the other night because I'm afraid. If what happened to my mother happens to—"

Sarah's arms came around him, and she held him tight. "It won't."

He resisted hugging her in return, desperate to keep some small part of himself guarded and safe. "You can't say that."

"I can believe it because I must. I believe in our future, in us, and if there will be tragedy or grief, I will still take what we have. I don't want the alternative. I don't want life without you, however long it might be." She pulled back and touched his face, her hand caressing his cheek. "I see that you're scared. And I think I can see why. Not because of love or loss—at least not just because of those things, but because, I think, you somehow don't believe you deserve to love and be loved. But Felix, you *do*."

He stared at her, the riot inside him quieting for the first time in the presence of another person. Because of the words and comfort of another person. "I don't think anyone has ever seen the real me. Not until now."

"Then it is my honor."

It couldn't be this easy. What if Anthony was right? What if he did devastate her? "I don't know how to do this, Sarah. Love. Trust." Felix glanced briefly toward the tomb. "He broke me."

A tear tracked down her cheek, but she still smiled for him. "We'll do it together." Her voice was steady and sure.

The dam inside him tore apart, and emotions, so many emotions, cascaded forth. He felt wetness on his cheeks for the first time in so long. He put his arms around her and brought her flush to his chest, then he kissed her, his soul seeking the solace he knew only she could give.

He picked her up and carried her outside. "I can't be in there with him anymore." He set her down a distance from the church, in the shade of a pair of trees. "I just want you, Sarah. I need *you*." He gently stroked the sides of her face, his palms resting against her cheeks. "I love you."

She smiled, and he feared his heart might burst.

He kissed her again, his mouth claiming hers with sweet

desperation. Touching her, feeling her was like air in his lungs after a lifetime underwater. She clasped his shoulders and pressed her body into his. He wanted to lose himself in her completely. No, he wanted to show her the depth of his emotions, the utter urgency he felt to possess her and be possessed.

He sank to the ground, pulling her with him. Kissing her, he scrambled to find the hem of her skirt, lifting it as her fingers found the buttons of his fall.

He pressed her back and rose above her, drawing in breath. "Is this terrible?"

She laughed softly and shook her head. "This is wonderful. Love me, Felix. Now."

She opened his breeches and he pushed her gown to her waist. His fingers found her sex, and she was more than ready. Her hand guided him forward, and he sank into her wet heat. Groaning low in his throat, he began to move.

She held him, one hand on his back and the other on his backside, pulling him deeper as her legs curled around his waist.

Passion, dizzying and reckless, consumed him. Her legs quivered, and her muscles tensed. She cried out as she clenched around him, and he drove into her, uncaring that he screamed her name when he climaxed. And uncaring that he poured himself and their future into her.

No, not uncaring. He did so with tender deliberation and boundless love.

She pressed her legs tighter around him, keeping him inside her. He kissed her cheek, her ear, and whispered, "I'm not leaving. Not ever."

She pulled his mouth to hers. "Good."

Several minutes later, or maybe it was an hour, Felix didn't know, nor did he care, he helped her to stand.

Somehow his hat had ended up several feet away. Sarah's was still atop her head, but quite askew.

"I'm amazed your hat is still in place," he mused. "Must be the excellent craftsmanship."

She laughed as she straightened it. "Must be. I hope people are willing to pay for them."

"They will, but even if they don't, I have it on good authority that you needn't worry about planning for a spinster future."

She paused in putting herself back together. "You know that's not why I'm marrying you."

He picked up his hat and returned to her. "I know precisely why you're marrying me. The same reason I'm marrying you—I can't live without you."

She kissed him again, and it was some time before she suggested they return to the house.

"Must we?" he asked.

She nodded, tucking her arm through his. "I'm afraid we need to get to a birthday party. If you're amenable."

Joy filled his soul. "I'm more than amenable. I can hardly wait."

◆క•3◆

AFTER A BRIEF stop at the house to organize Felix's birthday dinner, they went into Ware, where Felix purchased their marriage license. Then Sarah stopped to buy some hat supplies. Though it had started with uncertainty and apprehension, it had turned out to be the best day of Sarah's life.

When they'd returned the prior evening, Seales had informed her that Felix had gone into Ware. Though she'd waited for him to come home, she'd eventually given up some time past midnight only to awaken early and go in search of him.

Which was how she'd found him in the church. Seales had said Felix wasn't in the house, and a trip to the stables had revealed he hadn't taken a horse or vehicle. Catching sight of the steward's house, Sarah had thought of George and then of the church. History told her he wouldn't be there, and yet she'd gone anyway. Partly because if nothing else she wanted to pay her respects on the day their family had been torn apart.

"I don't think I'll stay for port," Martin said, drawing Sarah from her reverie. He stood from the table and gave Felix a somewhat pained look. "Felicitations again on your wedding—and your birthday."

Felix smiled up at him. "Thank you, Uncle. Remember, you're welcome to stay at the dower house for as long as it takes for you to find a new situation that meets your needs."

Martin's eyes, always bulbous, seemed to teeter at the brink of toppling from his head, but he blinked, and the risk was averted. "I appreciate your hospitality. Good evening." He bowed to the table and departed.

"How long do you think he'll stay?" Beck asked.

Felix shrugged. "I imagine it will grate him horribly. I never expected him to be so bitter, but that was foolish on my part. I have always known precisely what kind of man he is." He took a drink of wine.

"Shall we leave you to your port?" Sarah said, rising.

"No." Felix jumped up from the table. "It's my birthday, and I get to decide. Let's all go to the drawing room." He grinned at Sarah as he put his arm around her waist.

"I think I'm going to retire," Anthony said. He and Felix had made up that afternoon, but there was a still a dark, melancholy air lingering over her brother. Sarah suspected it would be there for some time. She wondered if she would feel the same if not for Felix and the happiness he'd brought her.

Sarah left Felix's side and went to press a kiss to her brother's cheek. "Sleep well."

He nodded and gave her a brief hug, whispering, "I'm glad you're so happy. Truly. If I wasn't in such a sorry state, I would have realized sooner how wonderful it is to have two of the people I love most find love with each other."

She hugged him back, saying, "I love you."

Anthony bade the others good night before he left.

Lavinia looped her arm through Sarah's as they made their way to the drawing room. "Have you chosen a date to get married?"

Sarah looked back at Felix. "Not yet. We'd like to have David and Fanny come if they're able. I wrote to her this afternoon to ask if they could come in a week. We're, ah, a bit eager to wed."

Lavinia laughed. "I know what that feels like. I'm sure Fanny will come. She's anxious to see you."

In the drawing room, Felix made sure everyone had a libation, and then he offered a toast. "To *my bride*, two words I thought I'd *never* say." Everyone laughed, and he grinned. "To Sarah, who has given me more than I ever imagined. But apparently, everything I deserve. According to her."

"She's right," Beck said. "She will always be right. Best to learn that now." He lifted his glass toward Lavinia and winked at her.

Sarah gazed at Felix with love and sipped her sherry, still amazed at how much her life had changed in such a short time.

Later, she stole into his room where he was waiting for

her with a kiss that curled her toes. "This feels rather naughty," she said as he led her toward the bed.

Felix, wearing nothing but a shirt that barely covered his erection, grinned at her. "Everything we've done has been naughty. And you're no stranger to my chamber or my bed."

"True, but we aren't married yet."

He undressed her, casting her dressing gown and night rail aside. "*Yet* is the key term there. We're as good as wed. In fact, I'm quite happy to race to London tomorrow and procure a special license. You can be my countess by sundown." He kissed her neck, and she closed her eyes with a sigh.

"While that is very tempting, I shall be patient for our wedding in Ware."

He lifted his head. "You're sure you don't prefer Harlow? I don't understand why you and Anthony wanted Ware."

"I think it's just easier," she said softly. "For Anthony in particular. Is that all right?"

"Of course." He kissed her and rested his forehead against hers. "Your brother is going to recover."

"Your father didn't." She pulled back and looked into his eyes, thinking about what she'd overheard him say that morning. "I can't believe what you endured. When I think about how your father treated you, what he did—"

"Shhh. It's all right. *I'm* all right. And Anthony will be too." He kissed her again. "As soon as he falls in love."

Sarah couldn't help but smile. "Is that right?"

"It's changed everything for me."

She clutched the hem of his shirt, preparing to tug it over his head. "For the better, I hope."

He cupped her face and smiled. "For the absolute best."

Chapter Sixteen

NINE DAYS LATER, Felix formally gave his heart and soul to the woman who already owned him. After marrying in the church, they returned to Stag's Court, a place where Felix had never truly felt at home but where he now looked to a future with his wife and the family they would hopefully share.

Fanny and David had arrived the day before, and watching Sarah with her friends made Felix smile. George had joined them, since over the last week, she and Vane had become a staple at the dinner table. If anyone found it strange that Felix dined with his secretary and valet, no one said anything. Felix was just happy to have this newfound sense of family and the intense feeling of love that seemed to permeate everything. Now that he'd embraced the emotion, he couldn't get enough.

Felix's aunt approached him in the drawing room following the wedding breakfast. She'd been thrilled to learn that Felix was marrying, and Felix suspected she took pleasure in her husband's plans being foiled.

Bridget patted Felix's arm with a smile. "Such a lovely ceremony. You truly could not have chosen a better wife. Your father would have been happy." Her forehead creased, and she dropped her arm to her side. "He did love you. Sometimes we parents are so focused on ourselves we forget to make sure—" She looked toward her son, who stood near the windows talking with Anthony. "Never mind." Her smile softened, as did her gaze as she transferred it back to Felix. "I did try to care for you as a mother ought, but perhaps I allowed Martin too much rein. He never wanted you to wed. He wanted the earldom for Michael."

"We needn't speak of this," Felix said. While he was making an effort to no longer hide his emotions, he didn't particularly want to display them for his aunt or uncle.

"No, I suppose we needn't. But I do hope you know that Michael is quite relieved. As it happens, he was petrified of becoming the earl."

"Then everything has turned out as it should," Felix murmured.

"Yes." Bridget glanced toward Martin and then cast her gaze to the ceiling briefly. "Martin won't agree, but ignore him. He'll recover. I actually think he's happy for you deep down. He's not good at showing his emotions. He could learn from you, my boy."

Felix coughed. "I doubt that. If you'll excuse me, I want to speak with Michael."

Anthony and Michael turned toward Felix as he came toward them. "Here's the happy groom," Anthony said.

"Here I am." Felix looked at his cousin. "Though you likely won't be inheriting the title, I should still like for you to come to London to stay with me and Sarah. Perhaps in the fall, if you're amenable?"

Michael nodded, smiling. "I would like that very much."

"Excellent. I will ensure you're settled, Michael," Felix said. "I give you my word."

"Thank you, Felix." Michael took himself off with a rather buoyant gait.

"You've made that boy's day," Anthony said. "Actually, you may have made his entire year."

"Perhaps," Felix said softly. He gave his full attention to his best friend, who was now his brother-in-law. "Thank you for allowing me to marry Sarah."

Letting out a sound that was part laugh and part scoff,

Anthony gave his head a shake. "As if I had anything to do with it. You were both going to do exactly what you wanted. I'm just glad you chose correctly."

"I am too," Felix said. "I did try to cock things up, but your sister is far smarter than me. I'm exceptionally lucky to have found her."

Anthony gave him a serious stare. "You are. Just as she is to have found you. But really, I'm the luckiest because I don't have to worry about my sister marrying a jackass I can't stand or my best friend taking an insufferable wife."

Felix laughed. "Well, we're glad to have satisfied your requirements. We shall expect you to do the same. I don't want you taking an insufferable wife either."

"There's no danger of that any time soon—insufferable or otherwise." He sipped his wine, and Felix knew he was still in pain and might be for quite some time.

Felix looked around the room at their friends and family. "Anthony, you will never be alone, even if you want to be."

Anthony arched a brow. "Is that a threat?"

"A heartfelt promise." Felix gripped the other man's bicep and gave it a quick squeeze. "Love is all around us. We just have to see it."

Felix joined his wife, putting his arm about her waist. She turned her head and smiled, and he wondered how he'd ever looked at her and not fallen instantly and completely in love.

"I understand we missed all the kissing fun at Darent Hall," David said.

Lavinia nodded. "Yes, Felix designs the best kissing games."

Sarah's eyes narrowed playfully as she linked her arm through Felix's. "Not anymore. The only kissing games he's playing are with me." She blushed as she shot an apologetic look toward Anthony. "Sorry."

Anthony shuddered. "Time for me to go. I'm off for Oaklands."

"You aren't going to stay to see the puppies?" Sarah asked. "We're bringing them home tomorrow."

"I met Poppy and Blossom just the other day," Anthony said with a chuckle. "When you nearly talked me into taking the last one."

"Nearly? You know I'm bringing that dog to Oaklands soon."

Anthony grinned and moved to press a kiss to his sister's cheek. "Come whenever you like, but without the dog. I wouldn't want him to be lonely. You should take him so he's with his sisters. Sisters are nice to have."

Sarah's answering smile was warm and full of love. "Maybe I will." She touched Anthony's hand. "Puppy or not, I'll come whenever you want me to. Truly."

He nodded, then inclined his head toward Felix before bidding everyone farewell.

Beck approached them. "He's going to be all right. A little darkness never hurt anyone. It might even make him more interesting." He waggled his brows and grinned, provoking most everyone to laugh.

"Yes, dear, why don't you teach him to pluck sadly at a guitar?"

Beck looked at Lavinia, aghast. "Is that what I do?"

She shrugged, then grinned, lifting a hand to her mouth to stifle a giggle. "Sometimes."

There was more laughter, and Felix marveled at how different it felt. He realized that as the planner, he'd often kept himself on the outside. That way, he hadn't been able to feel too deeply.

He leaned over and whispered in his wife's ear, "Thank you."

She turned, a tiny pleat creasing the space between her brows. "For what?"

"For everything."

Epilogue

❧❦❧

London, Late February, 1819

LADY EUGENIA SATTERFIELD wasn't sure how she managed to fit everyone in her town house year after year for her annual ball, but somehow she did. New people came; others did not. Some were removed from the invitation list.

Her daughter-in-law, Nora, stood nearby. She'd offered to host the ball if it ever became too unwieldy—her and Titus's house was much larger. Eugenia knew that day would come, but it hadn't arrived yet. For now, she was content to enjoy this night, beginning with watching her stepson start the dancing with his wife.

Eugenia and her husband typically started things off, but he'd turned his ankle riding the day before and was currently ensconced in the corner, holding court. She looked over at him and smiled, thinking he might well fake an injury next year too.

The music started, and Titus and Nora took to the floor, and Eugenia's eyes misted. They'd given her three beautiful grandchildren, and Nora was increasing again. After losing her only child years ago, Eugenia was incredibly grateful for all life had given her.

Soon others joined Titus and Nora, and Eugenia turned to mingle with her guests. Almost immediately, she encountered Nora's sister, whom Eugenia also counted as a beloved member of her family. Jo and her husband, Bran, were at last expecting their first child together. Long believing she was barren, Jo had been overjoyed. They were already parents to Bran's daughter, Evie, whom Eugenia considered another grandchild, and who was ecstatic about becoming a big sister.

"You are radiant tonight," Eugenia said, kissing Jo's cheek. "I hope you are feeling well."

"Thank you, I am. The sickness I've had the past several weeks seems to have passed, thank goodness." She sent an apologetic look toward her husband. "Poor Bran. He's been a dear to put up with me."

Bran adjusted his cravat. "I don't ever have to put up with you. It's you who put up with me. Now, let us find you some lemonade before you get overheated." He smiled at Eugenia and kissed her cheek before escorting his wife toward the refreshments.

Continuing around the dance floor, Eugenia encountered more of her favorite people. The Countesses of Dartford and Sutton stood together, and their husbands hovered behind them.

"Are you certain?" Lucy, the Countess of Dartford, asked.

"I know what it feels like," Aquilla, the Countess of Sutton, said.

"I know, but I feel completely different this time." Lucy was expecting her second child in a few months, and it seemed Aquilla was perhaps also increasing.

Eugenia wondered if there was something in the air. "Good evening," she greeted.

Lucy and Aquilla smiled in unison.

"Lady Satterfield, you look lovely," Aquilla said. "Your headdress is absolutely stunning."

"Thank you. I found it in the most cunning little shop in Vigo Lane. Farewell's, it's called. Have you been?"

The two exchanged a look and giggled. Lucy leaned

toward Eugenia. "Would you like to join us in a secret?"

"Of course."

"You know Lady Ware, don't you?" Lucy asked.

"Yes, she's a dear friend of Ivy's sister." Eugenia scanned the crowd but didn't see Ivy or her sister Fanny or Lady Ware.

Lucy nodded. "That's right." After glancing around, Lucy lowered her voice to a bare whisper, "Farewell's is *her* shop."

"How extraordinary."

Aquilla's forehead creased. "You must keep it to yourself, of course."

"Certainly." Eugenia understood why Lady Ware would want to keep it a secret. It would be a scandal if Society knew she was in trade. "You know how I am with those in my inner circle. They are like family."

"Which is why I told you," Lucy said. "I knew you'd appreciate and support her efforts."

"Her secret is mine, and now I must tell her how much I love this." Eugenia patted her head.

"Why are you all whispering?" Dartford asked, stepping next to his wife. "Are you discussing my excessive charm again?"

Lucy rolled her eyes. "No, Ned's." She looked toward Sutton, who gave Dartford a lazy smile.

"I *am* more charming," Sutton said.

Dartford scoffed. "Perhaps we should have a competition."

Eugenia laughed. Dartford wasn't called the Duke of Daring for nothing. "I will leave you to it!" She moved along and soon came upon more of her inner circle.

Three ladies were clustered together—the Duchesses of Kilve and Romsey as well as Mrs. Powell, who was the sister of the Duchess of Romsey. Eugenia had met her only a few times, since she lived far north in Lancashire, and expressed her pleasure at having her in attendance.

"It is my pleasure to be here," Mrs. Powell said. "And please, you must call me Verity. Titus was such an ally to my husband last spring."

When her husband had initially pretended to be her long-lost husband, the Duke of Blackburn, in order to protect her from her father before he'd been transported for a variety of crimes. It had been a bit of a scandal, but Eugenia had done her best to support the Powells and quash the gossip.

Verity looked toward her husband, who stood talking with Romsey and Kilve. They were an exceptionally handsome trio.

"It's her last event," Diana, Duchess of Romsey, said. "And ours. We're traveling to Lancashire tomorrow in advance of Verity's lying-in."

"My goodness, there *is* something in the air," Eugenia said. "It seems everyone is increasing. It's just splendid."

"I am not," Diana said. "But our daughter is just five months old, so I shall be grateful for that."

Violet, the Duchess of Kilve, nodded in agreement. "And our son is barely six months old." Her gaze traveled to her husband, who gave her a warm smile. "Though we are hoping to have another one soon."

Eugenia chatted with them for a few more minutes before she excused herself and carried on. She then came upon the Duke and Duchess of Clare.

"Good evening, Lady Satterfield," Clare said. "I was just speaking with your husband. He told me of his accident yesterday."

"Yes, he was rather clumsy," Eugenia said. "But I daresay he's enjoying holding court this evening."

Ivy smiled. "He seemed to. As usual, this is the premier

event of the Season. It doesn't really start, not officially, anyway, until your ball."

Eugenia touched her arm. She was particularly fond of Ivy, who had been companion to Eugenia's dear friend, Lady Dunn. "Thank you. I do enjoy seeing so many people I've come to know and love. Will you be in town long?"

"Just another week or so," Ivy said. "Then we must return to the country because I'm going to become an aunt."

"Oh, that's right, Fanny is expecting," Eugenia said, mentally counting the number of women here who were with child, and ultimately giving up.

Another couple joined them—the Marquess and Marchioness of Axbridge. Emmaline's state, that of rather advanced pregnancy, was quite obvious. "We wanted to come and pay our respects, Lady Satterfield," Axbridge said. "I'm afraid we need to be leaving. We probably should not have come, but Emmaline was adamant that she not miss your ball, even if we stayed only five minutes."

Ivy moved to put her arm on Emmaline's waist, her face creasing with concern. "Are you all right? Do you want me to escort you home?"

Emmaline waved a hand. "No, I'll be fine. I'm just a bit overheated."

Eugenia gazed at her in sympathy. "It may be time for me to allow Titus to host this ball. His house is so much bigger. He has a proper ballroom."

"No." All four of them said the word in unison, and Eugenia laughed.

"It's tradition," Axbridge said. "You host the first must-attend event of the Season. That's simply the way it is."

"You've convinced me," Lady Satterfield said with a

laugh. "Now, how about you go downstairs to our private library and put your feet up while your coach is brought round? I'll have lemonade and port sent down."

Emmaline's entire body wilted with relief. "You are an angel. Thank you."

"It is my pleasure, and do let me know when Axbridge's heir arrives."

"It's going to be a girl," Axbridge said.

Ivy looked at Clare. "You said that about Leah, and you were right."

He chuckled. "As right as I was about marrying you." He winked at his wife, and a moment later, Eugenia saw the Axbridges down the stairs.

When she returned, a new set had begun. She scanned the room—which was really two rooms opened up together—looking for Nora and Titus. Instead, she saw Ivy's sister Fanny and made her way to the young woman's side.

They embraced, and Fanny's husband, the Earl of St. Ives, bowed.

"I understand you'll be leaving for the country soon," Eugenia said. "I shall pray for your safe delivery."

Fanny's hand drifted over her abdomen. "Thank you. I'm a bit nervous, but Ivy says it will be fine."

"Of course it will, dear." St. Ives gave her an encouraging smile.

"I'm glad to have plenty of support," Fanny said. "Oh, here they come. Lady Satterfield, you've met my friends Lady Northam and Lady Ware, have you not?"

The two ladies arrived with their husbands, and it was evident that they too had breathed the childbearing air. There seemed to be an epidemic of exceptionally happy— and productive—unions.

"Yes, of course," Eugenia said, greeting the new

arrivals. "It looks as though many of my guests will be very busy over the next few months."

"Oh, you mean because of all the babies," Lavinia, Lady Northam, said. "I have to think that some of them will grow up and marry each other."

"I do think that's likely," Eugenia said. "Jo told me her daughter Evie has befriended the Duke of Blackburn." She looked toward Verity Powell, the duke's mother, and saw that Jo and Bran were now speaking with her and her husband, Kit. "Perhaps a match is already in the offing."

The conversation continued, and Eugenia waited for an appropriate moment to draw Lady Ware aside. "I understand I am to thank you for my headdress."

Lady Ware's gaze shot up to Eugenia's head, and she smiled. "Who told you? Not that I mind. It looks absolutely lovely on you."

"Lady Dartford. She was most complimentary. I hope you don't mind that she shared—I would never tell."

"I don't mind at all. I conceived of the shop when I was certain I would be a spinster."

"You, a spinster? Never. You're far too engaging and charming. You were simply waiting for the right man to realize you were standing right next to him." Eugenia looked to Felix, the Earl of Ware, who kept sending lovestruck glances toward his wife. She knew they had known each other for years, given Felix's close friendship with her brother.

"Lucky for me, that's precisely what happened," Lady Ware said, her eyes glowing.

Eugenia promised to visit the shop again soon, then saw Titus and Nora standing near her husband, whose audience had seemed to diminish, at least temporarily. Eager for a moment's respite from her circuit, Eugenia made her way to her family.

"Thank you for starting off the ball tonight," she said to Titus and Nora, her chest full of pride. "I'd begun to think that perhaps you should take over hosting the ball next year, but several people have disabused me of that notion tonight."

"And I'm glad they did," Titus said. "This is your ball. What makes you think I'd want to host it anyway?" He gave a shudder, then exchanged a small smile with Nora, who shook her head.

"He would host it if you asked him to," Nora said. "He would do anything you asked him to."

"No, he would do anything you asked him to, which is why I would ask you first." Eugenia winked at her daughter-in-law, who laughed in response.

"Oh, they're here," Nora said, looking toward the door.

Three ladies stood at the threshold. Eugenia recognized them, but then she recognized nearly everyone. What she didn't know, however, was why their arrival was noteworthy. "Have you been waiting for them?" she asked Nora.

"No, but I heard talk of them earlier. That's Jane Pemberton, Arabella Stoke, and Phoebe Lennox. They are, apparently, the ladies of Cavendish Square."

Titus groaned. "This isn't another nicknaming scheme, is it? Those bloody Untouchables names were finally beginning to die off."

"No, dear," Nora said patiently. "They are ladies, and they live in Cavendish Square."

"Together?" Eugenia asked. She thought they were all unmarried young women.

"That's why people are talking," Nora said. "Two of them are living together, and the other lives next door. Or so I heard." She wrinkled her nose. "I shouldn't repeat gossip."

"You aren't," Eugenia said. "You're sharing information with your hostess so she may be informed. Now, if you'll excuse me, I shall go welcome them and make sure everyone here knows they have my support."

Nora looked at her with love and admiration. "You are the champion of young women everywhere. You were certainly mine, and I shall never forget it."

Eugenia leaned forward and kissed Nora's cheek. "Everyone is worthy, my dear. *Everyone.*"

THE END

Author's Note

❦

Scott's Grotto is an actual place and you can view images of it at scotts-grotto.org. There is also a detailed map, but as you can see, there really isn't a hidden alcove. I took a bit of authorial license with that one.

The epilogue is a love letter from me to all of you who have read and enjoyed The Untouchables. Creating and writing these characters and telling their stories these past three years has given me incredible joy, but not as much as sharing them with you. It is very unlikely Lady Satterfield would discuss, gasp, pregnancy with any of the women at her ball, regardless of how well she knew them. However, I wanted to craft a scene in which you could see all your favorite people together, and Lady Satterfield's ball—the place where it all began—seemed perfect.

I hope you'll join me in the next chapter of The Untouchables in The Spitfire Society Series, coming soon!

Thank You!

❧❧❧

Thank you so much for reading *The Duke of Kisses*. I hope you enjoyed it! Don't miss the next Untouchable - Felix, the Earl of Ware in *The Duke of Distraction*!

Would you like to know when my next book is available? Sign up for my reader club at http://www.darcyburke.com/readerclub and follow me on social media:

Facebook: http://facebook.com/DarcyBurkeFans
Twitter at @darcyburke
Instagram at darcyburkeauthor
Pinterest at darcyburkewrite

I hope you'll consider leaving a review at your favorite online vendor or networking site!

The Duke of Kisses is the eleventh book in The Untouchables series. *The Duke of Distraction* is coming up next! Catch up with my other historical series: Secrets and Scandals and Legendary Rogues. If you like contemporary romance, I hope you'll check out my Ribbon Ridge series available from Avon Impulse, and the continuation of Ribbon Ridge in So Hot.

I appreciate my readers so much. Thank you, thank you, *thank you.*

Books by Darcy Burke

❄·3·❄

Historical Romance

The Untouchables

The Forbidden Duke
The Duke of Daring
The Duke of Deception
The Duke of Desire
The Duke of Defiance
The Duke of Danger
The Duke of Ice
The Duke of Ruin
The Duke of Lies
The Duke of Seduction
The Duke of Kisses
The Duke of Distraction

The Spitfire Society

Never Have I Ever with a Duke
A Duke is Never Enough
A Duke Will Never Do

Contemporary Romance

Ribbon Ridge

Where the Heart Is (a prequel novella)
Only in My Dreams
Yours to Hold
When Love Happens
The Idea of You
When We Kiss
You're Still the One

Ribbon Ridge: So Hot

So Good
So Right
So Wrong

Praise for Darcy Burke's

The Untouchables Series

THE FORBIDDEN DUKE

"I LOVED this story!!" 5 Stars

-Historical Romance Lover

"This is a wonderful read and I can't wait to see what comes next in this amazing series..." 5 Stars

-Teatime and Books

THE DUKE of DARING

"You will not be able to put it down once you start. Such a good read."

-Books Need TLC

"An unconventional beauty set on life as a spinster meets the one man who might change her mind, only to find his painful past makes it impossible to love. A wonderfully emotional journey from attraction, to friendship, to a love that conquers all."

-Bronwen Evans, USA Today Bestselling Author

THE DUKE of DECEPTION

"...an enjoyable, well-paced story ... Ned and Aquilla are an engaging, well-matched couple – strong, caring and compassionate; and ...it's easy to believe that they will continue to be happy together long after the book is ended."

-All About Romance

"This is my favorite so far in the series! They had chemistry from the moment they met...their passion leaps off the pages."- Sassy Book Lover

THE DUKE of DESIRE

"Masterfully written with great characterization...with a flourish toward characters, secrets, and romance... Must read addition to "The Untouchables" series!"

-My Book Addiction and More

"If you are looking for a truly endearing story about two people who take the path least travelled to find the other, with a side of 'YAH THAT'S HOT!' then this book is absolutely for you!"

-The Reading Cafe

THE DUKE of DEFIANCE

"This story was so beautifully written, and it hooked me from page one. I couldn't put the book down and just had to read it in one sitting even though it meant reading into the wee hours of the morning."

-Buried Under Romance

"I loved the Duke of Defiance! This is the kind of book you hate when it is over and I had to make myself stop reading just so I wouldn't have to leave the fun of Knighton's (aka Bran) and Joanna's story!"

-Behind Closed Doors Book Review

THE DUKE of DANGER

"The sparks fly between them right from the start... the HEA is certainly very hard-won, and well-deserved."

-All About Romance

"Another book hangover by Darcy! Every time I pick a favorite in this series, she tops it. The ending was perfect and made me want more."

-Sassy Book Lover

THE DUKE of ICE

"Each book gets better and better, and this novel was no exception. I think this one may be my fave yet! 5 out 5 for this reader!"

-Front Porch Romance

"An incredibly emotional story...I dare anyone to stop reading once the second half gets under way because this is intense!"

-Buried Under Romance

THE DUKE of RUIN

"This is a fast paced novel that held me until the last page."

-Guilty Pleasures Book Reviews

" ...everything I could ask for in a historical romance... impossible to stop reading."

-The Bookish Sisters

THE DUKE of LIES

"THE DUKE OF LIES is a work of genius! The characters are wonderfully complex, engaging; there is much mystery, and so many, many lies from so many people; I couldn't wait to see it all uncovered."

-Buried Under Romance

"..the epitome of romantic [with]...a bit of danger/action. The main characters are mature, fierce, passionate, and full of surprises. If you are a hopeless romantic and you love reading stories that'll leave you feeling like you're walking on clouds then you need to read this book or maybe even this entire series."

-The Bookish Sisters

THE DUKE of SEDUCTION

"There were tears in my eyes for much of the last 10% of this book. So good!"

-Becky on Books...and Quilts

"An absolute joy to read... I always recommend Darcy!"
-Brittany and Elizabeth's Book Boutique

THE DUKE of KISSES

"Don't miss this magnificent read. It has some comedic fun, heartfelt relationships, heartbreaking moments, and horrifying danger."

-The Reading Cafe

"...my favorite story in the series. Fans of Regency romances will definitely enjoy this book."

-Two Ends of the Pen

Secrets & Scandals Series

HER WICKED WAYS
"A bad girl heroine steals both the show and a highwayman's heart in Darcy Burke's deliciously wicked debut."
–Courtney Milan, *NYT* Bestselling Author

"…fast paced, very sexy, with engaging characters."
–Smexybooks

HIS WICKED HEART
"Intense and intriguing. Cinderella meets *Fight Club* in a historical romance packed with passion, action and secrets."
–Anna Campbell, *Seven Nights in a Rogue's Bed*

"A romance...to make you smile and sigh...a wonderful read!"

–Rogues Under the Covers

TO SEDUCE A SCOUNDREL

"Darcy Burke pulls no punches with this sexy, romantic page-turner. Sevrin and Philippa's story grabs you from the first scene and doesn't let go. To Seduce a Scoundrel is simply delicious!"

–Tessa Dare, *NYT* Bestselling Author

"I was captivated on the first page and didn't let go until this glorious book was finished!"

–Romancing the Book

TO LOVE A THIEF

"With refreshing circumstances surrounding both the hero and the heroine, a nice little mystery, and a touch of heat, this novella was a perfect way to pass the day."

–The Romanceaholic

"A refreshing read with a dash of danger and a little heat. For fans of honorable heroes and fun heroines who know what they want and take it."

-The Luv NV

NEVER LOVE A SCOUNDREL

"I loved the story of these two misfits thumbing their noses at society and finding love." Five stars.

–A Lust for Reading

"A nice mix of intrigue and passion...wonderfully complex characters, with flaws and quirks that will draw you in and steal your heart."

–BookTrib

SCOUNDREL EVER AFTER

"There is something so delicious about a bad boy, no matter what era he is from, and Ethan was definitely delicious."

-A Lust for Reading

"I loved the chemistry between the two main characters...Jagger/Ethan is not what he seems at all and neither is sweet society Miss Audrey. They are believably compatible."

-Confessions of a College Angel

Legendary Rogues Series

LADY of DESIRE

"A fast-paced mixture of adventure and romance, very much in the mould of *Romancing the Stone* or *Indiana Jones*."

-All About Romance

"...gave me such a book hangover! ...addictive...one of the most entertaining stories I've read this year!"

-Adria's Romance Reviews

ROMANCING the EARL

"Once again Darcy Burke takes an interesting story and...turns it into magic. An exceptionally well-written book."

-Bodice Rippers, Femme Fatale, and Fantasy

"...A fast paced story that was exciting and interesting. This is a definite must add to your book lists!"

-Kilts and Swords

LORD of FORTUNE

"I don't think I know enough superlatives to describe this book! It is wonderfully, magically delicious. It sucked me in from the very first sentence and didn't turn me loose—not even at the end ..."

-Flippin Pages

"If you love a deep, passionate romance with a bit of mystery, then this is the book for you!"

-Teatime and Books

CAPTIVATING the SCOUNDREL

"I am in absolute awe of this story. Gideon and Daphne stole all of my heart and then some. This book was such a delight to read."

-Beneath the Covers Blog

"Darcy knows how to end a series with a bang! Daphne and Gideon are a mix of enemies and allies turned lovers that will have you on the edge of your seat at every turn."

-Sassy Booklover

Ribbon Ridge Series

A contemporary family saga featuring the Archer family of sextuplets who return to their small Oregon wine country town to confront tragedy and find love...

The "multilayered plot keeps readers invested in the story line, and the explicit sensuality adds to the excitement that will have readers craving the next Ribbon Ridge offering."
-Library Journal Starred Review on YOURS TO HOLD

"Darcy Burke writes a uniquely touching and heart-warming series about the love, pain, and joys of family as well as the love that feeds your soul when you meet "the one."
-The Many Faces of Romance

I can't tell you how much I love this series. Each book gets better and better.
-Romancing the Readers

"Darcy Burke's Ribbon Ridge series is one of my all-time favorites. Fall in love with the Archer family, I know I did."
-Forever Book Lover

Ribbon Ridge: So Hot

SO GOOD

" ...worth the read with its well-written words, beautiful descriptions, and likeable characters...they are flirty, sexy and a match made in wine heaven."

-Harlequin Junkie Top Pick

"I absolutely love the characters in this book and the families. I honestly could not put it down and finished it in a day."

-Chin Up Mom

SO RIGHT

"This is another great story by Darcy Burke. Painting pictures with her words that make you want to sit and stare at them for hours. I love the banter between the characters and the general sense of fun and friendliness."

-The Ardent Reader

" ...the romance is emotional; the characters are spirited and passionate... "

-The Reading Café

SO WRONG

"As usual, Ms. Burke brings you fun characters and witty banter in this sweet hometown series. I loved the dance between Crystal and Jamie as they fought their attraction."

-The Many Faces of Romance

"I really love both this series and the Ribbon Ridge series from Darcy Burke. She has this way of taking your heart and ripping it right out of your chest one second and then the next you are laughing at something the characters are doing."

-Romancing the Readers

About the Author

❧

Darcy Burke is the USA Today Bestselling Author of hot, action-packed historical and sexy, emotional contemporary romance. Darcy wrote her first book at age 11, a happily ever after about a swan addicted to magic and the female swan who loved him, with exceedingly poor illustrations.

A native Oregonian, Darcy lives on the edge of wine country with her guitar-strumming husband, their two hilarious kids who seem to have inherited the writing gene. They're a crazy cat family with two Bengal cats, a small, fame-seeking cat named after a fruit, and an older rescue Maine Coon who is the master of chill and five a.m. serenading. In her "spare" time Darcy is a serial volunteer enrolled in a 12-step program where one learns to say "no," but she keeps having to start over. Her happy places are Disneyland and Labor Day weekend at the Gorge. Visit Darcy online at http://www.darcyburke.com and sign up for her newsletter, follow her on Twitter at http://twitter.com/darcyburke, or like her Facebook page, http://www.facebook.com/darcyburkefans.

37264566R00167

Printed in Poland
by Amazon Fulfillment
Poland Sp. z o.o., Wrocław